BRANCH

DATE DUE

RECEIVED

NOV 6 1997

By

BRANCH

THE RIVER AT SUNDOWN

By Earl Murray from Tom Doherty Associates

EARL MURRAY

THE RIVER AT SUNDOWN

A TOM DOHERTY ASSOCIATES BOOK
NEW YORK

THE RIVER AT SUNDOWN

Copyright © 1997 by Earl Murray

This book is printed on acid-free paper.

A Forge Book
Published by Tom Doherty Associates, Inc.
175 Fifth Avenue
New York, NY 10010

Forge® is a registered trademark of Tom Doherty Associates, Inc.

Design by Lynn Newmark

Library of Congress Cataloging-in-Publication Data
Murray, Earl.
The river at sundown   /   Earl Murray.—1st ed.
p.   cm.
"A Tom Doherty Associates book."
ISBN 0-312-86124-9
1. Frontier and pioneer life—Montana—Fiction.   2. Women
pioneers—Montana—Fiction.   I. Title.
PS3563.U7657R5   1997
813'.54—dc21   97-13321
CIP

First Edition: November 1997

Printed in the United States of America

0 9 8 7 6 5 4 3 2 1

Again, for my loving wife, Victoria,
with whom I'm living happily ever after.

THE RIVER AT SUNDOWN

One

FOUR MONTHS after Lee's surrender at Appomattox and no word of her husband left Holly Porter certain he had been killed. But she knew he had returned when Jess, the family bloodhound, raised his old ears and struggled to his feet. He stared out at the roadway and let out a series of low, coarse barks, the kind reserved for Isaac's return from long journeys.

Holly turned from the stove and peered out the window. From the foggy Tennessee River bottomland there appeared a thin man in a tattered gray uniform, shouldering a scarred Springfield rifle.

He drew closer, passing the cluster of willow near the pump house. Holly stepped out of the cabin, brushing her long black hair from her face; her trim body trembled with anticipation.

From behind the cabin appeared a boy of ten, carrying a set of traps.

"Is it Pa? Is it really him?"

She peered down the road. "Isaac! Is that you?"

The man stopped on the road and looked up. "Holly, Justin. I'm home."

Justin dropped his traps and broke into a run, the dog struggling to keep up.

Holly began to run behind him, tears streaming down her face. Isaac Porter, his breath labored and painful, fell into the arms of his wife and son.

"Dry your tears, Holly," he said. "I've come back. They whupped us, but I guess you already heard."

"It's over, that's all that matters," she said. "Thank God you're alive."

Holly studied her husband. He had come back alive, but he wasn't the man who had left home four years before, solid as oakwood and able to carry a hundred pounds of feed on each shoulder. There was pain written in the way he held himself. His eyes and cheeks were hollow and his frame was little more than skin and bone.

Isaac coughed, a spasm of pain crossing his gaunt face. "It don't matter if they say it's over. Folks are still at war. It won't never be the same here. Never."

"How long have you had that cough?" Holly asked. "It sounds like you've a pleurisy."

"Just a little cold. No bother."

"You've been shot through the lungs, haven't you?" Holly started to open his shirt and he pulled away.

"Don't fuss over it. The doc says I'm healed up good enough."

"It doesn't sound like it to me. Let me have a look."

Holly opened up his shirt to see a round, dark spot halfway down his left side. On the opposite side she found a small, linear scar only half healed.

"They cut me open there," Isaac said, "to take out the slug."

Justin's eyes widened. "It don't look good, Pa."

Isaac rearranged his shirt. "It didn't kill me. To look at the both of you, a man would think he was done in."

"You're going to have to go easy until you get your strength back," Holly said.

"What do you know about such things, Holly?" he asked.

"I've seen it, Isaac. I helped nurse during the fighting in these parts. I couldn't see staying at home while folks was in need."

Holly had seen more than she cared to remember. She had

left Justin for days at a time, hidden in a cellar with an older neighbor woman on the other side of the river, while the fighting moved back and forth along the bottomland. She attended soldiers in both uniforms who fell at Chattanooga and Lookout Mountain, watching boys die in the arms of other boys.

Then, when the old woman had died suddenly, she had kept herself away from the fighting, caring for Justin and trying to answer questions that had no answer.

"There's a great many of those soldiers told me they'd make it, then took their dying breath," Holly said. "You don't fool with bullet wounds."

"I tell you I'm good as new," Isaac insisted. He pulled an envelope bearing a Union seal from a pocket of his uniform. A physician had signed a letter saying he had been properly cared for at a military medical facility and was now "healed and fit for work."

"What kind of 'medical facility' was this?" Holly asked. "A Bluebelly farmer's barn?"

"It was a barn, all right. I was there a couple of months. That's all I needed. I'll mend proper."

Holly shook her head and crumpled the paper into a ball. "This will start a fire in the stove. That's about all it's good for."

"Holly, I got to work this land," Isaac said. "It's all I know how to do."

"Just listen to me." Holly's voice rose. "You'll be able to work in time, just like always. Until then, let me help you get your strength back."

"I'll help, too," Justin said, offering to relieve his father of the rifle.

"You're near a man, son," Isaac said, handing over the rifle. "I'll teach you to shoot that Springfield."

"Ma already taught me to shoot." He studied the rifle. "She even lets me use the old Hawken once in a while. When she's with me."

"You still got that old relic?"

"You just wish it was yours," Holly said, "and that we all lived in the Western mountains, like my own father did."

"I 'spect your right."

The Hawken, a fifty caliber, had been given to Holly by her father just before his death. He had used it during his years as a trapper in the Rocky Mountains. She had done well by the gun, even though her mother hadn't approved. Now that her mother was also gone, there was no one who complained about her hunting and tramping the woods when she felt like it. Justin was always by her side, and during the war the Hawken had kept them both supplied with small game and an occasional deer.

"Lot's changed since I been gone." Isaac's eyes were hollow. He looked out to a field in front of the cabin. "I see you got a crop in, and your garden. You always could do for yourself, couldn't you?"

"I missed you, Isaac," she said.

Justin hated seeing his mother upset. It seldom happened, but when it did, it meant something important was going on. He knew his father had come home from the war sick and weak and that maybe his healthy days were gone forever.

He resolved to make the best of things and assure his father that he thought no less of him.

"Tell us about the war, Pa," he said as they went into the cabin.

"There's not much about it that's good to tell, son," Isaac said. "I'd rather we talked about you and your ma."

"I'll fix some breakfast," Holly said. "We've got a lot to catch up on."

Over eggs and biscuits, she described the changes that had come to the area. Isaac wanted to hear the news but found himself breaking in often to talk about all the bad decisions that had cost the Confederacy, and how the country was going to change because of the outcome. Justin couldn't understand half of what his pa was saying. He wanted to hear about the battles.

"Just a lot of blood, son," Isaac told him. "You don't want to hear about it. It'll give you bad dreams."

"You have bad dreams, Pa?"

"Sometimes. I don't see this country the same no more. In fact, I have the urge to get us out of here. There's apt to be more bloodshed and I don't want us near it. Not anymore."

Isaac's first week home brought adjustment for Holly, and confusion for Justin. She didn't have the same husband and he didn't understand what his father had become. He had expected his father to be fearless like a soldier should be, not nervous and irritable about every little thing. He often heard yelling in the middle of the night, and the sound of footsteps at the fireplace, where the rifles were hung.

Holly fretted and bit her lip often, pacifying Isaac with hot cider while she rubbed his shoulders to settle him back into fitful sleep. She wished against hope that it would all get back to normal, but it only got worse.

The following morning, three men dressed in business suits arrived in a carriage. Isaac met them with his rifle.

"I don't intend to sell my land to the likes of you," he told them, "and I want you to turn around and get out of here."

"We'll give you a fair price," one of them said. "You'd best take it while you've got the chance."

Isaac lifted his rifle. "You heard me. Scoot on out of here."

When they were gone he told Holly, "Them carpetbaggers are everywhere. They think we've got nothing and will settle for nickles and dimes."

"I can see what you're saying about change," Holly said.

At the end of the week Isaac announced he was going up to Missouri to see how his family was doing. "I ain't seen any of them for a long spell."

"They didn't take to your choice of fighting for the South," Holly reminded him. "Are you sure they'll welcome you?"

"I've got to find out how they fared through the war," he said. "I can't just let it ride."

"But couldn't you wait until you're stronger? Just another month, maybe?"

Isaac promised to wait two more weeks but left at the end of four days. He took a flatboat up the Tennessee River and then caught a ride on a grain barge up the Mississippi, walking cross-country to the woods east of Springfield. He was gone for the rest of the month. All he could say when he returned was that his parents had died and that he and his brother, Harlan, couldn't see eye to eye any better than they ever could.

"Harlan turned Bluebelly Yankee," Isaac said. "He lost the family farm and now he's slopping hogs for a neighbor. Still, I feel I owe him something, him being younger and all."

They had talked about it often, but Holly voiced her opinion to deaf ears.

"Harlan don't care about you, Isaac. It never mattered to him that your ma wanted you to get along. Harlan wants whatever he can get."

He ignored her, saying, "I should have figured there'd be nothing left up there. Maybe Harlan and me can start fresh somehow."

"How do you mean?"

"There's talk that folks are doing themselves proud by going West. We should think about that."

"You've got to be strong to do that."

"I'm strong enough!" Isaac said, pounding the table. "I don't want to hear you say that no more."

The next morning he insisted on working one of the fields

behind a pair of mules. Holly tried to dissuade him but succeeded only in rekindling his anger. She watched as he stumbled and coughed behind the plow, and later found him lying in the field, doubled over in pain. "Will you listen to reason now?" she said. "You're going to kill yourself if you don't slow down."

Isaac spent the next month wandering up and down along the river. At first, Justin followed along with the dog but they seldom spoke more than a few words. His father had a faraway look in his eyes, and when he talked, he spoke of the damned carpetbaggers coming in for the spoils.

"I pray to God I don't end up shooting one of them," he commented to Justin one afternoon. "You see me lift the rifle, you stop me. Hear?"

The autumn months rolled past, and with rest, Isaac regained sufficient strength to use his Springfield. He brought down deer and turkeys for the table. Justin accompanied him often and found his father more talkative, although he would still never tell him anything concerning the war. He decided it was something his pa would hold inside him for the rest of his life.

With time and growing strength, Isaac grew more restless. Just after the new year Holly and Justin sat down to an evening meal without him. He had gone into town, as he had begun to do on occasion, always returning in time to eat. Holly began to wonder if he hadn't left for good, when he finally showed up just as they were finishing.

"What happened?" she asked. "It's not like you to be gone for supper."

"I've made a decision," he told them. "We can't stay here, not no more. I want all this behind me forever. I heard tell in town today that there's folks digging a fortune in gold way up in the mountains. Montana Territory. I aim to go and find some for us."

Holly's breath caught in her throat. "Why, that's just

wilderness out there. We can't take Justin into that country."

"Folks say it's changed out there," he said. "A lot of folks are moving to those diggings. Going in wagons. I heard the gold camps got more folk in them than a lot of the towns around here."

"When we going?" Justin said.

"You just hold tight. I've got this figured out."

"How will we get there?" Holly asked. "We haven't the money to even buy what we *need,* much less any extra for a wagon."

"I figure to go out first," Isaac said. "There's a number of men from these parts and we'll all band together and go out to St. Louis by the rivers and then onward a-horseback. We'll move faster than wagons for sure. When I get out there I'll file a gold claim and then send for you."

"How do you know you'll find gold?"

"He will," Justin said. "I'll help."

"No, son," Isaac said. "You've got to stay here and help your ma, like you did while I was off fighting."

"You didn't answer my question," Holly said. "What if you don't find gold?"

"It's all over in that country, is what they say," he said, his enthusiasm unshaken. "I'll find us some gold, don't you worry. When I'm ready to have you come, I'll send a letter to my brother, Harlan. We talked about it some when I was up there. He'll help you come out and maybe work the claim with us, if he don't find his own."

Holly grew more disappointed. Harlan was three years younger than Isaac. She had met him one time, just before she and Isaac had been married. The only thing he had said to her was, "You ain't really much of a woman, are you? Too small." His breath had reeked of whiskey.

"How do you know Harlan will want to go West?" Holly asked. "If he's got a jug, he's settled."

"Don't carry on like that."

"It's the truth. He's not going to help us any."

"Still, he's my brother and he's got nothing up there where he's at."

She saw that there was no question that Isaac was going and that he wanted Harlan to share in his fortune.

"If you find gold, how will we find you?"

"The men in town who're all going told me about a fort they call Laramie. That's where the trail splits from the one that takes all the people to Oregon and California. When the time's right, I'll meet you and the boy there."

Justin's eyes were filled with tears.

"Get brave, son." He turned to Holly. "Don't fret none. I'll send for you. And don't put a crop in this year."

"Why not?"

"You won't have time to harvest it."

Within three days Isaac was packed and gone. Holly heard nothing from him until a letter finally arrived at the end of April:

Last Chance Gulch

Montana Territory, 3 April 1866

Dear Holly and Justin,

Made it and am looking for gold. Virginia City is full up and all good claims are gone. Came here with five men and we all put stakes on Prickly Pear. A lot of folks here and food is high. Don't need much to live on. Will find gold and rite agan.

Your husband,

Isaac

Holly noticed that his handwriting had changed. She began to worry that he was losing strength again and that he was working himself too hard. No amount of gold was worth anything if you were buried in the ground.

In the middle of June, a neighbor delivered a small wooden box. Beneath the faded HORSESHOE NAILS label was her name and address in charred tracings. Holly loosened a slat with her skinning knife and poked in among the packing of dried leaves.

She found a small but heavy skin bag with a letter wrapped around it.

"What's that, Ma?" Justin asked anxiously.

"I think I know," Holly said, barely able to control her enthusiasm.

She took the skin bag over to the table and pulled the letter off, shoving it aside. She worked feverishly to cut the rawhide thongs that held the top of the bag shut. Dear Lord, he's done it! she thought to herself. He's realized his dream. We *will* be able to start over.

She worked the bag open. Her eyes widened as she stirred the fine metal with a fingertip.

"Is that gold?" Justin asked excitedly.

She nodded. "It looks like we'll be going West."

The letter suggested they sell the farm to Nate Whipple, whose place was just a short distance upriver. He was a young man who could use the land to feed his growing family, and he wouldn't give in to any carpetbaggers.

Isaac wrote further that he would meet them at Fort Laramie the end of September. That would give them time to buy a wagon and the goods needed for the trip. "You will have to have three or four good milk cans with tight covers," he wrote, "for carrying good water. Lots of alkali along the way and not good to drink. Bring vinegar, crackers, and lots of yeast. Bring Frazier's Lubricator to grease wagons."

There was more than enough gold to purchase what they needed; Holly had no worry about that. Her concern centered on Isaac. His handwriting had gotten noticeably worse. She would turn thirty-three in two months and didn't want to celebrate as a widow.

"Ma, can I get me a real rifle?" Justin asked. "Maybe a squirrel gun?"

"We'll wait awhile," she said. "One rifle's enough for the both of us for now."

Isaac's letter also mentioned that he had notified his brother and told him to meet them at Independence, Missouri, in a month's time. Holly knew she would worry enough about her husband on the way out, but now there was the added burden of having his worthless brother along. Unless Harlan had changed a great deal, the trip with him wouldn't be pleasant.

"You excited?" Justin asked.

"Yes, I am." She tied the bundle back together.

"It's going to be a lot different living out there, ain't it?"

She nodded. "A lot of things will be different from now on."

Two

WITHIN A week Holly had the farm sold to Nate Whipple. The young neighbor would take possession just as soon as she and Justin were gone. Everything was packed except for one sentimental item, which she carried out onto the porch.

"Grandma, you know I'd never leave you behind," she said, wiping the dust off an old mirror her grandmother had given her. She glanced at her own reflection and began wrapping a blanket around the mirror.

Justin came around the corner, leading Jess by a rope tied loosely around the old dog's neck. Tears rolled down the boy's cheeks as he looked up at Holly.

"I won't be the same without him," he said.

"You know it's best," she told him, working to hold back her own tears. "Jess could never make it on a trip way out to Montana Territory. He's better off here with the Whipples."

"I know it's best. It ain't that easy to leave him behind, that's all."

She knelt beside him and lifted his chin, drying his tears with the corner of her apron. "You'd best get him over to the Whipples now. Your pa is on his way to meet us out there and we don't want to keep him waiting."

Justin led the old bloodhound a short distance down the main road and veered off onto the well-used path that went through the woods and came out at the Whipple place. He knew the Whipples would look out for the old dog; Nate and

Lorraine were good folks. They had a boy, Eli, three years older than Justin, for Jess to play and hunt with, and a girl, Aggie, a year younger.

The Whipple place came into view and Justin wiped his nose with his shirtsleeve. Jess followed along, his head down as if knowing he was seeing the boy for the last time. Lorraine met him at the door.

Justin bit his lip. "I come to bring Jess to you folks. You promise to do good by him?" He couldn't hold back his tears.

"Oh, Justin." Lorraine put a hand on his shoulder. After a moment she said, "Why don't you go down to the barn? Nate is there with Eli and Aggie."

Justin led Jess down to the barn and met Nate coming out the door.

"What brings you over?" he said.

Justin held up the rope. "Jess is too old to go with us. He's yours."

Nate Whipple squatted to pet Jess. "You're a right smart boy," he said. "Old Jess likely wouldn't stand a trip like that. We'd be proud to take him for you, and we'll treat him right. Why don't you take him to the barn and tell Eli and Aggie? They're with the puppies."

"Puppies? Your tick hound had puppies?"

"I guess it's been a spell since you've been by."

"I was with Pa mostly, when he first got back," Justin said. "Now I've been helping get ready to go. We're going to meet Pa out at the mountains, you know."

"Well, you go right on in there." He pointed through the barn door. "You tell Eli how you want Jess cared for."

Justin led the dog into the barn, where Eli and Aggie were arguing over a long-eared puppy that was chewing on an old harness strap. They both turned when they heard Justin enter, and Aggie picked up the puppy and held it against her breast.

Justin handed the rope to Eli. "This here is a smart dog I'm giving you. Promise you'll take good care of him?"

Eli took the rope and knelt down to pet Jess. "You ain't taking him along with you?"

"He's too old. But he can still hunt and he'll keep the coons out of your crops."

"Pa has said good things about your dog," Eli said. "We'll take right good care of him. I promise."

Justin noticed Aggie staring at him. She was holding the puppy tightly.

"That puppy looks sorta like Jess," Justin said. "Can I hold him?"

She hesitated, then held out the pup. Justin took the scrambling ball of ears and legs and pulled him close. The dog began nosing around Justin's arms and neck, then licked him on the cheek.

Eli and Aggie looked at each other and came to a silent conclusion.

"Being as how you gave us such a good dog, it wouldn't be fair that we don't give you something in trade." She pointed to the pup. "Do you want to keep him?"

"You'd have to promise to train him good," Eli said. "That's the best dog of the litter."

"You mean it?" Justin asked. "I can have him?"

Eli smiled. "Only if you train him good."

"Me and Pa will train him just like Jess," Justin promised, the puppy snuggling into his arms.

"Then it's a fair trade," Eli said, and held out his hand.

Justin shook Eli's hand, then Aggie's. She was close to tears but held them back.

"You heard Eli," she said. "You take good care of him."

Justin nodded. Aggie wasn't so bad, for being a girl. "I think I'll call him Nozer," he said. "On account of he's nosey all the time."

Justin turned and bent down to hug Jess one last time. Tears streamed down his cheeks. He stood up and quickly rubbed his face with his free arm and rushed out of the barn.

He ran all the way home, holding the kicking puppy tightly, and entered the cabin breathless.

"What took you so long?" Holly asked, turning from the stove. She saw the puppy in Justin's arms. "What have you got there?"

"It's a fair trade, Ma," Justin said quickly. "I named him Nozer. He looks just like Jess, don't he?"

Holly knelt down and pulled the boy close to her. "If he's your pup, you're going to have to take care of him."

"I promise I will. Me and Pa will teach him to be just as good as Jess."

After nearly two weeks of travel—first across country to the Mississippi and then by riverboat—Holly and Justin found themselves in Independence, a bustling jumping-off point for emigrants headed west. Rows of log saloons lined the trail leading into town, mixed with blacksmith shops and dry goods stores and a few new hotels.

The edge of town was crowded with wagons and teams of oxen or mules. Livestock roamed everywhere, including cattle, sheep, and hogs, as well as ducks, geese, turkeys, and chickens. A number of farmers were toiling to load scythes and sickles and even plows into the backs of wagons, alongside beds, butter churns, and carefully wrapped china dishes.

Holly learned that most of the emigrants were going south along the Sante Fe Trail to settle in California. She bought a wagon and team of oxen at a good price from an older couple who had turned back from a wagon train that had left a week earlier. That evening she and Justin crossed the Missouri on a ferry and camped with fifty-two other wagons, the last wagon train heading toward the northern mountains that year.

The wagonmaster, a burly middle-aged man named

O'Brian, welcomed her by name. He had been expecting her.

"How did you know I was coming?" Holly asked. "And how do you know my name?"

"Someone's been asking about you." He pointed to a man dressed in a greasy shirt and trousers sprawled under a nearby tree, his sweat-stained hat tipped down over his eyes. "Says his name's Harlan Porter. He got in about three days back and has been trouble ever since. You know him?"

"He's my brother-in-law," Holly said. "He's come along to help me."

"Good luck," O'Brian said.

"Has he really been that bad?"

"I've seen it before. When you're so bad off you'll steal from other folk to trade for a jug of rotgut whiskey, you're asking to get yourself shot. I just hope you learn how to handle him."

Justin adjusted Nozer in his arms and frowned. "That man over there is Uncle Harlan?"

"A word of advice, ma'am," O'Brian added. "You'd best have your oxen hitched and your wagon in line up front way before the pink shows in the sky. The first folks up get the best places, and I'll guarantee you one thing: You ain't seen dust until you've been back in line a spell."

"Thank you. We'll be ready."

"We're going out to meet my pa," Justin said. "Nothing is going to hold us up."

O'Brian laughed and clapped Justin lightly on the back. "You two pups will make it just fine, I'll bet."

After O'Brian had left, Holly and Justin approached Harlan. She waited until he had lowered his jug.

"What is it you want, lady?" he asked gruffly. He was drooling from the corners of his mouth and his eyes were only half-open.

"Don't you recognize me?" Holly said. "I'm Isaac's wife. We met just before Isaac and I got married."

Harlan squinted and propped himself up on one elbow.

He tipped his hat back over a thatch of graying hair and scratched his unshaven face. "You look older than I remember. Guess that's why I didn't know you." He struggled to his feet. "That your kid?"

"This is Justin, our son. Justin, shake hands."

Harlan waved him back. "Just keep him out of the way. I don't want to be tripping over no suckling kid and his dog."

Justin looked to his mother. "Do we really need him, Ma? Can't he find his own way?"

Harlan's eyes narrowed. "I'll take no sass from him, either. I'll whup him good."

Holly stepped in front of Justin, her face suddenly hard as stone.

"What did you say?"

"You heard me," Harlan snapped. "I'll teach him some manners."

"You so much as lay a hand on this boy and I'll cut your fingers off, one at a time. I've got the knife to do it, back in the wagon."

Harlan's eyes widened. "You're crazy."

"I don't care if Isaac wanted you to come with us," Holly said. "You aren't going to make any trouble for us. Do you understand?"

Harlan grunted. "That ain't very friendly."

"You just remember what I said. Justin doesn't make trouble for anybody. He never has. You just stay away from him."

Harlan tried to stare Holly down but failed. It left him angry and resentful, but also respectful. He wondered if she knew how to use a knife. Better not to test her. He would go into Independence and celebrate a late night before departure and deal with the two of them when the time was right.

The sun was pushing up into a cloudless sky and the entire eastern horizon was shot with changing shades of red and pink. Holly washed the breakfast dishes and put out her campfire. The trip west across the plains was about to begin.

The conversations among the travelers had been anxious; they all were wondering what lay in wait along the trail to Fort Laramie, seven hundred miles distant.

The night before, they had gathered together around campfires and listened wide-eyed to any number of tales about rampaging Indians and thundering war drums that pounded all night.

Justin had listened to one man who had made the journey ten years before. He was going out again to try and find his lost son. He was certain the Sioux had him. Though others told him the boy was likely dead, the man denied that and was determined to find him.

His name was Clyde Wambolt, a tall, thin man near forty years of age. The combination of sorrow and bitterness from losing his son made him appear much older.

In the summer of 1855, on their way along the Platte River, Wambolt and his son were gathering wood with some other men from the emigrant party. The Sioux had come and were stealing horses. After his father and the other man had turned to run, the boy had fought bravely to get back his favorite pony.

Wambolt had rushed to try and stop the raid, only to take an arrow in the arm. He had watched from the ground while the Sioux rode off with his son.

Some who heard the stories were planning to turn back. Holly could understand their fears, but not how they could decide to go back now. Some of them had come from as far as New York and Pennsylvania.

The worst hazard she and Justin would face was Harlan, she thought. He had returned from Independence late and had made all kinds of drunken noise. He had made his bed under the wagon and was sleeping when Holly began hitching up the oxen.

"You going to move, or do I have to run over you?"

"Can't you leave a man in peace?"

"We're moving out."

Harlan sat up. "Can I sleep in the wagon with the boy?"

"No," Holly said flatly as she climbed up to the wagon seat and took the reins. "It looks like you're going to have to wait until tonight to sleep. Either that or stay behind."

The camp was ready to head west, and up at the front, O'Brian gave the order to move out. Leather creaked and whips popped as the wagons lurched into motion.

By daylight they were rolling smoothly across a broad flat beyond the Kansas River, along a trail worn deep by nearly thirty years of continuous use. Dogs yapped at children's feet, and men swore at mules and oxen as the dust boiled into a blue and cloudless sky.

Harlan walked alongside the wagon, never looking up at Holly. Justin, holding Nozer tightly, finally plopped down on the wagon seat next to Holly and began to ask a thousand questions, to none of which Holly had answers.

They reached the crossing on the Kansas River and the wagons were fitted with logs tied with ropes along the sides to make them more buoyant. The mules trudged into the water and pulled their loads and the oxen did the same, standing lower in the water and blowing it from their noses as they worked.

A number of Kansas Indians watched and rode up and down the shoreline. Some wanted to assist the emigrants in getting belongings across in crude dugout boats. O'Brian warned everyone to pay close attention to their belongings and barter with the Indians first, or risk having things taken from them in payment.

In all, the crossing was easy and there was no real trouble. The biggest problem was keeping provisions and belongings dry. The current splashed up over the rafts and the wagons and the few hide bullboats that some of the Indians were using to transport goods.

After the crossing the journey resumed, reaching onward into what was now a vast sea of rolling grass that stretched toward the horizon. Along the river there were thick groves of maple as well as wild plum and Indian thorn apple, their branches covered with fruit.

Scattered here and there were the crude log dwellings of the Delawares, moved from their homelands farther east, who seemed to be making a halfhearted attempt at farming. But for these small settlements the land was open, and Justin wondered how it would change once they reached the mountains.

The days passed uneventfully. Harlan kept well away from Justin and barely spoke with Holly at all. If he could maintain this type of behavior for the rest of the trip, she thought, there would be fewer problems to deal with.

O'Brian checked in on her occasionally and could see that she and Harlan had come to a quick understanding.

He rode up alongside the wagon. "You handle things pretty well," he told her. He turned to Justin and gave Nozer a scratch under one ear. "How you two pups doing so far?"

"Good," Justin said with a big grin. "Ma shot a turkey last night and Nozer thinks that's pretty good."

"You're fitting in good with this country," O'Brian said.

"But where did all the trees go?" the boy asked. "There ain't no trees anymore but along the river. What happened to them?"

"It doesn't rain out here near as much as back where you're from," O'Brian said. "When we hit the Rockies, you'll see plenty of trees."

Late that evening, the wagons were circled while a brisk wind buffeted them from the west. The sky in the distance was filled with rain clouds that rolled out from the mountains.

Holly took tinder and dry wood from the wagon and, with her back to the wind, used a small flint to spark a fire.

Justin held Nozer and watched while Holly cut small cubes of venison and dropped them in a kettle. She and another emigrant family were sharing a deer she had killed with her Hawken the night before. They traded her a large bag of dried tomatoes for stew and she in turn gave them half the deer.

"Got a piece for Nozer?" Justin asked, watching his puppy's nose twitch and sniff continually.

"He'll get this bone when I'm finished here," Holly said. "Why don't you and your pup go find me some wood?"

Holly had the stew steaming when Justin returned with an armload of cottonwood branches. Nozer trotted at his heels, stopping to sniff at nearly everything he saw.

He dropped the wood next to the fire and took a seat with Nozer near the kettle, watching his mother stirring the stew. He picked up a piece of wood and probed the coals of the fire.

"I think that wood is a little damp," Holly told him. "We'll let it dry some before we burn it. We don't want a lot of smoke."

"Hope it dries fast. This fire is just about gone and it's almost total dark out. I think Nozer's getting cold."

Holly smiled and went to the wagon for a blanket. She returned with the down quilt her mother had given her and shared half with Justin and the pup.

"Suppose we'll see Indians before long?"

"Don't worry about Indians. Hold your bowl out and I'll dish you some stew."

Justin nodded. "I could use some, all right," he said. "Will Pa be at Fort Laramie for sure when we get there?"

She ladled the stew and took a deep breath. "I hope so. I want him to be there as much as you do."

"Does he have a long way to come?"

"Almost as far as us, I imagine."

Holly broke a branch of wood over her knee and placed the pieces in the growing blaze, wishing they had already reached the fort. She knew that the other emigrants were as anxious as she and Justin to reach the mountains, still a long distance away.

She thought momentarily that if she had it her way, she would give the order to just push on, to forget about camping for the night. But there was little sense in that, she realized.

She filled another bowl of stew and called under the wagon, "Harlan, come out and get some food into your stomach."

A head of tangled graying hair poked out from under the wagon. "I don't want food. I want another bottle." He slid back into the shadows behind the wheels.

"Drunk again," Justin said matter-of-factly through a mouthful of food. "Drunk and sick, like he always is."

"Don't talk about your uncle that way."

"Even if it's true?"

"Even if it's true."

"Don't fight with him, Ma," Justin said. "I hate it when he yells."

"I'll just leave him be," she said. "Finish your stew and get to bed. It's getting late and we have a big day ahead tomorrow."

"But it's not hardly dark yet," Justin said. "Nozer won't be able to go to sleep."

"Yes, he will. Off to bed with the both of you."

She allowed him to get into the wagon by himself, as he always insisted, then made certain he was covered with the blue wool blanket his grandmother had made for him before he was born. The sharp wind was bringing a chill into the camp and she wondered if rain was coming.

As she sat back down at the fire, Holly felt chilled and wondered if the late start had been foolish. They would have to travel without any delays or winter would set in on them before they reached Montana.

Three

THE LITTLE and Big Vermillion rivers came and went and they pushed into Nebraska Territory. The days were brisk and windy; sunsets laced the horizon with red. The prairie rolled on and on, a spreading sea of grass.

Two days before they reached the Big Blue River, O'Brian came to Holly's wagon.

"There's some trouble ahead," he said. "Not Indians."

"What, then?"

"Cholera. A train ahead of us got wiped out. Some of our folks have decided to turn back. I thought I'd give you the choice."

Holly's stomach tightened. "You're sure it's cholera?"

"The graves are shallow," O'Brian said, "and there's a lot of abandoned clothes and bedding that's been set on fire. My scout says the graves are lined up alongside the trail for nearly ten miles. What would you say that meant?"

Holly had seen the disease ravage military camps and field hospitals during the war. It came like a fog in the night and left just as quickly, clearing out vast numbers of people in its wake.

She wondered now if the disease would get her this time. As often as she had seen it and yet been spared, her luck couldn't last forever. It frightened her to think she might pass on and leave Justin to fend for himself.

"What do you plan on doing?" O'Brian asked.

"We'll be going ahead."

"May God be with you."

O'Brian left and Harlan appeared. It was clear he had been sharing a jug with someone.

"You hear the news?" he said.

She nodded.

"You plan to turn back?" Harlan asked.

"No," Holly replied. "Do you?"

"Hell, no. There's gold up ahead and nothing's going to stop me from getting to it. That's what Isaac would want."

By first light those who elected to turn back were already on the trail—nearly a third of the wagons. Holly tied a kerchief around Justin's nose and mouth, fitted herself as well, and waited for the wagons to roll.

"This is too tight, Ma," Justin said.

"You don't touch that scarf, unless you want to end up in a grave," she said.

He held Nozer close. "Maybe you'd better fit him with one."

Holly did her best to cover the puppy's nose, knowing he would paw the scarf loose. It would give Justin something to do, keeping his dog's nose covered.

By midmorning, the wagons reached the first graves. Much of the clothing and bedding still smoldered, sending an acrid smoke into the air. Crude wood crosses stood over mounds of rock and soil hurriedly thrown over the bodies. Here and there the wolves had found the digging easy, and partially devoured corpses were exposed.

One small grave had been marked with a piece of headboard from a bed. The carved epitaph read:

MARY JEAN FLYNN

AGE 3

GOD REST HER LITTLE SOUL

SEPTEMBER 20, 1866

Justin stared at the graves. "I feel sorry for those folks who lost their families."

"They'll carry on," Holly said. "The Lord gives and the Lord takes away."

"And it don't take long to do either one," Justin said. He pointed. "What's Uncle Harlan doing out there, looking at those graves? He don't even have a kerchief on."

"He does what he pleases," Holly said. "One day he'll learn. Maybe."

The wagons rolled on. For a time the people rode in silence, but finally gave in to their hopes and dreams, discussing the good things they believed lay ahead for them. To the west, the mountains waited, promising a new life for them all. If the rumors were true, gold made the slopes a sparkling paradise.

They crossed the Big Blue and followed the Little Blue to the Platte. They passed Dobey Town, a collection of mud structures housing whores for the soldiers and bullwhackers from nearby Fort Kearney. Harlan considered visiting the place but had no money and abandoned the idea.

Fort Kearney was named for a commander who gained notoriety in the war for California. Established in 1848 to protect the early Oregon Trail travelers from Indians, the fort bustled with activity. Bullwhackers unloaded goods at the sutler's store while soldiers marched across the parade grounds. At the corrals, newly acquired horses were being branded and broken for use, kicking up dust that drifted over a flatboat moving slowly downriver.

The last leg of the journey to Fort Laramie would soon begin, and Holly welcomed the two days they were taking to rest the livestock and repair wagons and gear. It seemed they had left Tennessee a long time past and there was still the biggest part of the journey left ahead.

That evening, while Justin took Nozer and joined some other boys to explore the river, Holly washed clothes. It was hard to keep up with the work with the long hours traveling, and she had spent many a sleepless night worrying about Isaac and his health. She wondered if he would be at Fort Laramie when they arrived; then she wondered if she and Justin would even get to the fort themselves.

Since passing the graves of the cholera victims they had met a large emigrant wagon train headed back from the mountains. They were referred to as "Skedaddlers" by those who felt they were not cut out for the hardships. Holly sympathized with them. They told of terrible deaths along the Bozeman Road at the hands of the feared war chief Red Cloud and his warriors, who had attacked travelers and left them in dismembered heaps while their wagons and provisions were burned.

Holly now wondered what she would do in such a desperate situation. She would keep her wits about her as they corralled the wagons and have Justin crowd in close to her under the wheels. She could use the Hawken and hold her own with any of them, soldier and civilian alike.

But how would she deal with Harlan? He had no common sense about him and might just run crazy. Lately, he had become quite testy again. He had found others of his kind with whom he could share complaints about life in general. They almost outnumbered the Sunday people, those who insisted the wagons remain still on the Sabbath, so that proper observance of the day could take place. O'Brian had his hands full, continuously separating those with a bottle and those with a Bible.

But now there was no whiskey left among them and the urge for drink was building within Harlan. He had nearly gotten himself into a fight just after crossing the Big Blue, a dispute over a horse he claimed he had a right to, since he had helped save it from drowning. O'Brian had stepped in and settled things and considered telling Harlan that when they reached Fort Kearney, he would have to go back with the next wagon train headed east.

Then O'Brian heard news that made him change his mind. He approached Holly while she scrubbed clothes on a washboard.

"We've got three weeks left to Fort Laramie," he said. "You're holding up good, considering that brother-in-law of yours. I thought about telling him that he was going to have to stay here at the fort and wait for another group to travel with."

"I was in hopes the trip might change him," Holly said, wringing the water from one of Justin's shirts. "If you have to, you tell him to go back."

"I won't need to. He'll have to watch himself now, or he won't last a day. I just got word that a detachment of troops will be escorting us from here to Fort Laramie. Everyone will have to stay in line. The commander's name is Lieutenant Hodges, and he's not one to take a lot of guff."

Holly looked at O'Brian with concern. "Does that mean there is a problem with Indians?"

In talking with women, O'Brian usually liked to find a way to soften such issues, but he kept a stoic look about him.

"We've heard a lot about what Red Cloud has done already, but there shouldn't be much to worry about between here and Fort Laramie. It's farther north where the real problems are."

Holly thought about Isaac. "What kind of chance do people have coming through there from the gold camps?"

O'Brian knew she was referring to her husband and his attempt to get to Fort Laramie to meet them. "From what I've been able to learn," he said, "the wagons going north are the ones the Indians want to stop. They like it when they see someone going back where they came from. I doubt if your husband will have much trouble getting through . . . if he's traveling fast and with a good-sized group."

He didn't sound certain enough to make Holly feel any better.

"Another thing," O'Brian added. "The Indians are on their fall hunts right now and their main concern is killing buffalo before the snow flies. That might take some of the pressure off."

"I hope you're right," she said. "I hope to God that you're right."

Leaving Fort Kearney, they continued along the Platte and, though they saw no Indians, the soldiers made the atmosphere much more comfortable. The country spread flat in all directions, the trail winding along the riverbank into the endless distance. Holly thought about the lives of the people who had gone before: Where had they gone and what were they doing? Many had left dressers and other furniture along the trail, lightening the load. To some it had proved of no avail, as there were plenty of ox skeletons to break up the continuous scenery of dried grass.

Scattered among the oxen remains were the skulls of buffalo. The huge skulls with black, upcurved horns seemed to stare at the travelers, warning them that their mortality was fragile.

Finally, Chimney Rock came into view, a hundred-foot column of stone and clay rising from a conical hill, and a day later Scotts Bluff, a series of steep and rugged clay walls that marked the western edge of Nebraska.

Here the high grass had given way to shrublands and shorter grasses that came nowhere near a rider's stirrups. Justin had never seen forage so short or country so boring.

"Some of this land ain't none too pretty," he remarked.

"All land has its own beauty," Holly said. "You remember that."

"Yeah, well, some land's got a lot more beauty than others."

O'Brian explained that the land was sloping higher on its way to the mountains and that the trail, clear to the foothills, would be in a "rain shadow."

"The mountains catch most of the rain first," he said. "Not much left by the time it gets here."

They passed Scotts Bluff and, as the afternoon wore on, Holly could think only of Fort Laramie. People were already talking of reaching the fort. Holly wanted to see Isaac in the worst way, to rush into his arms and hug him for remaking their lives. He had taken a big chance and it had paid off. A lot of people were searching for gold but only a lucky few had succeeded in finding it.

With the sun falling, they camped for the night and Holly called to Justin for help in gathering wood. To pass the time he had consumed himself with a volume dealing with King Arthur that he had found back along the trail.

"I didn't know lands like this existed," he said. "They cover their horses with special saddles and chain coverings to keep them from getting hurt in battle."

Holly hesitated to tell him it was all make-believe. She herself had found dreams in books as a child, and they had been dashed often by her own mother.

"There's a lot of the world out there that we haven't seen," she said.

Justin returned with the wood and Holly built a fire. As she prepared a cut of antelope for the evening meal, she let herself dream of the glorious future she would share with Isaac and their son. Their house would be among the finest built along Last Chance Gulch, a home with a French Gothic flair, the furnishings imported and of the finest quality.

And as for social events, surely the growing culture of a

gold-rich community would demand stage dramas, possibly even opera.

"Ma, are you going to dish me some stew?" Justin asked. "Me and Nozer, we're hungry."

"That's good," Holly said. She watched Justin eat hungrily from the cut of meat, sharing bites with the pup. He was old for his age, having seen a lot of undesirable things during the war, but he had come through it well and would make a fine man.

Learning, Holly realized with pride, was something Justin thrived on. He already read adult literature and easily comprehended it. Though he loved the woods, his future seemed to be of a more sophisticated calling.

"What about Uncle Harlan?" Justin asked when he had finished. "Shouldn't he eat something?"

"You take Nozer and hurry off to bed," Holly said. "You want to be fresh when you meet your pa."

When Justin had gone, Holly shook Harlan awake and got him, grumbling, out from under the wagon.

"Wake up and eat something."

"Why can't you leave me sleep?"

"You need something besides whiskey in your stomach," she said.

Harlan plopped down and crossed his legs in front of the fire. He wiped his nose against a torn and greasy shirtsleeve and leaned over a bowl of stew.

"This don't taste so good."

"Get it down," she said, feeding wood to the fire. "You need it."

"You know," he said, "you're a foolish woman. You think Isaac's going to be at the fort?"

"Why wouldn't he be?"

" 'Cause he's near a dead man, that's why. You ever think of that?"

"Yes, I've thought of it."

"You know, he might be dead and buried by now."

"What is the matter with you? He's your brother."

"Facts is facts." He slurped a mouthful of stew and talked while lines of brown liquid streamed down both sides of his unshaven chin. "And that being the case, I think you ought to write me a note that says if he's dead, I get his half of the claim."

Holly took a moment to recover. "You want me to do what?"

"Write something down that says I got a share in that mine."

"I'm not going to do anything of the kind. That's up to Isaac."

"You ain't listenin'. I said what if Isaac ain't alive no more? If that's the case, then half that claim is rightfully mine. I'm his closest kin."

"We're not going to bury Isaac yet," Holly said angrily. "I won't have you talking that way."

Harlan grunted. "If he's going to die, I got a right to his diggin's, and that's the whole of it."

"Listen, Harlan, I brought you along because Isaac asked me to. No other reason. As far as I'm concerned, you don't deserve anything from anybody."

Harlan threw his bowl of stew to the ground and stood up. "I told Isaac when he was courtin' you that he'd be sorry. He ought to have found a woman who would listen to reason. But, no, he had to go and marry the likes of you. I'm not Isaac and I don't have to put up with your mouth." He turned and stumbled off.

Holly glared into the fire. She had felt like striking him and wondered what would have happened had she given in to her anger. She took a deep breath to calm herself and turned when she heard a voice behind her.

"Ma, you should just keep away from him," Justin said.

"You climb back into the wagon and get to sleep. It's getting late."

"You going after him? You'd better. You know he'll be trouble to somebody. He always is."

"I'll go after him," she said. "Now, go on like I asked."

She followed him to the wagon and helped him in. Nozer, tied inside to a dresser, licked Justin's face as he climbed up.

"I'll be back soon," she said.

Holly began her search for Harlan, checking among the wagons. Soldiers were mingling with the emigrants, discussing the trail ahead, but Harlan wasn't at any of the campfires.

Finally, she discovered a small fire out from the wagons, near the river. Upon approaching, she saw Harlan seated with three emigrant men and a young cavalry soldier. At first none of them noticed her.

"You men don't know what you're getting yourselves into," the soldier was saying. "You wouldn't stand a five-minute fight against Red Cloud."

"We fought in the Rebellion, against Bluebellies like you," one man said.

"You might have fought good," the soldier said, "but you didn't fight Injuns. I heard tales about what's happened on that Bozeman Road. You never heard of such things in your life."

They finally noticed Holly and fell silent.

"Harlan, it's time we turned in," she said. "You and Isaac have a lot to discuss tomorrow."

"Leave me be," Harlan said angrily. "I'm learning things here, and it might do you good to listen in for a spell."

She took a seat on a stump in back of the circle. The men were brimming with plans to reach the gold fields and make their fortunes, caring little about what stood in their way. The soldier could hardly be twenty yet, Holly guessed, yet he appeared more calloused than the others, hardened well beyond his years.

He was huddled in an off-blue overcoat a full size too large. Near one of the buttons on his chest was a neat, round hole with dark stains in the fabric. He looked at Holly quickly, then stared into the fire and blew steam off the top of his coffee.

One of the young emigrant men cleared his throat. He didn't appear to be much over sixteen or seventeen, but he had a thick growth of blond hair and a rugged build.

"As for me, I'm like the others. I ain't afraid of no Injuns," he said. "I wouldn't mind fighting one, just to see what it was like."

"You ain't about to fight just one," the soldier said. "They ride in big bunches, all painted up, and come down on you when you don't know it's going to happen."

"I still ain't scared," the young man said.

Harlan spoke up again, turning to the soldier. "Word is going around that your commander won't guarantee escort from Fort Laramie up the Bozeman Trail. Is that true?"

The soldier shrugged. "I'd be the last to know."

"Well, he'd best change his mind. We don't stand a prayer against Injuns if we got no soldiers to fight for us."

The soldier agreed. "That's why these forts are out here."

"Can't they send soldiers down from Fort Reno or that new Fort Phil Kearny to take us up?" Harlan asked.

"Not likely," the soldier said dryly. "We've all got to have the right orders to go to the outhouse, and in proper order. By the time you waited for the paperwork, it would be Christmas. Take my word for it, you don't want to travel these parts anywhere near Christmas. Injuns or not, this country will kill you."

Harlan spat into the dirt. "I thought there was an army out here to escort us through to Montana. That's what we were told. It sounds like all we get is excuses."

"I've got no say in how things are run," the young soldier said. "I just do what I'm told and get paid damn little for it."

Harlan glared at the soldier. "I don't think you've got the stomach to fight Injuns."

"Harlan," Holly said, "don't make trouble here."

Harlan ignored her. "If I was you I'd hate for people to think I was called a soldier."

The trooper glared at Harlan. "What the hell did you just say?"

"You heard me."

The soldier rose slowly. "Say it again, so I'll have good reason to kick your ass from here to Kingdom Come."

"It's time to go," Holly said. She took her brother-in-law by the shirt and dragged him to his feet.

"Not so fast, lady," the soldier said. "He's going to make an apology."

"Please," Holly begged. "He really doesn't mean it." She tugged on Harlan as he tried to thrash away from her.

A strong voice rose from nearby. "What's going on here? I'd better have a good explanation or I'll put you both under arrest."

Four

A GROUP of soldiers appeared from the shadows, led by their commander. Holly recognized him as Lieutenant Lane Hodges.

She had noticed him back at Fort Kearney, assuming his command and ordering his troops into formation. He was nearly six feet tall and well built, with sandy hair that offset deep blue eyes. The uniform fit him well and she could see why men would want to follow him.

She watched while the lieutenant stood back and surveyed the scene. He told the young soldier to get himself back where he belonged, and told the others it was time for them to return to their wagons.

The lieutenant dismissed the soldiers who had come with him and approached Holly and Harlan. He acknowledged Holly with a slight tip of his hat and turned his attention to Harlan.

"I trust you're headed back to your wagon now, and with no stops along the way."

"You got no call to order me around, you yellow-bellied bastard."

"Have you ever been under military arrest? Ever worn a ball and chain across the prairie?"

"You wouldn't do that."

"Just try me."

Harlan looked to Holly. "Ain't you going to say something?"

"I think you'd better do what he says."

Hodges said, "I'm losing my patience."

Without another word, Harlan started back toward the wagon.

"I'm sorry, Lieutenant," Holly said. "He's not the best-mannered person you'll meet."

She had heard a lot of positive things about Lieutenant Hodges from O'Brian and the emigrants, many of whom had come from the South. He was soft-spoken and courteous to those who needed advice and harsh to those who pushed his patience too far. He wasn't one to flaunt his command; his troops respected him and spoke highly of him, which wasn't always the case among frontier military leaders.

In fact, it was said that Hodges often spoke in behalf of his soldiers, at the risk of annoying his superiors. There were stories of how he argued over orders to move against the Indians when there was no real need, working for a peaceful solution to the problem. There were those who said he had friends in high places, for he usually won all his arguments.

The lieutenant turned to Holly. "May I have a few words with you?"

"Certainly. What about?"

"Your brother-in-law. It's important."

"I think I know what you're going to say."

"Just hear me out," he said.

The lieutenant walked beside her back toward her wagon. "I assume you know who I am," he said, "but I'll make it proper. I'm Lieutenant Lane Hodges, at your service, ma'am."

"I see. I'm Holly Porter, and I'm pleased to meet you."

"Let me say first of all that I'm not going to worry about being called a yellow-bellied bastard," the lieutenant continued. "I fought proudly in the Rebellion and I've had some skirmishes with Indians. So you'll appreciate that I'm not picking on your brother-in-law. But he's headed for real trouble, and soon, if he doesn't stay put at your wagon."

"I'll do the best I can to keep him there. But if he won't listen, I won't be disturbed if you're forced to do your duty."

"I'm glad to hear that." He paused. "I certainly don't want to pry, but I don't know how you put up with him, or why you even allow him in your company."

"My husband will soon tend to him," she said.

"That's good to hear. At least you've got someone to look out for you."

"I've looked out for myself all my life, Lieutenant. Isaac is my husband, not my keeper."

"I meant no offense, ma'am. I'm just not used to seeing a woman hold her own with a drunken man."

"Like I said," Holly told him, "that should end soon."

At the wagon, Hodges tipped his hat. "A pleasure to talk to you."

"I can offer you a cup of coffee before you go back to your men, if you'd care for one."

"Yes, maybe a quick one," he said with a smile. "The nights out here have gotten downright cold. It's going to be an early winter."

"Lord willing, we'll all be someplace warm when the snow flies," Holly said, pouring his coffee. "I believe I have some cream, and just a day old."

"I'll drink it black, ma'am, thank you," he said. "I appreciate the hospitality."

Holly poured herself a cup. "I didn't mean to be short with you, Lieutenant."

"Think nothing of it. I shouldn't have assumed you needed caring for. In fact, I should have known better. You're a brave woman to be out here with a young son, and a troublesome brother-in-law as well."

"I'm meeting my husband at Fort Laramie tomorrow. He'll go with us from there up into Montana Territory. He has a gold claim, and we're going to settle and start a new life."

"I see. There are a lot of folks hoping to make their lives

better up there. It can't come true for all of them. I'm glad to hear your husband has already staked a claim."

"That's how we bought our wagon and supplies," Holly said with pride. "Isaac sent us the gold dust to get ourselves what we needed to make the trip. I just didn't have any idea it would take so long."

"It's a big land out here," Hodges said. "I first saw this place as a kid. My dad was a fur trapper out here until the day he died."

"Your father trapped in the mountains?"

"He trapped beaver from the Missouri clear down to the Gila. Later he guided some Englishmen on a hunt out here and brought me along. That was just after my mother died. I wasn't much older than your son, maybe eleven or twelve. I learned a lot about this country, and I've always been grateful I had the chance. But my dad just didn't want to go back to where people lived in towns. He died just before the war broke out."

"Maybe your father knew mine," Holly said. "My father trapped out here for five years."

He smiled. "There's a good chance. Those men saw a lot of country in those days."

"Did he ever tell you about the Bozeman Road?"

"It wasn't the Bozeman Road back then," Hodges said. "There wasn't a Bozeman or any town when they were out here."

"They say the road is very dangerous," she said. "Do you know anything about an escort?"

"I don't. I wish I could be of more help." He stood up. "I'd best get back to my command." He tipped his hat again. "Thank you for the coffee, and I wish you and your family luck and good fortune."

She stood up with him. "Thank you. And I'm sorry about Harlan. I'm hoping he'll get himself into a better frame of mind once we join my husband."

Hodges passed into the shadows and Holly crawled up into the wagon. She nestled in next to Justin and Nozer, and tucked them both in against the cold night. Out the back end of the wagon, the stars hung in the black sky like far, distant jewels. She watched them and found herself thinking about Lieutenant Hodges.

Of all the men she had met, he somehow touched something deep within her. It wasn't something she could readily understand, but it certainly was something she could feel.

Watching him at the fire and listening to him tell of his past, so similar to hers in many ways, it seemed they had known each other for a long time. She felt momentary guilt; Isaac had never given her such a feeling, and that troubled her.

She had met Isaac when she was eighteen. He was twenty-five and yearning to make a new start somewhere other than Virginia. Isaac's uncle had arranged the meeting with her mother at a holiday dance, as her father had yet to return from the mountains.

Holly's mother had been delighted to hear that Isaac approved of her and would consider marrying her. No one else had come forward, and Holly saw no reason not to marry him. He was considerate, if not talkative, and his family had a reputation as good farmers. Six months after their meeting, she became his wife.

She had learned to love Isaac after a fashion, but he never understood her deepest needs and desires, try as he might. Though he had met her at a dance, they rarely went dancing, and he expected her to learn to work in the field as well as the kitchen, so she could keep the farm going when he was away.

When Justin had been born, he paid no attention to the baby until he was nearly two. "No sense in getting attached unless I'm sure he's going to live," he had said. He had in fact been gone much of the time, looking for a better place to settle.

To him there was always a better place to settle. Holly suspected he had never been a happy person and was likely trying to find happiness somewhere down the road. It had always bothered her to think he couldn't find contentment with her. Now he had found gold, and she hoped that would bring him what he couldn't otherwise seem to find.

Holly turned from the stars and closed her eyes. Fort Laramie was so close, yet still very far away. A lot of things could happen even in the space of just a single day. Even if things went well and they arrived safely, Isaac might be there and he might not. He might be alive and he might not.

The wagons rolled through a foggy dawn. Clouds settled in, obscuring the surrounding hills in mist. The oxen, their breath blowing in clouds, churned along the trail. Holly held the reins, a blanket draped down over her arms to keep her hands shielded from the chill.

Justin rode in the front of the wagon, reading. He spent a considerable part of the morning popping his head out to ask, "Are we there yet?" Holly finally gave up answering him and by noon he was asleep, with Nozer snuggled against his chest.

By late afternoon the clouds began to lift and the rain stopped. Fort Laramie came into view: starch-white buildings around a large parade ground, gleaming in the distance.

Hodges rode up alongside the wagon and enjoyed the view with Holly.

"Quite a sight, isn't it?"

"I'm so glad we're here at last," she said, her anxiety over Isaac mounting.

Justin was sitting next to his mother. He stood up on the wagon seat with Nozer to get a better look, and Holly made him sit down again.

"I just wanted to see if Pa was coming out to meet us. I don't see him, but there's a bunch of *Indians*!"

Hodges chuckled and told Holly about an encampment of Sioux who had come to the fort to prove they weren't hostile, to show they had no association with the Sioux to the north, no connection at all with Red Cloud, whose forces were terrorizing the Bozeman Road.

"You say they're friendly?" Holly asked, noting their dress. "How can you tell the friendly ones from the hostile ones?"

"You can't. Not until they prove themselves."

Hodges rode back to his troops and led the wagons into an encampment just outside the fort. Emigrants from another train of fifty-three wagons already settled in along the river gathered to watch the newcomers' approach.

Harlan, who was walking alongside the wagon, looked up at her. "I hope Isaac ain't here," he said. "Then you'll for sure have to figure on cutting me into the gold claim."

He increased his stride and walked ahead to join some other men headed toward the river.

Holly felt lost. She knew she should be elated for having gotten to Fort Laramie with both herself and Justin in good health, but the thought of not seeing Isaac made her feel strange. She knew that he loved her in his own way and was doing all he could to make a new start, but her feelings for him were changing. Still, he was the only man she had ever known, and the thought of him having died brought tears to her eyes.

She dismissed the notion and credited her worry to Harlan's constant badgering.

She halted her team of oxen in line along the river and began to release them from their traces. The men were beginning to drive the loose livestock out to drink and graze.

Justin stood on the wagon seat, Nozer sitting beside him, peering out toward the fort grounds.

"Can't you hurry?" he said. "Pa's waiting for us."

Holly worked feverishly, her mind on Isaac the entire

time. She looked often toward the fort, hoping that he had noticed their arrival and was headed out to greet them.

But there was no sign of him, and Holly determined to look on the fort grounds. On their way past the wagons, Justin stopped where Harlan was standing with a group of men, sharing a jug of whiskey.

"Uncle Harlan, will you help us find Pa?"

Harlan pushed him away. "I'm busy here. Can't you see that?"

Holly pulled Justin back. "Don't treat him that way," she said angrily. "How many times do I have to ask you?"

"Don't he want to see Pa?" Justin asked as they started for the fort grounds.

"Don't concern yourself," she said.

She held her dress above her ankles as they crossed a short stretch of open grassland to the fort. On the parade ground, soldiers drilled in formation to the calls of their commanders. Men down from the hills—buckskinners and old trappers from a lost era—loitered about.

Holly could visualize her father among men like these. She wished she could have gotten to know him better, but he had come back only a few times during her childhood and she hadn't seen him since she was fifteen. She wondered if he was even still alive.

Justin stared at the mountain men. A large group had gathered in front of the sutler's store, where frontier gossip was passed back and forth between jugs of corn and rye whiskey. Since the coming of the wagons, the sutler was selling as much liquor as he could make or acquire by whatever means available to him.

"Can I talk to some of them?" he asked as he viewed the scene. "They might know something about Pa."

"There's not much chance they'd know your father," she said.

She led Justin past the trappers to a group of travelers who had come from the north. None had seen or heard of Isaac Porter. She moved to other travelers with the same result. No one was of any help. She tried a gathering of soldiers, who shook their heads, telling her there were so many travelers coming through all the time there was no way to keep track of everyone.

She had given up hope when the young soldier who had been with Harlan the previous night stopped her.

"Ma'am," he said, "it might be of help if you'd talk to those buckskinners in front of the sutler's store. I heard one of them say he came clear from Last Chance Gulch."

"I told you, Ma," Justin said.

Holly thanked the soldier and gripped Justin's hand. They hurried over to where five grizzled frontiersmen were grouped around the store's steps.

Justin marveled at their dress—the beads, animal teeth, and bird feathers used to decorate their hats and garments. One of them even wore a necklace made of large seashells.

Centered among them was a chunk of a man, broad as tall, whose smile split a gray beard fringed with white. He wore a faded red woolen cap with the dried bodies of two small birds tied onto the front.

As Holly and Justin approached, he rose to his feet and removed the cap. His eyes took in everything in darting glances.

"A good evening, ma'am," he said. "My name's Burnham Hess. I wasn't certain who you were 'til you got up close. Like as not you'd be Isaac Porter's wife, or would I be wrong?"

"I am," Holly answered. "But how did you know that?"

"Why don't we step over yonder," he said. "I've got some news for you."

She took Justin by the hand and followed the buckskinner to a hitching post, where a small mule stood packed with belongings.

"Do you know Isaac?" she asked impatiently. "Do you have news of him?"

The buckskinner smiled and pulled a bag from the mule's back, searching through it until he found a worn photo that showed Isaac seated on a chair with Justin on his lap. Holly was standing beside him, a hand on his shoulder.

"Ma!" Justin said. "That's our picture!"

Something was wrong, Holly knew. Isaac never parted with that photo. The lower left-hand corner was wrinkled and stained with something dark.

"Oh my God," Holly whispered: She looked into the eyes of the mountain man. "Is that blood? Has something happened to him?"

"That ain't his blood," he said quickly. "I got this picture from old Josh McFarland last night. He said your husband give it to him up at Fort Phil Kearny."

"Isaac's up the trail somewhere? He's alive?"

"I figure he is. But he ain't well. Josh said he took sick and couldn't come down. He wanted Josh to watch for you here and give this to you if'n he saw you. Well, Josh can't do that now. Three nights back he got himself shot up in a card game over at a hog ranch and he told me to see you got this just before he died. That's his blood."

Holly held Justin tightly as she listened, relieved to hear that Isaac was still alive, but wondering where he was.

"When Josh got shot and told me this story about the picture," Burnham Hess continued, "I thought he was just talking out of his head. But when I saw you and the boy, I knew the story was true."

"Thank you so much for your help," Holly said. "Can I pay you something for your trouble?"

"No trouble. Just go north and find your man and live happy."

"What are we going to do now, Ma?" Justin asked as they walked back toward the wagons.

She held the picture in one hand and Justin's hand in the other. "We've got to get up to Fort Phil Kearny."

"When do we go? Tomorrow?"

"I don't know. If we can find Lieutenant Hodges, maybe we can find out about an escort. One way or the other, we'll get there."

Five

HOLLY AND Justin returned to the wagons to find a group of people celebrating their arrival at Fort Laramie. Two men were playing fiddles while people danced on the riverbank. But Holly's thoughts were not festive. Getting started along the Bozeman Road was all she cared about.

Justin pointed to Harlan, standing with a group of soldiers away from the dancing. As they approached, Holly could see there was some kind of trouble.

"Looks like he's in another fight," the boy said.

"You just keep a good hold on Nozer and stay back here with me," she said.

Holly and Justin watched while Lieutenant Hodges and his soldiers broke up a confrontation between Harlan and a Sioux Indian. The Indian was of medium height and very slim. His right jaw, having once been badly broken, was sunken deeply into his face. His arms and legs were covered with red paint, and his hair, long and unkempt, held two black feathers.

Even though the lieutenant and his soldiers were there, Harlan continued to yell insults at the Indian, who though weaving from excessive drink, stood ready to fight.

Nearby, another group of Indians watched with their arms folded, angry over what was taking place.

"Maybe this time Harlan will learn something," Holly said.

"He ain't one to learn too fast," Justin said.

They continued to watch as Lieutenant Hodges positioned

his soldiers and stepped between Harlan and the Indian. He took Harlan by the arm and pulled him away.

"Why are you taunting him to fight?" Hodges asked.

"I told you before," Harlan said, "I don't have to listen to no yellowbelly."

"You'll talk to me or find yourself in the stockade," the lieutenant warned.

"You can't do that. I ain't in your army."

"Talk to me or go to the stockade. It's your choice."

Harlan pointed to the tall Indian. "He wants to fight. So I'll fight him."

"No," Hodges said, "you won't fight him."

One of the Indians who had been watching stepped forward. He spoke to Hodges in English.

"My friend, the tall one named Bad Face, gave this man a gun for some whiskey. This man broke his word and didn't come back with more whiskey."

"More whiskey?" Hodges said.

"Yes," the Sioux said. "He already gave Bad Face some whiskey. Bad Face gave him the gun to get more."

"That's a lie," Harlan said.

"No lie," the Indian said, and moved back with his group.

Hodges used sign language to speak to the tall Indian. "Did this man give you whiskey?"

"Yes," he answered. "I, Bad Face, swear it's true."

Hodges turned to Harlan. "Do you know what can happen to you for supplying liquor to Indians?"

"You going to believe them over me?"

"Yes, I am."

Harlan looked away and then toward the crowd that had gathered to watch. "I don't know anything about no liquor."

"What about the rifle?"

"I don't know about no rifle, neither."

"I don't have time to find out the truth here," Hodges said. "This is my last warning. If I find you involved in any more trouble while I'm around, you're going to the stockade. No questions asked, you're going to be locked up. You understand?"

Harlan opened his mouth to protest, but thought better of it and took a step back. He turned around quickly and stomped away.

"What about my rifle?" Bad Face asked.

"I'll look into it," Hodges said.

Bad Face turned to stare after Harlan, still weaving, holding the handle of his knife.

Hodges quickly made sign. "Don't go after him. I'll get your rifle back."

As everyone moved from the scene, Justin tugged on Holly's dress.

"Look at this, Ma. Look what Nozer found. Is it gold?"

The boy was holding a small buckskin bag he had found in the dust. He noted that it was tied together securely at the top. Curious, he loosened the strings and opened it.

Bad Face noticed and rushed for him but stumbled and fell. He began to crawl toward Justin on his hands and knees.

"Justin, wait!" Hodges yelled.

Justin had already opened the bag and was dumping its contents into his hand. What he discovered startled him and he spilled the items onto the ground.

The boy bent down and picked up a small bird's head, two smooth, reddish-colored stones, and four small feathers. Bad Face lunged and Justin dropped the bag and items, and hurried to his mother's side.

Bad Face picked up the small buckskin bag, singing a high-pitched chant while he fumbled to place the items back inside.

"What are those things?" Holly asked Hodges.

"It's his medicine. Sacred articles given to him for protection in battle. Didn't your father ever discuss with you the things he learned in the mountains?"

"No, my mother wouldn't allow it," she said. "She was angry that he taught me to shoot the Hawken. Why is that Indian so angry?"

"It's an insult to handle sacred items."

"It couldn't have hurt anything," Holly said.

"In his mind, a lot of damage was done," Hodges said. "He no longer feels safe in battle."

He explained that Bad Face had been exiled from his band of Sioux for accidentally running down one of the chief's sons with his horse. The boy had lingered through the night and died the following morning.

"The chief spared his life but banished him from the tribe. Now, with this, he's liable to believe that the spirits aren't protecting him any longer."

Harlan had returned and was standing to one side, watching with interest. The other Indians moved forward toward Bad Face, who clutched the bag to his breast, glaring at Holly and Justin.

"He looks like he wants to kill us," Holly said.

"That's exactly what he wants to do," Hodges said.

The lieutenant ordered his soldiers into formation and held up his hand in peace toward Bad Face.

"What's going to happen?" Justin asked his mother.

"Don't worry," Holly said. "The lieutenant will handle it."

Hodges turned to Bad Face, speaking further in sign. Bad Face glared at Hodges and shook a fist at him.

"I told him to keep his medicine bundle in a safer place from now on," Hodges told Holly. "He didn't like to hear that."

"Would you apologize to him for us? God knows we meant no harm."

"What's done is done," Hodges said.

Suddenly Bad Face hurried over to Holly and Justin. He pointed at Justin and made a sign to Hodges.

"Just shake your head no," Hodges said. "And don't stop.

He wants to take Justin to the chief in exchange for the boy he killed."

Holly shoved Justin behind her. Bad Face reached for Justin but Hodges grabbed his arm. He pulled away from Hodges and stormed off, the others following.

"The only way he would make peace with you is if you gave him Justin," Hodges said.

"You wouldn't expect that of me, surely?"

"Of course not. Bad Face is a renegade and has always been trouble. He shouldn't have lost his medicine bundle in the first place."

"Will he make more trouble for you?" Holly asked.

"Probably. But things can't get much worse than they already are."

Bad Face and his followers vanished in the night and Holly saw no sign of him the following day. She turned her attention to organizing a wagon train headed north. Burnham Hess, the old buckskinner, said he would go, as he wanted to try his hand in the gold fields. But most of the emigrants had decided to join a train that had arrived from Denver that morning, on its way to Oregon.

"I'm sorry, Mrs. Porter," O'Brian said. "I can't in good conscience take people through Red Cloud's hunting grounds now, since he's been on the prod. It's worse than I thought. Besides, winter's soon to cover that country with snow."

"We've got to go on," Holly said. "We've come so far."

"There's another bunch of wagons due in from Denver in a couple of days," O'Brian said. "The word is they're headed up the Bozeman Road no matter what."

Two days later an even twenty wagons arrived on the Overland Trail. They also had plans to reunite with relatives in the gold fields and wanted to reach Montana Territory before the harsh weather set in. Holly and five other wagon parties joined them. They all believed that with a cavalry escort, the chances of a Sioux attack would be diminished greatly. Only after Holly talked with Hodges at length did he go to his commanding officer for orders to lead the wagons.

"You got your wish," Hodges told her that evening. "I have orders to take you up the trail."

"You don't know how much I appreciate it," Holly said.

"Still," Hodges said, "if I were you, I'd consider going south, down the front range of the Rockies to LaPorte, on the Cache la Poudre River, and waiting out the winter there. You can travel the Bozeman Road next spring."

"Spring is not an option, Lieutenant. I intend to join my husband as soon as possible."

"I think you should reconsider. You and the others are putting yourselves in a lot of danger."

"I thought you said you had already been given orders to take us."

"I think my commander was worried that you and the others would go whether or not you had an escort."

"We talked about it," Holly said.

"There's another reason he gave me the orders," Hodges said. "There's not enough provisions here at the fort to keep all the wagons over the winter. That's why I'm suggesting you head south."

"North is where we're going, Lieutenant."

"Begging your pardon, but you're a hard-headed woman, Mrs. Porter."

"I have to be," she said, "or I'd never make it in this world."

That evening, as she prepared the evening meal, she considered the upcoming journey. There would certainly be dangers, especially the Indians, whom everyone talked about endlessly. She wondered if they wouldn't be a bother no matter how many wagons there were. She hoped they might be off hunting or stay away because of Hodges's soldiers.

Burnham had decided to go along, to "see the gold roll off the hills," as he put it. It made Holly feel better, somehow, knowing that he was going along.

Harlan, more of a bother than a concern, crossed her mind. She wondered where he had gone and if he would return drunk again.

She turned her thoughts to Isaac, wondering if he would still be alive when they reached Fort Phil Kearny. Maybe he had already passed on. It left her wondering what she would do if he had, and how Justin would take it.

She had wondered about Justin all during the meal. Something hadn't been quite right, yet she hadn't been able to put her finger on it.

Now she realized the difference. Justin was without Nozer, highly unusual for him.

"Where's your puppy?" she asked.

"I gave him away."

"You *what?*"

"There was a boy and girl about my age who came in with the Denver folks. They told me they'd lost their ma to sickness on the trail. I figured Nozer might help them some. He took right to them. I think they'll feel better now."

She sat down beside him. "That was a brave thing to do."

"I figure they need him more than I do."

"We'll get you another dog just as soon as we get to the gold fields," Holly said, an arm around his shoulder.

"It'll be kind of hard to sleep without him to snuggle with and all."

A voice from behind said, "I'd bet my last penny some warm milk might just help that."

They turned to see a plump, middle-aged woman walk into the light of the fire, carrying a pitcher of steaming milk.

She wore a blue print dress with a large rosary around her neck. Her smile covered her broad cheeks and her blue eyes sparkled like jewels. Liberal streaks of gray twined through red hair fashioned into a bun on the top of her head.

"My name's Tillie McGivern," she said. "I'm aunt to the lad and lass your wonderful son gave his puppy to. A right manly thing to do."

"Happy to meet you," Holly said. "My name is Holly Porter and this is my son, Justin."

"Good to meet you, and you as well, Justin," she said. "You're a right fine lad."

He smiled. "Thank you for saying so, ma'am."

"If you'd care to, you can call me Aunt Tillie. For what you did to help Jenny and Jeb, I feel a wee bit like kin already. How did you come to be such a brave lad, giving your own dog away and all?"

Justin shrugged. "I just figured it was the right thing to do."

"Well, God bless your soul, so it was." She held out the pitcher. "If you got a cup I'll fill it for you."

He held up his cup. Accustomed to water mostly, he found the warm milk a treat.

"I remember that I saw you with Jenny and Jeb after I gave Nozer to them," he said. "They feeling better now?"

"Much better. They'll do fine with that dog. I don't know about their pa, though. He's taking it awfully hard."

"I'm sorry to hear that," Holly said.

Tillie McGivern went on to explain that the children's father was her only brother and that his wife had fallen to consumption a week north of Denver.

"I told her she wasn't strong enough to make the trip, the poor lass," Tillie said. "But she said she was every bit as strong as Giles. That's my husband." She fingered her rosary. "He's in a bad way himself. Consumption as well. But he says he wants to lay a pan into a stream full of gold before he meets his Maker. God bless him, I hope he can." She held her rosary tightly and brushed a tear from her cheek.

"It'll be a hard go," Holly said. "But if we all keep together, we'll make it."

"That's the way I see it," Tillie said. She set the pitcher of milk down, then reached into her apron pocket and produced a small, flutelike instrument. "And I intend to make things as merry as I can along the way."

Tillie withdrew a pennywhistle, as she called it, with notched holes in a slender wooden stem.

"I learned to play it from an older brother, who didn't make it across the big ocean," she said. "God rest his dear soul."

She began playing "The Irish Washerwoman," bobbing her head as the notes flowed out. Justin watched wide-eyed.

"Maybe you'd care to learn, lad?"

Justin smiled. "I sure would."

"I'd be glad to teach you along the way." She stuffed the whistle back into her pocket and picked up the milk pitcher. "More?"

"One more cup." He noticed his mother's stare. "Please."

After filling the cup, Millie said, "I'd best get back to Giles. He can't be for long without me, the poor man."

"If there's anything we can do to help," Holly said, "don't be afraid to ask."

"I thank you, I do," Tillie said. "We'll be talking along the trail, I'm sure."

"Yes, we will," Holly said. "It was good to meet you."

Justin saluted with his cup. "Thanks for the milk."

Holly settled the boy into the wagon and he quickly fell asleep. She had just placed new wood on the fire when Lieutenant Hodges approached.

"I've got two cottonwood stumps to sit on and a little coffee left," she said. "Be my guest."

"I don't want to sound improper," he said, "but I enjoy your company. You're easy to talk to."

"Thank you for saying so. I find you to be a gentleman. And though you wear the uniform well, I don't see you as a soldier."

"You're very observant," Hodges said. "It doesn't fit me well. After the war I thought that I might further myself, but I'm beginning to think that I don't follow directions well enough to climb the ladder."

"The army's filled with a lot of silly rules," Holly said. "I know that for a fact."

"A lot of rules that could cause disaster," the lieutenant said. "I've got a set of instructions for every occasion and I'm obliged to follow them to the letter, no matter what."

"What if the occasion calls for something different?"

"The army believes *all* occasions are covered in their regulations."

"And what if you chose to make a different decision?"

"Then I could be court-martialed." He peered out into the night. "I saw a good friend of mine hang for making a decision that saved a lot of lives. He was supposed to charge an enemy position, but they knew he was coming. He chose to wait until the following morning, hoping for reinforcements. The enemy left and when the commanding officer arrived, my friend was tried on the spot for cowardice and desertion."

"What kind of commanding officer would try a man for saving lives?"

"The officer's name was Custer, George Armstrong Custer. He'd better hope I never catch him alone somewhere."

"So why did you stay with it? Why didn't you take a discharge and do something else?"

"I had hoped to make a difference out here," the lieutenant replied. "I thought I could take a command and make my own decisions. But that's not the way it works."

"You sound bitter."

"I'm sorry, but I can't help it. I was promised two companies of cavalry to escort this train. Earlier today I was told that I would get one, and not to argue about it."

"What happened to the other company?"

"They're being detailed to another command. It seems a senator from Washington sent his niece and her family up from Denver to follow the Oregon Road. That way is not nearly as dangerous, yet they're sending four times as many troops as they gave me."

"Are you saying that you don't think we ought to go ahead?"

"That's about it, Mrs. Porter. I'd advise against it."

"The others are every bit as anxious to get up the trail as I am," Holly pointed out.

"It's likely you could talk them out of it."

"I don't believe that. As you already know, there are those who'll go without an escort."

Hodges studied her. "I presume you're still among them?"

"You presume correctly, Lieutenant."

"It will be an experience you won't forget."

"It already has been. A few more hardships won't mean the end of things."

Hodges stood up. "I hope not, Mrs. Porter. I certainly hope not."

Six

AT DAWN they began their journey north along the Bozeman Road, a set of wagon ruts that crossed the open plains and foothills, twisting through draws and winding up steep slopes, across creeks and flats covered with salt.

The Bozeman was the home of wind and sagebrush, of soil that when wet stuck to the wagon wheels in clumps. The evenings brought on a deep chill and clouds gathered in huge formations over the distant mountains, laying heavy snows atop the peaks.

Despite the awesome distance ahead, the settlers seemed eager. Many sang songs as the wagons rolled; Tillie McGivern could be seen driving her team of oxen with one hand and fingering the beads of her rosary with the other, her lips moving in prayer, while in the wagon her husband coughed incessantly. In the evenings, she would sit beside her wagon and play her pennywhistle. Everyone believed she hoped it would bring new life back into Giles, that maybe the music would stir him and he would throw off his sickness.

One night Justin asked her to teach him a tune. After three full days of practice, he was able to play a few lyrical notes in succession.

"You keep with it, lad," Tillie told him. "One day you'll play with the best of 'em."

They passed the Natural Bridge and, at the end of the small Laramie Range, reached the North Platte River. A ferry took the wagons over and the men swam the herds, chilling themselves in the cold water. There was no time for drying out and they moved onward to the fork where the Mormon Road broke off to the west, toward Salt Lake City.

Here they stopped at a trading post for provisions. French Pete's crude log shed held—among many other things—tack for the horses and grease for the wagons. His only rule: No one was to speak English.

Burnham Hess and Hodges both communicated in sign, assuring him there was no need to worry.

"He's afraid of the Sioux," Hodges explained to Holly later. "He says there was a group of renegades through here the other day and they warned him about trading with whites. He's even married to a Sioux woman."

"Even with the new forts along the trail, there's need for worry?" Holly said.

"There's need for worry *because* of the forts," Hodges said. "A peace commission was sent out from Washington to Fort Laramie to get the Sioux and Cheyenne to allow wagons across their hunting grounds. They brought beads and guns and all kinds of gifts. Right in the middle of the peace ceremony, what should show up but an army of soldiers coming out to build forts."

"So, naturally, that enraged the Indians," Holly said.

"Of course. One of them stood up and said his people were being made fools of. 'You bring us offerings of peace,' he said, 'but you send soldiers at the same time to force us to your wishes.' I can't say as I blame them for being angry."

"It seems like you're in the wrong profession," Holly said.

"That's the way I see it." Hodges contemplated. "Maybe after I get back to the fort I'll resign and start over."

"Start over?"

"Maybe become a peace officer, a U.S. marshal or something. That will give me the authority to make my own decisions for a change."

"I don't think you'd make a marshal," Holly said. "You're not hard enough."

"What do you mean?"

"Most peace officers I know would have thrown Harlan in irons the first time he caused trouble. I'm not saying you're not fair, as you gave him another chance. I'm just saying that men with authority are usually hard cases."

"I can be hard when I want to," he said. "There may come a time when you'll see just how hard I can be."

The Bozeman Road led on over endless sagebrush hills and past spires of rock sculpted by the relentless wind. Holly saw each uneventful day as a blessing, bringing them that much closer to finding Isaac. She and Justin watched the sun rise, opening the day's warmth, and watched it set, huddling against the evening chill. They watched geese fly over and the last of the meadowlarks trill from their perches atop rocks and tree stumps.

Harlan complained continually. To keep him quiet, Holly allowed him to sleep in the wagon during the day, as Justin preferred to be out most of the time. When it rained, all three would sit under the canvas, Harlan in sullen silence.

"I wish he'd stayed back at the fort," Justin told his mother one evening. "He ain't no good for nothing."

"Watch your tongue, Justin. It does no good to talk bad about anybody, no matter what you think."

Two days from the South Fork of the Powder River, the weather turned unusually mild; the wind stilled and the sun shone warmly. Everyone enjoyed the reprieve.

As they neared the South Fork bottom, Burnham, who had been riding out ahead as a scout, returned with news that sparked excitement along the entire train.

"Buffalo!" he said. "A big herd."

The wagons pulled forward and topped a rise. Below,

across the open valley, spread a huge mass of brown and black. Burnham proclaimed it the biggest herd he had seen in years and wondered at its size.

"You don't see herds like that so close to the trail," he told Holly and Justin. "Most of them have been run off from here. That's why the Sioux are so ornery."

Holly leaned back into the wagon. "Harlan, wake up. You need to see something."

"What?" he asked groggily.

"Buffalo. A huge herd."

"Leave me to sleep," Harlan said. "I don't care about no damned buffalo."

"You likely won't ever see anything like it again," Holly said.

"You hear me? I don't give a damn."

"Why don't you go out and ride one of them?" Justin said. "I'd like to see that."

"You shut up, boy. You hear?"

"He's only funning you, Harlan," Holly said. "What can a little fun hurt?"

"Just keep him shut up."

They watched the herd for a good part of the afternoon, waiting for the animals to move on. But they continued to graze up and down the valley, blocking the trail.

Tillie McGivern came over to Holly's wagon, holding her rosary tightly.

"I'd love to have Giles see this," she said. "But he's taken right sickly, the poor man."

"Anything I can do?" Holly asked.

"Say a prayer for him. He'll be needing all of them he can get."

Late in the afternoon, clouds rolled over the mountains and brought heavy thunder.

Harlan looked out of the wagon. "Those the buffalo? What's the big deal?"

"Have you ever seen anything so beautiful before?" she said. "Look at them, a sea moving across the grassland."

"Don't matter to me one way or another," Harlan said. "We've got gold to find. No sense sitting here." He yelled for the lieutenant.

Hodges rode over. "What is it, Harlan?"

"You should be doing your duty."

"My duty?"

"Yeah. Move those buffalo."

"Nothing can move them until they want to move themselves," Hodges said.

Harlan pointed into the hills. "It's bound to rain soon. We've got to get going."

"All the better reason to sit tight," Hodges said. "With lightning and thunder, no telling what the herd might do."

Harlan left the wagon and began roving among the other emigrants, talking up the idea of moving on. He got three wagons to pull out of formation and begin to advance across the bottom toward the buffalo.

One of them, a young settler named Kestler, invited Harlan up on the seat next to his pregnant wife.

Hodges rode up to them. "Where do you think you're going?"

Kestler glared. "Harlan's right. We've got to keep moving. Besides the gold, I don't want my wife having our baby on the trail."

"You should have thought about that before you came out here," the lieutenant said. "You can't go across that bottom. Not yet."

Harlan yelled, "You've got no right to do this!"

"I've given you your last warning," Hodges said. He called the sergeant forward. "Place this man under arrest and tie him up."

Harlan bolted from the wagon seat and ran down into the

bottom toward the buffalo, yelling and waving his hands in the air. The herd turned and broke into a run, thundering through the sage and greasewood. A number of them broke off, coming dangerously close to the wagons, but when the dust had settled, they were again grazing peacefully in the far distance.

Harlan stood at the stream bank, yelling for everyone to hear.

"I did it! I did it!"

"You going to arrest him now?" Kestler asked Hodges.

"I should."

Burnham Hess, who had joined Hodges during the stampede, shook his head.

"God protects fools, and that's a natural fact."

With the sun nearing the horizon, the wagons started across the bottom. Overhead, lightning flashed and the rain began to fall in large drops. Holly and Justin pulled out of line to help Tillie McGivern with her husband, who was having a coughing fit.

"I don't know what to do for him," Tillie was saying. She held a towel over her husband's mouth while he coughed blood. Finally exhausted, he fell back.

Hodges arrived and asked about the holdup. "You can't stay here," he said, pointing into the hills. "There's a big thunderstorm up there."

"Giles McGivern is very ill," Holly said.

"Get on out of here," Hodges said. "We'll tend to him up above."

Holly and Justin went back to their wagon while Tillie urged her oxen out of the bottom and up onto the hillside. Holly followed at a distance, the last wagon.

While crossing the creek, the right front wheel hit a sharp

hole. The axle popped and the wheel tilted sideways. The front of the wagon fell awkwardly and Justin had to clutch the seat to keep from falling out.

The oxen jumped in their traces, pulling the wagon nearly onto its side. They pulled to exhaustion and stood with their heads down and their sides heaving.

Thunder rolled overhead as Holly eased down into the current. She released the oxen from their traces and they stumbled out of the stream.

"Hand me the rifle and my bag of dresses," she called to Justin. "We've got to save a few things."

Suddenly the sky opened up and rain poured in torrents. From the hills above came the sounds of rushing water.

"Get down from there and run for it," Holly yelled, pulling the boy into her arms.

"What about you, Ma?"

"I'll be right behind you. Now, go. Go!"

Justin struggled through the rising water to shore, Holly right behind him. The water from the hills began to descend upon them, pushing the creek to overflowing. They struggled through the bottom, the water gaining on them steadily.

"Ma! We can't make it!" Justin yelled.

"Keep going!" she screamed. "Keep running!"

Through the downpour, Holly watched as Burnham and Hodges rode off the hill and into the bottom. Justin pulled himself up behind Burnham and they set off toward higher ground. The water had now reached them and the roiling current threatened to drag Holly off her feet.

Hodges rode up to Holly, fighting to control his horse. "Grab my hand!" he shouted.

Holly reached but fell. She pulled herself up, struggling through the mud toward Hodges's horse. The pony sidestepped and she fell again.

"Steady!" Hodges told the horse. "Steady, now!"

With the water rising, Holly grabbed the lieutenant's hand,

but slipped from his grasp a third time. She fought to regain her feet, the rain coming in sheets, obscuring her vision.

Then Hodges was there again, steadying his horse. Holly lunged and clutched a stirrup with both hands, holding on tightly as he pulled her to safety.

Behind, the water rushed through the bottom, swallowing the wagon and dragging it downstream.

On the hill, Justin ran to Holly's arms.

"You all right, Ma?"

"I'm fine, Justin. Thank God you're safe."

"We lost everything. Even my book."

"We'll get you another book," Holly said. "We'll get you as many as you'd like."

Harlan stood nearby, pointing at her. "Look what you've gone and done," he yelled.

Holly ignored him and thanked Hodges and Burnham for their efforts. Tillie McGivern, her bonnet on tight against the last remnants of the storm, approached.

"I'd be pleased to offer you room in my wagon, being as there's one less of us now."

Holly wiped muddy water from her face. "What? Is it Giles?"

"He passed away at the top of the hill," she said.

Holly held her as she sobbed. "I'm so sorry."

Tillie dried her eyes. "It was for the best. He's not suffering now. He'll rest easy in the Lord's arms."

They found a suitable burial spot along the side of a hill, between two junipers, where the soil was loose and not as muddy as in the bottom. Burnham, who had buried a number of good friends, quoted a passage he remembered from the Bible, the passage about ashes to ashes, dust to dust. Then, in the twilight, Holly helped place a wooden cross over the mound of dirt and stood back while Tillie wrapped her rosary around the cross and stood up.

"I've said a good plenty of prayers with those beads on

his behalf," she said. "He gave them to me at the altar, the day we were married. It's best if they stay with him."

As darkness settled in, Tillie took firewood from her wagon and they sat in a circle around the coveted flames, eating warm stew. Holly had removed her ruined dress and now wore a hat and a pair of Giles's boots and some of his clothes. They fit well, as Tillie's husband had been a very small man.

"Don't you go gawking at her, now," Tillie told the others. "Unless one of you has a dress for her, she'll make do with what I've got."

Harlan stared at her for a time and walked off into the darkness.

"I think you look good, Ma," Justin said. "Now you can ride a horse better."

Holly laughed. "I feel like I belong in clothes like these, strange as that sounds."

"You've had to do a man's part ever since you started out here," Tillie said.

Later, as the group broke up to retire for the night, Hodges told Holly, "You're right. That outfit seems to suit you fine. But, then, you'd look good in just about anything."

Seven

THE WAGON people called Montana Territory the Promised Land and believed it was filled with gold and glory. But the road getting there seemed like hell itself.

As they neared the army post called Fort Reno, there had been nothing but continuous rain and bogs filled with mud. Nights of heavy frost and biting winds that slid down off the mountains were daily indications that snow would soon come.

Holly and Justin rode with Tillie, Holly taking her turn with the oxen. Harlan had taken to riding with the young settler Kestler and his pregnant wife, "the only others here of a sane mind," as he put it.

They stayed at Fort Reno but one day. The post, little more than log buildings dirt-packed by driving winds, sat on a high bench overlooking the Powder River. Holly listened to soldiers talk about their homes and how boring their lives were. They spoke about getting away from their isolated quarters, even if it meant having their lives threatened chasing Indians.

Hodges told her that the fort was manned by Confederate soldiers taken from Union prison camps during the war. "They were given the choice of either rotting away or coming out here to fight Indians," he explained. "They're called 'Galvanized Yankees' by some, and 'Whitewashed Rebs' by others. Either way, they don't like being here."

Holly wondered momentarily why they hadn't deserted, but after gazing across endless miles of desolation, where the

Sioux waited in ambush, she realized that staying within the fort walls would be a better choice.

"What's the chances of getting some of them to join your soldiers?" she asked Hodges.

"I already checked on that. They're shorthanded here as it is. The commanding officer is not about to part with a single trooper."

"That means we go ahead with what we have," Holly said.

"Yes, but the hardest part is just ahead."

They left the following morning, making slow time through the rocky foothills. In the far distance stood the top of the Bighorn Mountains. At their summit rose Cloud Peak, as Burnham pointed out. "I crossed that way a few times, when I hunted beaver," he told Holly and Justin. "It's a pretty place up there."

Justin lamented the loss of his book but felt fortunate at not having lost his life. He passed the time with Tillie Mc-Givern, learning tunes on the penny whistle. Evenings found him playing along the creeks, the sound carrying out across the plains.

Though the going was hard, nothing threatened them, and Holly hoped the peace might last. Then near the upper reaches of Crazy Woman Creek they came upon the charred remains of a previous wagon train. Little remained of the victims, for the attack had taken place some time in early summer. Still, it was obvious they had been cut to pieces, their arms and legs hacked off and left for the wolves.

Hodges called a halt to bury the remains, a detail that lasted the rest of the day. As the sun dropped, many began to believe they had made a mistake in leaving Fort Laramie. Emigrants and soldiers clustered together around fires, arguing their concerns. Even Tillie's penny whistle couldn't calm any nerves.

With Justin taking a lesson from Tillie, Holly left the circle of wagons and walked down to the creek to watch the sunset. She sat on a log and listened to the rushing water, thinking of Tennessee.

Before meeting Isaac, she had spent her time learning what she could from books, reading by lantern. During the day she often took long walks in the woods, nurturing herself beside springs and flowing streams, listening to the birds and watching the deer.

Her mother frowned on her journeys. "You're just like your pa, through and through," she often said. "Always wandering off to nowhere." Holly often thought about Elam, her younger brother, who had died of influenza as a small boy. She realized how much her mother missed him by the remarks she would make. "He's the one who should have been the woodsman," she often told Holly. "Not you."

They had all shared sorrow over Elam's death. Holly wondered if that hadn't been what had driven her father into the mountains for such long periods of time, leaving her mother at home to try and teach her a woman's ways.

Perhaps, Holly thought, that was why her mother had been so anxious to marry her off, so she wouldn't have to worry any longer about long trips into the woods. "A good wife stays at home and cares for her man" were her words.

Though she had never felt anything deep for Isaac, they had always enjoyed the same things. Riding horseback along the Tennessee River used to be a favorite pastime. But during their rides he never seemed intent on her, just what lay ahead in the distance.

She had gotten used to his aloofness over the years and, she believed, had actually come to love him. She owed him a great deal for providing for her and Justin. Though meager, it had been enough. And now, with gold in his hands, he would be a happy man to greet.

She hoped there would be a big river where they were

going in Montana, one with broad banks good for sitting and watching sunsets. It was the only thing in the world that gave her peace of mind. Everything about war and death and dying could be put in the background while the day ended on a beautiful note.

Behind her the night brought arguments out from camp while here the breeze rustled loose the few remaining gold leaves from the giant cottonwoods. They fell as huge soft flakes that twisted circles in the breeze and settled in piles along the water's edge. Besides the Indian threat, there was no question the land was closing down on them and would soon trap them in frozen days and nights.

She had a lot to consider now, since losing everything in the flash flood. Her future now lay in the hands of Tillie Mc-Givern and the others. She would make it, as she always had, and she would have Justin beside her. But it wouldn't come as easy as she had hoped.

The sun fell in a blaze of cold crimson, giving her a little fulfillment. She made her way back to the wagons, where the discussions concerning the future of the train had become more heated. Hodges stood near a gathering of men, making certain that the arguments didn't break out into fights.

She reached Tillie's wagon and found Justin at the fire, toying the coals with a stick. She sat down beside him and drew him close to her.

"Where's Aunt Tillie?" she asked.

"She said she had to say a prayer for her husband, and asked me to go to bed."

"I see you didn't take her advice."

"I can't sleep."

"You need the rest," she said.

"All them folks want to turn back," he said. "We ain't going to, are we, Ma?"

"We'll have to see what they decide," she said.

"We don't have to follow them. Pa wouldn't want us to."

"I want to see him as badly as you, but we can't do it alone."

"I've never heard you talk that way before."

"We have to realize that we've too much to face out here. We'll find your pa in the spring."

Tears rose in Justin's eyes. "I'll go it alone if I have to."

Holly turned as footsteps approached. Justin quickly wiped away his tears. Burnham Hess appeared from the shadows.

"Good to find a fire where nobody's fightin' and screamin'," he said. "That coffee of yours can sure drift to a man's nose."

"Have a seat," Holly said. "You're welcome."

Justin made room beside the fire while Holly filled a tin cup with coffee. Burnham took it with a weathered hand and slurped a mouthful, then set the cup down and rubbed his hands together.

"This sure ain't Californy," he said.

"You've been there?" Justin asked. He had heard a lot of people discussing California, where there had been a gold rush nearly twenty years before.

"I've seen the likes of it all," Burnham said, his eyes flashing in the firelight. "From Frisco all the way down. Put a pick or a pan in every hill and stream. Yep, I filled a poke or two in my day."

Justin shifted himself to get a better look at the man. This was the first time he had sat and listened to him.

"Are you after gold again?"

Burnham laughed. "Ain't we all? I hear them Montaner hills is solid nuggets. A man just has to bury his pick and they roll out like marbles. Yep, I'd say we'd all like a taste of that. That is, if Red Cloud don't take our hair for lodge fixin's."

"You figure he'd scalp us?" Justin asked.

"Sure as the day you were born, if he caught you."

"I ain't scared," the boy said. "Red Cloud and the rest of them Sioux won't come at us with you and Lieutenant Hodges with us."

"I'd like to think that myself, son, but I'm none too sure of it."

"Justin," Holly said, "it's time for bed."

"It's not that late."

"We have a hard day ahead. Now, scoot."

Justin reluctantly left the fire and climbed into the wagon. Holly leaned closer to Burnham.

"What do you really think our chances are of getting through?"

Burnham sipped his coffee. "Slim to none, for what I think. Not many of these folks can travel hard and bear up. Just you and Justin, and maybe a few others. If there was a lick of sense left in my old brain, I'd have stayed back at Laramie for the winter."

"I've been talking to the lieutenant," Holly said. "He says we might have some advantages."

"What might they be?"

"I understand Indians won't fight if they think they'll lose a lot of their men. Is that right?"

"They don't like to lose their own, no."

She felt a surge of confidence. "We're somewhat small in number but we've got guns and men that can use them. Besides, there's the soldiers."

Burnham wiped his chin. "Those soldiers boys don't worry them as much as we do. That lieutenant can handle men and he might have caught your eye, but he's never fought the likes of Red Cloud's Sioux."

"I'm a married woman, Mr. Hess," Holly said.

"Yeah, I just meant he's a kind sort, is all," Burnham said. "I meant nothing more by it."

"I'm sure you didn't," Holly said.

"I just hope them soldiers can fight." Burnham's tone was serious and his quick smile had vanished. "I'll tell you, times have changed. Way back, I trapped among Blackfeet mean as hell and got by Utes on the Bonneville. There was 'Paches and Comanches down south, just as bad. Back then a man could save his hair by maybe a trick or standing up to them with gall showing in his eyes. They thought a man had medicine back then. Not no more. These Injuns want their hunting grounds back. No talk. No parley. No tricks. They're out to kill, and that's the whole of it."

"How do you know all this?"

"I had a Sioux wife for a spell. She took sick and died, so I left the village. I learned a lot while I was among them."

Holly remained hopeful. "Maybe we can make it to Fort Phil Kearny and wait the winter out there."

"Not a good idea either," Burnham said. "Kearny's smack dab in the middle of Sioux hunting grounds and they'll be on the back porch all winter. Nobody can keep 'em away."

"But I heard the fort has field cannons," Holly said. "Is there really any concern about an attack?"

"There's a few things you ain't thought of," Burnham said. "The Sioux will make it tough all winter at Kearny, what with stopping supply trains from coming through and all. And they'll make it tough on woodcutters going out from the fort. It won't be an easy time there."

Holly realized that even if they reached Fort Phil Kearny, their troubles would be just beginning. Feeding soldiers and emigrants alike through a long winter would be extremely difficult if not impossible. From his days with a Sioux wife, Burnham thought like an Indian, it occurred to Holly, and he had no doubt listed in his mind everything that was going to happen to this emigrant train from here on out, weighing the odds on what choices should be made.

Burnham finished his coffee. "If we get out of this, I'll be taking no more chances. I'll settle down and leave the fighting to younger men." He rose to his feet. "Get a good night's sleep while you can. Come the next few days, we'll all be awake all the time."

Burnham lost himself in the shadows and Holly finished her coffee. Most of the fires around camp were manned only by soldiers now, sentries on duty, each taking his turn, watching the shadows carefully.

Holly had just lay down in the wagon next to Justin when the pounding of drums sounded in the distance.

"I ain't never heard them at night," Justin said. "Does that mean they aim to come at us in the dark?"

"Burnham says no," she replied. "They dance at night and fight in the early morning."

"How can he be so sure?"

"He knows their ways, son. He was married to one once."

"He said that?"

"Yes, he's had quite a life."

"Maybe he could talk them out of fighting us, then."

"I wish he could," Holly said. "I surely do."

The night wore into a thin film of gray light that gradually grew into a flaming streak across the horizon. To the west, heavy clouds were rolling over the mountains.

Everyone had remained awake during the night, and Hodges had posted his entire command on watch. Holly and Justin stood with Burnham, looking out into the distance, while Tillie McGivern sat on the wagon seat.

Justin blew into his hands to warm them. He pointed out below the base of a hill where a group of riders were hidden in the shadows.

"Indians!"

"You've got a keen eye, son," Burnham said.

"Are they Sioux?" Holly asked.

"Sure as glory be."

Harlan, who had come to eat breakfast, said, "Did I hear something about Injuns? Time for that yellow-bellied lieutenant to earn his keep."

The sun climbed into full view, and twenty warriors eased their horses out into the open. They seemed out for a leisurely morning ride, moving their ponies at a walk through the thick stand of gray sagebrush that plugged the flats above the stream.

"They've got something planned," Burnham said. He studied the hills, eyeing each shadow and stand of trees.

"Do they want to fight us?" Justin asked anxiously.

"I'd say so," Burnham replied. "They ain't dressed for no Sunday social."

Harlan continued to complain, kicking the dirt with his heel. He walked back to the Kestler wagon, mumbling to himself.

"Why'd he take up with that young couple?" Justin asked.

"I don't rightly know," Holly replied. "I guess he feels more kinship with them than us."

The sun rose higher, its light yielding to a heavy mantle of clouds that slid out from the mountains. The warriors continued their slow march down from the hills.

All the emigrants were gathered inside the circle of wagons, watching the Sioux boldly approach the camp. Mothers rushed their children under the wagons while the men checked their rifles and carbines, loading extras and placing boxes of ammunition near the wagon wheels.

Holly held Justin close while Burnham checked his rifle.

"They're mighty brave for a cold morning," he said. "Maybe they figure to soon be warming things up around here."

Tillie McGivern got down from the wagon seat, clutching her husband's rifle.

Harlan, at the Kestler wagon, stood holding a Springfield carbine.

Hodges had his soldiers at the ready, hurriedly tightening saddle cinches and forming their lines.

"I hope he keeps control of those men," Burnham said. "Half of Injun fighting is keeping from getting too anxious."

Eight

THE SIOUX approached to within a long stone's throw of the wagons. Burnham studied them and said that he was certain they were Oglala, a subtribe of the Lakota nation, led by Red Cloud.

The air, now filled with light rain, brought a deep chill to Holly, yet the warriors were stripped to breechcloths and painted for war.

Each warrior had his own individual designs and colors. Most bore combinations of stripes and jagged lines along their legs and upper bodies, and facial bars across their cheeks and foreheads. Nearly every horse was painted similarly.

"Do they mean to fight us?" Holly asked. "Just those few?"

"There's more of them somewhere," Burnham said. "They've got war in their eyes for certain."

"Why are they painted?" Justin asked.

"It's what they do when they get ready to die," Burnham replied. "Each paint mark means something special to the one wearing it. Those jagged lines, that's lightning, to give them speed and strength. There's other meanings for the other designs, too."

Hodges ordered his men to mount and face the advancing line. Young soldiers, their eyes wide with fear, took position as ordered. The Sioux broke into a clamor of shrill war cries, raising their rifles and bows into the air.

"They don't stand a chance against the soldiers and us too," Justin said.

Burnham scratched his scraggly beard. "We'll just wait and see what they do."

Tillie handed her rifle to Holly. "I figure you can use this better than me."

"You going to fight, Ma?" Justin asked.

"You keep your head down, Justin. Hear me?"

"I'll keep down, but you just don't go getting too brave yourself."

"I'm as afraid as I've ever been right now," Tillie said. "I wish I hadn't left the rosary back there with Giles."

The warriors continued to scream at the wagons, their weapons raised. A few of them had broken from the line and were riding their ponies back and forth, shouting oaths.

Justin noticed a length of rope trailing from each warrior's horse, the end formed into a noose.

"That's a special rope for hauling off their wounded in battle," Burnham explained. "They ride by and slip it around a fallen warrior. It means a lot to them to save their dead and wounded from the enemy."

One of the warriors edged his horse toward the line of troops, riding sideways, his right arm hidden behind.

"Watch him close, Hodges," Burnham whispered to himself.

The rain fell harder as the warrior drew closer. Some of the soldiers edged their horses forward.

"Hold the line!" Hodges ordered. "Hold that line firm!"

The warrior drew closer and suddenly reined his horse to a stop. He brought his hidden arm into view, aimed a Springfield carbine at the line of soldiers, and fired.

In the line, a soldier grunted as the slug slammed into his chest. He writhed in the saddle and pitched sideways from his horse.

The warrior turned his pony and, with a loud yell, kicked

it into a run. When he reached the line of Sioux, they all turned and rode hard toward the hills.

Hodges yelled, "Charge!" bringing his saber down. A bugle blared and the column swept out across the bottom after the fleeing warriors, mud and grass flying from the horses' hooves.

The Sioux stayed together in a close group, leading the soldiers into the foothills beyond the bottom.

"Why didn't he leave any of his men with us?" Holly asked.

"I told you," Burnham replied, "he don't know Injuns."

"Maybe he had orders from his superior to give chase to any hostiles."

"It don't matter what his orders were," Burnham said. "Now we're in trouble for certain."

The rain fell harder, pooling on the ground. Two of the emigrants ran to the fallen soldier, where he heaved blood down the front of his uniform.

To the west, the Sioux challengers had disappeared into the hills. The rain and mist had swallowed Hodges and his cavalry. The settlers stood dazed, looking in all directions.

"Damn, he'd best get back here," Burnham spat. "He's left us bare-ass naked as the day we were born."

Harlan was pacing back and forth, cursing the soldiers and Indians both. Kestler and his pregnant wife stood out in the pouring rain, wondering what might come next.

Suddenly the hills to the north came alive with screaming Sioux warriors. They rode full speed toward the wagons, their weapons raised high.

Burnham untied his horse and handed the reins to Holly. "Take your boy and go!"

Harlan quickly ran over and grabbed the reins from Burnham's hand. "I'm taking this horse," he said, starting to mount.

Burnham tried to pull him down but Harlan, seated firmly in the saddle, kicked the old trapper square in the jaw, knocking him to the ground, then whipped the horse into a dead run away from the wagons and oncoming Indians.

Holly tried to revive Burnham, but he wouldn't move.

"Is he dead?" Justin asked.

"He's just knocked out," Holly said. She became aware that the air had turned colder, her breath clouding as she spoke.

As the war party approached, the camp became a chaos of screaming women and children. Terrified animals bolted among the wagons. Holly caught a loose horse and pushed Justin into the saddle. She pointed to where Hodges and his troops were nearing the hills.

"You ride toward Lieutenant Hodges just as fast as you can," she said. "You get him back here."

"Ma, I can't leave you here!"

"You have to, Justin. Now, go!"

Justin rode out, tears streaming down his face. The Sioux reached the camp and, after circling once, began to pour in between the wagons, shouting and firing their bows and rifles. They looked surreal and ghostlike, painted faces and bodies on painted horses, galloping through the gray mist.

Arrows made a hissing *zip* through the rain, and smoke belched from carbines. Holly stood her ground and cocked the Hawken as emigrant men and women scattered around her. Warriors poured in from every direction to intercept them, eager to ram a lance through them or chop them down with a battle ax or club.

While the attacking warriors fought settlers on all sides, Tillie McGivern, with a superhuman effort, dragged Burnham beneath her wagon, between the front wheels. She lay down over him, pulling blankets over them both.

Holly trained her Hawken on a warrior who rode toward her, his lance leveled. She felt the jolt of the rifle butt against her shoulder and saw red gout splatter the painted chest. The warrior's lance tilted down and buried itself at Holly's feet. He sprawled headfirst into the mud and slid for a distance, coming to a stop against a fallen horse.

Holly threw the Hawken aside and grabbed a Henry repeating rifle from the grasp of a fallen emigrant man. Her hands shook as she levered a round into the chamber and shot an attacker who had just turned his bow on her.

Two more Sioux fell from their ponies as Holly continued to fire. She slipped in the mud and fell, then quickly rolled aside as a warrior lunged at her, the blade end of a lance burying itself right next to her.

She lurched to her feet as he drew his knife and came at her. She slammed the stock of her rifle against his face, breaking his nose and driving wood splinters into one eye.

As he fell back, blood streaming from his nose and eye socket, Holly saw that it was Bad Face.

She turned as the Kestler woman clutched at her, screaming, an arrow protruding from her back. Another arrow thumped into her and she fell next to her husband, who lay sprawled with his face to the sky, his forehead smashed by a war club.

Through the screaming and the pounding rain, Holly heard the blare of a cavalry bugle. She stood on a wagon tongue and peered through the storm, barely able to make out the coming tide of blue uniforms.

Justin was among them.

Holly screamed his name. A bugle blared as Hodges and his troops drew nearer. The warriors turned from their killing and began to ride out from the wagons.

All but one.

Holly screamed as a rope flew over her head and shoulders, tightening up under her armpits. Bad Face yelled in triumph as he kicked his pony into a run, dragging her along behind.

Holding the rope to keep her head up, Holly slid through the mud, bouncing off clumps of sagebrush and raking over pads of cactus. Almost instantly her entire body was shot through with pain. She struggled to breathe, to keep her face out of the splashing mud and water. She felt herself being dragged through a creek, but by now her entire body had gone numb.

Close to fainting, she became aware that she was no longer being dragged. She heard warriors yelling and the sound of Bad Face shouting back at them. She felt the sudden, heavy pain of an arrow enter her lower back, more yelling, and Bad Face's pony pounding away from her.

Holly wondered if she would die. The pain again brought her to the brink of passing out. She reached back and felt the arrow protruding from her back. Luckily, the head had not fully penetrated her ribs. But it was stuck fast and she couldn't budge it.

She tried to crawl and gasped as pain shot through her. She heard the sound of someone screaming, seemingly distant and unattached. But when her mouth closed, she realized that the sound had come from deep within her, and she found herself in total silence with a wet, heavy snow touching her face.

Holly was never aware of the old Indian woman who knelt down beside her, checking to see if she was still alive, probing her wounds. She didn't feel the arrow being removed from her back or herself being rolled onto the travois, then being tied securely for the trip into the far reaches of Crazy Woman Creek.

The only thing she remembered about the journey was coming to consciousness and being aware that her body was moving, somehow, across a bumpy expanse, and that the snow fell continuously into her face.

For three days she babbled insanely, fighting the efforts of the old woman to splint her broken leg and arm, to pull cactus needles from her body, and pour warm herb broths into her. Never during that time did she become aware that she was among the living.

All the while she dwelled in a misty place, filled with floating beings and splotches of blood that haunted her day and night. She often saw Justin's face—anxious, wondering, often very sad—and she wondered if her son was alive or dead.

Within this floating world came intense pain mixed with periods of a strange bliss, a sensation of no discomfort or worry. Each time this occurred, she felt herself drifting closer and closer to its source.

Her drifting turned into a journey that each time brought her to an old wooden door, similar to the one at the cabin where she grew up. This door would open and a man who might have been her brother, Elam, had he lived to adulthood, would appear, saying, "Go back, Holly. You can't come in here yet."

"Who are you?" she would say each time. "Where am I? Why can't I come in?"

"Go back and wait until it's time," the man would always say. "I love you, Holly."

Then he would close the door, and each time she found it hard to go back. She would turn and retrace her steps to the old wooden door and each time the man who looked like Elam grown up would become more forceful in his insistence that she go away.

Finally, desperate to find her way out of the strange suspension, Holly retreated from the door, farther and farther from it, turning into the pain, forcing herself into the unbearable misery. Maybe it would bring her death, and relief.

"Ah! You have awakened at last. Can you understand me?"

She nodded.

"Good," she said. "I learned the white man's tongue as a little girl, but I haven't spoken it in many years."

Holly stared and wondered if she might still be dreaming.

"I thought you might decide to cross over," the old woman said. "But maybe it's not your time yet."

Holly knew she wasn't dreaming. She blinked and tried to rise. The pain nearly knocked her out.

"You must be still. It's better that you move very little."

Holly saw an old woman leaning over her, her back stooped, her face like ridged rawhide. Her thick hair, bright and clean, white as newfallen snow, hung in long braids over her shoulders.

She was short and heavyset, dressed in doeskin, with a necklace of blue beads around her neck.

"This is my little cabin," she said. "It isn't much, but I hope you like it."

Holly forced the words. "Who are you?"

"I am Old Calf Woman. I am Blackfoot and grew up in the lands to the north, at the place along the Big Muddy River, called Fort Benton, where the white traders live. I was left here some years ago by my people, who thought I had died. It's a long story I will tell you in time."

Holly took several deep breaths. Her memory began to return.

"My son! Justin! Where's my son?"

"Ah! You must lay still. It will only bring you a great deal of pain."

"I must know where he is."

"You can't know. Not yet. You must be content to wait."

She lay back, tears streaming from her eyes. "But he was with me."

"I saw no one but you," Old Calf Woman said. "The Sioux warrior was dragging you behind his pony. Some of the others saw me coming down the hill toward you and yelled to him. They want nothing to do with me, for they know my medicine and think I'm a crazy woman. So the warrior who dragged you tried to kill you with an arrow and then rode away with the others who called for him, all of them afraid of me."

"There were wagons," Holly said. "What about the others at the wagons? My son, Justin?"

"As I have said, I saw no one but you. I could hear the fighting and yelling, but it was a good distance off. That warrior's face was covered with blood and still he dragged you a long way. He must hate you a great deal."

"I must thank you very much for saving me," Holly said. "But in a few days, I'll have to be going."

Old Calf Woman laughed. "You won't be going anywhere, my strong one, not for a very long time."

"But I must. I have to find my son."

"The Creator has plans for him, whether he is in this world or another. There's nothing you can do."

The tears came again and Holly couldn't bear the thought of losing Justin. She continued to sob though it brought pain to her entire body.

"The best thing you can do," Old Calf Woman said, "is to rest and listen to me. I'll take care of you until you're strong enough to leave here. But that will be the passing of two or maybe three moons. If you go any sooner than that, you will surely die."

Holly wondered if she wasn't still dreaming. But the touch of the old woman's hand against her arm assured her that she had revived fully.

"You must drink this now," the old woman said, holding out a cup. "You haven't taken much since you came to me, and it's time you began eating again."

Holly leaned up and tasted a pasty broth made from herbs and meat. It was strong and seasoned with sage.

"Ah!" the old woman said. "That's good. You're going to come back to life fully very soon. You might not like the road ahead, but you've been chosen to follow it."

Nine

JUSTIN SAT on the Indian pony, his hands tied behind his back. The snow and cold bothered him much less than wondering what had happened to his mother. Had she died? Had there been any survivors? He hoped that was the case and that she would soon come with Lieutenant Hodges to find him.

There had been no chance to find her, so swiftly had he been snatched from his horse. He had reached Lieutenant Hodges and his soldiers, already turning back to the wagons, and had been told by the lieutenant to stay back out of the fighting. But he had ridden with them to find his mother. Nothing else mattered.

Now he could remember calling for her through the storm, while watching the battle raging around him. But then he had suddenly been jerked from the saddle, kicking and screaming, by an Indian whose arms felt like iron clamps.

The harder he fought, the tighter the warrior's grip had become around his middle, until finally he felt he would pass out. Then he had been told, in a language he couldn't understand, to stop resisting or die. Still, he knew what the words meant, for the warrior had held a knife to his throat.

Then, as they rode out to escape the soldiers, they were joined by other warriors, one of whom had lost an eye in the fight. Justin remembered seeing him before: Bad Face, who had been at Fort Laramie, the one with the little bundle that had looked so much like a pouch of gold.

Bad Face, wearing his medicine bundle around his neck, had ridden over to Justin and had looked him over carefully. He had nodded to the others and had whooped loudly, all of them yelling and whooping with him.

Now, as the snowstorm ended as darkness fell, they rode out from the mountains into a vast land of hills and gullies that carried endlessly into the distance. The moon rose and wandered into midsky and still they rode, on and on until Justin thought they were headed to the end of the earth.

The Indians stopped to talk and Justin decided to make a break for it. He jumped from his pony and ran into the darkness while the warriors laughed and Bad Face ran him down, knocking him sprawling into the cold mud.

It didn't stop there. Bad Face dismounted and, in the light of the moon, flailed him with a willow cutting, the sting of which he would never forget.

He hoped then that maybe he would die and join his mother, if she were where the dead live. He hadn't given it much thought until now, but something told him he could be very close to that place.

But he asked himself what would happen if he died, only to find out afterward that his mother was still among the living. He decided to stop feeling sorry for himself. The next time he made a break for it, he would have it better planned, and he would make it work.

As the sun rose, Justin fought to keep himself erect on the pony. Fear, cold, and fatigue had drained him of strength as he rode in the midst of his captors into the Sioux village.

It was a large camp, filled with women and children and barking dogs, all lined up to watch the war party's return. Over a hundred cone-shaped lodges were set in formations along a riverbank. Smoke rose lazily into the morning sky from holes at the top.

Bad Face led the group directly to a lodge in the middle of the village. Their chief, tall and long-faced, with a single eagle feather in his long, loose hair, emerged and spoke to Bad Face.

Justin wondered if this might be Red Cloud, the feared leader of the Oglala Sioux. He discovered his guess to be correct when a white woman dressed in buckskins, carrying a baby, was brought forward to interpret.

"He says that he, Red Cloud, wants you to know that you are his new son," she said.

"Tell him," Justin said, "that I don't care to be his new son."

"He won't want to hear that," she said. "You'd best behave and do what's asked of you."

Justin felt overwhelmed with fear as Red Cloud walked over and pulled him from his pony. He stood defiant, his eyes blazing as the tall leader untied him and looked at his eyes and teeth, then felt him all over his body, testing the muscles in his arms and legs.

He tried to push away, but Red Cloud held him fast.

The crowd roared with laughter. The chief smiled and clapped Justin on the back, then took him into his lodge.

Inside, Justin was offered a bowl of stew. He refused it, and the Indian woman, one of three who stared at him, set the bowl down. They looked at one another and shrugged, then went to work sewing clothes and moccasins.

He sat in the warm lodge, saying nothing, staring at the three Sioux women, who busied themselves and paid him no mind. The tall warrior studied Justin's droopy eyes and left.

For a time, he fought sleep, wondering what would happen to him if he let himself rest. His fears were soon overcome by exhaustion and he slid sideways, unaware that one of the women laid him out on his back and covered him with a blanket while he drifted into deep sleep.

* * *

During the next two days, Justin remained defiant toward Red Cloud and his three wives. The only person in the entire village he could relate to was the white woman he had met the first day.

Justin motioned to the woman on the morning of the third day and made it understood he wished to speak to her. She met him outside the lodge, carrying her baby, and he was allowed to accompany her to the river for water.

"My name is Ella Clark and I came from Illinois," she told him. "I've been a captive for nearly four years. But now I'm married to a warrior and have a child. Still, I'll never be as important as you, being his new son and all."

"I don't understand. Why would he want me as his son?"

"To fill the vacant place in his heart for the son he lost." She pointed. "That warrior over there, the one who lost his eye, brought you here. He was banished for running the chief's son down with his horse."

"I know who he is. His name is Bad Face," Justin said. "I heard that story when I saw him back at Fort Laramie."

"For bringing you to Red Cloud, Bad Face has been given his place back among the people," she said. "There are a lot of us who don't want him back."

"Why couldn't he take an Indian boy my age?" Justin asked. "I mean, I'm not Indian."

"It doesn't matter to Red Cloud," she said. "You are young and strong and of good spirit. He wants you to be his son now and to bring him great honor when you come of age."

"Honor?"

"He will expect you to become a strong warrior and bring honor to the Sioux nation."

Justin listened carefully to Ella Clark while she explained his future.

"As a chief's son, you will be given many privileges. You will be given a good pony and you will learn the ways of hunting from Red Cloud's relatives, all of them fine warriors. For this reason, the other boys will resent you and test you."

"I don't care about any of that," Justin said. "I don't want to be the chief's son. I want to find my ma and go on to Fort Phil Kearny, where my pa is."

"How do you know she is still alive?"

"It would take a lot to kill her and I don't think she's dead."

"You are just wishing. Maybe you should think about a new life. You could do worse than being a chief's son."

"No, I'll leave here as soon as I can. I'll go to Fort Phil Kearny first, and then on to Montana if I have to."

"Do you even know where you are? You're in Montana, far down on Powder River."

"I could still find my way back."

"No, you couldn't. Even if winter wasn't coming on, this land is so big you could get lost and no one would ever find you."

He remembered what it had been like to travel the vast expanse at night and concluded it wouldn't be any better in the daylight. He knew that if he followed the river he could get back to the mountains, but where would he go from there?

"Besides being strong, you have to know the country well to survive here," Ella added. "Listen to me. I know."

"Is that why you never tried to escape?" Justin asked.

"I never wanted to," she said. "I've been treated better here than I ever was by my white husband. They can say what they want about savages, but they respect their women."

"So you'd rather stay here than go back to Illinois?"

"There's nothing for me back there. My husband was killed in the raid, and my kin back home would likely turn me away for living with Indians, especially with the little one."

"I'm sorry you lost everything."

"I didn't lose all that much," she said. "They've given me a name, Whistling Woman, and a good warrior has taken me as his wife. This is a better life than I'd ever hoped for."

"Well, it's not a good life for me," Justin said. "One day I'll find a way to get out of here."

"You'll need a lot of good luck," Ella said. "An awful lot of it."

The cold autumn gave way to an early winter. The snow continued to fall and the days blended one into another. Holly's physical pain began to decrease with time, but her mental anguish grew with each passing day. Her dreams, haunted by the loss of her son, tormented her endlessly.

Old Calf Woman did what she could to ease Holly's suffering, telling stories throughout the days and tending to her with herbal broth by night.

During the times when the pain lessened, Holly listened while Old Calf Woman spoke of her past. She told of running away from her people at a young age to escape punishment for having slept with a young fur trader while married to a Blackfoot warrior.

"That young Long Knife was strong and kind," she said. "He gave me a beautiful shell necklace, and I couldn't resist him."

"Was that enough to run away over?" Holly asked.

"I had to," she said. "The way we were getting along, my husband would have likely killed me, or certainly cut my nose off."

"That's a harsh punishment," Holly said.

Old Calf Woman continued. "I found my way to a Crow village and was taken in, then married soon after that. But he was killed in battle and I went off on my own, until another band of Crow people took me in. Then I began having children with my new husband and the hard times began."

Despite her own pain and desperation, Holly could only wonder at the old woman's fortitude and her ability to cope with having lost not one but four children to disease or accident or battle, and an additional one to abduction by an enemy tribe.

"The smallpox took two of them at an early age," she told Holly. "Another drowned in a river, and my eldest was killed during a battle with my own people, the Blackfeet."

Old Calf Woman explained that her sorrows had really begun when her first child had been taken in a raid by the Assiniboin, who took the small boy far to the north.

"I was picking berries with some friends and left my baby son with one of the elders, a woman I admired greatly," she said. "A war party swooped into camp and stole some horses and three small children. We were never able to catch those raiders, so I had to let my child go."

"You didn't go after him?"

"It's a very big land up there. My husband wouldn't let me go. 'You need to stay here and have more children,' he told me."

"Do you ever wonder what happened to your son?"

"There is a saying that the Creator owns all children until they reach the age of ten. Only after that can you call them yours. No matter how I feel inside, I have to believe that the Creator took him for a good reason."

"That would be hard to live with," Holly said.

"I'm just a simple human being, grateful to be alive," Old Calf Woman said. "I have long since stopped questioning the Creator's ways."

Holly respected the old woman greatly and was grateful to her for saving her life, but she knew that she could *never* give up her search for Justin. It wouldn't come soon, she realized, for the severity of her injuries wouldn't permit it. She wouldn't walk for some time, much less ride a horse.

In addition to a fracture in her left upper leg, her right ankle had been badly broken. Old Calf Woman had set it as best she could, but the ankle would always be weak.

Two ribs had broken inward, puncturing a lung. Along

with breaking her right forearm, her left shoulder had been badly dislocated. Merely being alive was a miracle.

Yet she grew restless and impatient. The days dragged by and her pain and weakness nearly drove her insane. She had no means by which to find her son and was not comforted by the old woman's suggestions that Justin was likely living well and in good hands.

"You can't worry about him endlessly," Old Calf Woman said. "You're robbing yourself of the strength that you need to get well."

"But I don't care to get well if I don't have my son," she said.

"It is foolish to think that way. You have to believe he's being cared for."

"How could that be? Unless he somehow got to the fort and found my husband, he can't be doing well. Maybe he's dead."

She fell into a depression that lasted several days. Old Calf Woman, concerned about Holly's will to live, went outside behind the cabin and entered a small, dome-shaped structure covered with horse and buffalo hide.

Inside the sweat lodge, Old Calf Woman poured water over river rocks she had heated white-hot in a fire. She prayed through four sessions inside the lodge while the steam seared her body.

After the fourth and final round of prayers, she left the lodge and rolled in the snow, and prepared herself for the remainder of the ceremony, to be held inside the cabin, with Holly's involvement.

Inside the cabin, Old Calf Woman arranged a buffalo robe on the floor near Holly's bed. She placed a rock bowl in front of her and filled it with dried sage leaves, bringing them to a flame with the flint from an old rifle. The strong aroma brought a coughing fit from Holly, whose lungs were still weakened from injury.

Holly watched from her bed while the old woman sang and rocked back and forth, spreading the sage smoke over herself with an eagle feather. She sang a song four times and asked for Holly's hand.

"I'm going to give you sage leaves," she said, "and then I want you to let me hold your hand in mine."

Old Calf Woman placed four dried sage stalks in Holly's hand, then held it tightly and began to sing. Her strong voice filled the cabin.

After a time, Holly's arm began to ache badly, but she said nothing. The old woman continued the ceremony until well into the night before finally releasing her grip.

"You can rest now," she said. "And if you don't mind, I will go with you wherever you take me."

Groggily, Holly said, "I don't understand."

"We will have a medicine dream together. You will find your son and I'll be with you."

The old woman lay next to her and Holly drifted to sleep, waking the following morning with a start.

"I thought I saw Justin," she said.

"You did see him," Old Calf Woman said. "I saw him as well, in our medicine dream."

"But I can't remember where he was."

"That doesn't matter," the old woman said. "I've learned where he is. He has not been harmed and will never be harmed where he is."

"How do you know that?"

"Believe me, it's true."

Holly studied her. "Where is he? Did Lieutenant Hodges take him back down to Fort Laramie?"

"I saw no Bluecoats in my dream. Did you?"

"I can't remember."

"Well, I saw him. He was sitting among people he has never met before. But they are glad he's there."

"Did he make it to Fort Phil Kearny? Is he with his father?"

"No, he's not with white people."

"Indians? He's with Indians?"

"I believe they are Sioux."

"Is he a captive?"

"Not in the sense that he's a slave. As I told you, he's being treated very well."

Holly rose halfway up in her bed. "If you could make me a pair of crutches, I could go out and look for him."

"Ah!" Old Calf Woman said. "You must be stronger than the spirits."

"What do you mean?"

"Not even the strongest warrior, if he was hurt as bad as you, could rise up and go out. You would have to be a very strong spirit to do that. So, lay back down and rest."

"Why did you tell me where Justin is if you knew I couldn't go to him?" Holly asked.

"I didn't learn right where he is. I only know that he's safe. Isn't that what you wanted to learn?"

Holly's eyes filled with tears. "I wanted to learn where he is, so I can go to him. I thought you understood that."

"I understand," Old Calf Woman said, "but you couldn't go now anyway."

Holly clenched her fist. Pain shot up her fractured arm.

"Do you see?" the old woman said. "You can't even make your arms work, let alone your legs. How do you think you could go anywhere?"

"Maybe I can't do it now," Holly said. "But the day will come. I promise you, Justin, I'll find you. Just hold on, son. I'll find you."

Ten

WHILE THE snow fell, Justin sat in Red Cloud's lodge and thought about the battle at the wagons. He wondered about Burnham Hess and Aunt Tillie, picturing them dead with Sioux arrows in them. And what about Uncle Harlan? He'd taken a horse and run off, but somehow he must have gotten caught. He hoped so, for that man had caused more problems than anyone he had ever known.

He also wondered how he might have avoided being captured, but the more he thought about it the more he realized it was foolish to concern himself: He couldn't change what had already happened.

But he would never give Bad Face any satisfaction. The one-eyed warrior often tried to make conversation, but Justin ignored him. There would never come a day when he would acknowledge that Bad Face even existed.

As time passed he thought most of all about his mother. He missed the sound of her voice and the feel of her gentleness, her holding him and reassuring him that everything would be fine and that they would some day find his father when they reached Fort Phil Kearny.

He often heard the white woman, Ella, talk about the fort, the hated Bluecoat stronghold that stood alongside the wagon road.

"Like as not you'll go along to watch the fighting one of

these times," Ella said. "Maybe you'll learn why these Indians hate that place so badly."

"I know why they hate it," Justin said. "They don't like the soldiers and they don't like the wagon people."

Justin had talked with Ella at length about his father's dreams of striking it rich in the gold fields. Ella's husband had shared that dream, but his fate had been the same as many others who had taken the Bozeman Road.

"I don't think about him much no more," Ella said. "And I don't think about gold at all. I used to, but I don't care no more."

"You and I don't think alike, then," Justin said.

"I suppose not. But if they take you to watch the fighting, you'd best go and say nothing about your pa. You see, you've got a new pa now."

"I don't see it that way."

"Take this for what it's worth, Justin," Ella said. "You'd best behave well and take what you're given. If Red Cloud ever decides he doesn't want you any longer, you're as good as dead."

He thought about the advice and decided he would take it. After all, she had survived among these people for four years, so she must know something. Maybe he would go along with things and in the meantime, he would plan his escape. He would learn what he could from the Sioux and make use of it later.

"You've got some tough times ahead of you," Ella said. "Come spring, you'll likely begin your training as a warrior. You'll get sent out alone, to face the country by yourself. You'll have to fight the cold and the rain and the heat, not to mention hunger and, most of all, loneliness."

"You went out on your own?"

"Not into the hills. But I got plenty lonely here, until I learned to turn to these people. I see that you're staying back and keeping to yourself. It's a mistake."

"That's the way I like it. As soon as they send me off by myself, I'm gone. I'll run as far and as fast as I can. They can't stop me if I'm alone."

"You won't be entirely by yourself," she said. "You'll think you are, but there'll be a warrior or two watching from a good distance, just to see how you do."

"What do they want of me?" Justin asked.

"You're the chief's son, and since you belong to Red Cloud, he wants to see if you've got that inner power that makes a good warrior and a strong leader. You look to have it, but only by being out by yourself can show it for real."

"I still don't see why you've taken to this place so well," Justin said. "The food's nothing like what Ma makes."

"You'll get used to the food, and you'll learn to like it. Especially the buffalo, come spring after the cold lets up. After you've gone hungry, a good chunk of fresh buffalo meat can satisfy you like nothing else."

"I don't want you to take this wrong, Ella, but it seems to me maybe you've gone a little crazy."

"Maybe so," she said, "but this is the best place on God's earth to be that way."

Ella's words came to pass. Even though the coldest weather had yet to come, Justin, as the days progressed, began to learn the ways of the young Sioux warrior. He was given a breechcloth to wear and a good buckskin shirt. He showed Red Cloud he could already shoot a rifle, which pleased the chief greatly, and was then given a knife and bow.

He realized that to resist his training would mean real problems for him. Ella had said that should he show a stubborn streak, he would be relegated to a lower class or maybe killed.

So he stayed with it and, despite the weather, rode daily and cared for a stocky buckskin pony named Smoke that Red

Cloud had given him. He rose with the sun to join other boys his age, who watered and cared for the horse herd, breaking holes in the ice along the river and watching the ponies as they searched the hills for dried grass.

And also true to Ella's prophecy, the other boys cared little for him, with the exception of one, a gangly mixed-blood boy named Germain.

It was this new friend who offered advice and encouragement, and made Justin feel welcome when the others showed their resentment. Speaking in broken English, some French, and some Sioux, Germain had been born at Fort Laramie, where his mother later left his father and married a warrior in Red Cloud's band.

"It's a hard life for a boy like me," he told Justin. "As you can see, I'm not like any of the others."

He had been born without a left arm, resulting in his inability to shoot a bow or hold a rifle. Despite this, he thought highly of himself and often said that he must be special for the Creator to make his life so difficult.

"You must be special as well," he told Justin. "You are white and are pushed into a camp of Indian people. That would be very hard for someone who had never been around us before."

"But you're part white."

"That doesn't count against me as much as having just one arm."

"You seem to be able to do more than some with two arms."

"When you're not whole," Germain said, "you have to do things a lot better than ordinary people."

"I guess I am pretty lucky, at that," Justin said. "I'm whole and being the chief's son gives me chances the others can never get."

"But as you can see," Germain pointed out, "it also brings hate to you. Can't you feel the others staring at you?"

"Yes, but it don't bother me."

"I don't know if I believe that."

Justin wanted to tell Germain that he wouldn't be around long enough for any of it to matter, but he held his tongue.

"Their hatred of you is deeper because you're white, and also a chief's son," Germain said. "If you were just white and lived with an ordinary family, you'd be fighting all the time. Since you're Red Cloud's son, the other fathers will keep their sons from ganging up on you."

"I don't care if they gang up on me," Justin said. "I can whup them."

Germain smiled. "You might be tough, but you can't fight everyone at once."

Justin saw the wisdom in Germain's words: If he meant to survive, he would be better off to fit in, until the time he decided he knew enough to leave.

Both Germain and Ella began to teach Justin the Sioux way of life, including the Lakota tongue and sign language. At first he cared little about learning any of it, but he soon became convinced that understanding their language and the signs they were making would better help him to know their plans for Fort Phil Kearny.

He realized that very soon Red Cloud would be leading his warriors against the fort. He knew they talked about it daily and it frustrated him not to understand their plans.

"If you care about your pa like you say you do," Ella told him one day, "you'll learn what you can from Germain and me. Then, if you're so hell-bent on getting out of here, you'll have the tools to survive and find the fort."

"You told me before that it would be foolish to try and escape. You said the country was too big."

"The time when Red Cloud will be taking you with him is

getting closer," she said. "The more you know before then, the better off you'll be."

"You mean, you think he'll take me out into the country around here with him?"

"Yes, I figure he will."

"So, if I learn the country well enough, I can find my way to the fort and warn Pa and the others. That right?"

"I figure you've got the spunk to do it," she said. "But I ain't telling you to, understand. I'm just saying you'd best learn what Germain and I have to teach you. Then you can make up your mind for yourself."

Over the days, Justin painstakingly learned basic Sioux dialogue and sign language. He began to pick up on words and phrases, especially those among the men when they talked of war.

The warriors began leaving the camp in large groups nearly every morning, returning in late evening. Bad Face went along but never in the lead. No matter that he had captured a replacement for one of Red Cloud's sons, he would never gain the status he felt he deserved.

Red Cloud often went with the war parties, but Justin was never asked to go along. He began to wonder if Ella had any idea what she was talking about.

"I thought you said Red Cloud would take me out on a war party," he said to her one afternoon.

"Be patient," she said. "He will. Soon."

"How do you know this?"

"Because that's how it works. He'll take you along when he thinks you'll be true to the Lakota people and not your own."

"I'll never do that."

"Maybe he knows it."

Justin thought a moment. "What could I do to make him think I want to go?"

"I don't know that you can do anything. Just wait."

"What if they attack the fort and kill everyone?"

"There's too many soldiers and Red Cloud would lose too many warriors," Ella said. "What they'll do is go after the woodcutters, who leave the fort for firewood, and try to stop the hunters from getting game. Sooner or later that will bring the soldiers out of the fort. Nobody can fight if they're hungry and freezing."

Justin thought about what she had said and wondered if he shouldn't plan his escape sooner. But it would be a hopeless effort, as he still didn't know the country.

A few days later Ella asked Justin, "You know that it's close to Christmas?"

"I thought it might have passed," he said. "I can't keep track of the days."

She pulled a notched cottonwood twig from under her blanket.

"I've got one of these for every year I've been here," she said. "Each one has got every day that passed cut into it. Like I said, I'm near in the middle of my fourth year."

"Why do you keep track of the days?"

"There's some things about my white upbringing I can't let loose of," she said. "These people keep track of time by the moon, but I've got to know day by day."

Justin went off to the river to ponder the news. He sat near the bank, watching the current flow under a thin film of ice. The thought of Christmas both invigorated and saddened him. Back home, it had been a time of festivity, and even though they had had little, they always celebrated with a big pie and candied apples.

It seemed unfair that he had to spend the holidays without his mother. He had gotten used to Christmas without his pa, as the war took no time off for family life. He wondered what other changes he would have to face and if he would ever see any of his family again.

Germain came through the willows and stood beside him. "I think you should come see this," he said. "Red Cloud is getting ready to lead a war party against your people."

In the village, Justin stood with Germain and watched a circle of painted warriors dance around a fire, Bad Face among them, as they all yelled war cries and raised their weapons into the air.

Nearby, a group of women danced around a pole decorated with enemy scalps. They charged the pole, slashing at the scalps with skinning knives, singing songs as loud as the warriors.

"It is a preparation for a big battle," Germain said. "Everyone is getting ready."

"Are they going to charge the fort?" Justin asked.

"I heard them say that a lot of soldiers will die, that some of the villagers have had visions."

Justin continued to watch the dancing, wondering what it all meant. He had heard about the vision many medicine people had and how all the villagers held great respect for their abilities to see into the future, a concept Justin had a great deal of trouble grasping. But these people took full stock in the belief and were readying themselves for a big fight.

Caught up in watching the dancing, Justin failed to notice that Germain had left his side. He saw the reason when Red Cloud walked over, leading Smoke.

"I will tie your pony up in front of the lodge," Red Cloud said in sign. "Tomorrow you will go with us. It's time you learned how a warrior goes to battle."

The trail from the village cut through draws and over passes filled with snow. The wind bit deeply and sang a frigid song of mourning.

As he rode next to Red Cloud in silence, Justin thought of escape. The more he considered it, the more he realized that with the number of warriors present, his chances of success were next to none.

The following morning they reached a high hill overlooking the fort. Smoke curled from fires within the walls. All else was still.

"You will stay with me and watch," Red Cloud said.

Justin felt sick. There would be a fight and maybe his pa would die. He could do nothing but watch.

The warriors broke into three divisions. With Bad Face among them, a large force took cover over a hill in the brush and dried grass, while another force rode up toward the mountains, where a band of woodcutters felled trees.

A third force then rode down close to the fort, staying back just far enough to be out of rifle range.

Justin heard distant shots and yelling as the first group of warriors surprised the woodcutters. He then watched while the group who had gone down near the fort taunted the soldiers who rode out through the gates.

The troopers halted at the commander's order, their horses snorting steam in the cold air. They watched while the Sioux began to ride slowly up the hill away from the fort.

Justin strained to identify the troopers' commanding officer, thinking it might be Lieutenant Hodges. But he was too far away.

"Watch carefully what happens," Red Cloud told Justin. "My warriors will trick the Bluecoat leader into believing he can catch them when he cannot."

The soldiers dismounted and fired at the Sioux, the balls from their muzzle-loading Springfields falling short. On the hill, the warriors laughed and made obscene gestures, even building fires to warm themselves. Frustrated, the commander ordered his troops to mount their horses.

"It will happen now," Red Cloud said. "You will see."

Even though the troopers had mounted, the Sioux on the hillside appeared unconcerned, continuing to warm themselves by the fires, telling stories and laughing. In the distance, the shooting at the woodcutters' fight grew more sporadic.

"Did they get all the woodcutters?" Justin asked.

"The woodcutters do not matter," Red Cloud said. "It's the Bluecoats who must die."

The warriors continued to taunt the soldiers while the commander led his men up the hill. The warriors mounted their ponies very slowly, as if in no hurry, and some of them rode downhill to zigzag their ponies back and forth in front of the cavalry.

The fight at the emigrant wagons replayed before Justin's eyes in full force. He again saw the young soldier fall from the bullet fired by the Sioux warrior who had ridden his pony in close to show his bravery. And he heard the screams and cries of the wounded as the warriors attacked in the storm.

He wanted to turn his pony and ride away as fast as he could, but he remained still, watching, listening while the trap for the soldiers slowly began to close.

The commander continued to remain calm while Bad Face, riding his best pony, ventured closer to the soldiers than any of the others. With a loud scream, he fired an arrow at a cavalryman, hitting him in the shoulder.

The commander ordered the line held, as Lieutenant Hodges had at the wagons.

From out of the fort's gates appeared a column of infantrymen, who took position behind the cavalry.

"The Bluecoats are ready to fight," Red Cloud said with a smile. "Now they'll make a mistake."

The Bluecoat leader drew his saber and gave the order to charge. A bugle blared through the cold air. Bad Face, laughing in his glory, turned his pony and joined the other Sioux riding over the ridge that separated the fort from the brush and grass concealing more warriors, all waiting patiently for the soldiers to follow into the trap.

But the soldiers halted at the ridge, at least for a time. The

commander waited for the infantry to arrive and then gave the
signal to continue in pursuit. A cavalry bugle again sounded
and the troopers rode over the hill into a frenzy of crazed
Sioux warriors, who fired at them from all angles.

"You know what is happening," Red Cloud said. "I can see
it in your eyes."

Justin watched as the warriors who had attacked the
woodcutters arrived and rode to the top of the ridge, blocking off any escape the soldiers might have had. The sky above
the ridge rapidly filled with blue smoke and the air carried the
sounds of yelling mixed with rifle fire.

"They're all being killed," Justin said, "just like those people who had the visions said."

"You need not ride over there, if you don't wish to," Red
Cloud said.

"I'll stay here," Justin said. "Are you going to attack the
fort as well?"

The chief looked into the sky. "It is late in the day. Our
wounded must be tended to. Another day we will come."

Eleven

WITH THE aid of two crutches Holly stood at the edge of the creek, looking down from the timber into the expanse of foothills and plains below. Snow covered everything in a thick mantle of white, and frost covered the trees and the tips of the sage that stuck out of the snow.

To keep warm she wore a wolfskin coat, complete with ears and eyeholes, that Old Calf Woman had given her as a gift. The old woman had received the coat from her grandmother and had been wearing it the day of the Great Fight, as she called it, when she had been left in the foothills to die.

"He was a prime male wolf when my grandmother killed him with an arrow," she said. "She tanned it with the head skin still on so that she could wear it over her face and look through the eyeholes when she wished. She always wanted to be a wolf. The coat has remained in good condition all these years. Now it will be yours to keep."

Holly thought it the best gift of her life. The coat, a mixed black and gray, fit tightly and kept out the cold wind. She wore it often, looking out across the white landscape, wondering about her husband and son.

She knew it to be close to the new year, for Old Calf Woman had said that soon the moon would have changed twice since her arrival. Holly wept as she looked across the expanse of winter, realizing she had spent a Christmas without Justin and Isaac.

Holly leaned her crutches against a tree and took a few steps on her own. She could balance herself well, but the pain remained with her.

Frustrated, Holly batted the crutches with her open hand, knocking them into the snow. She had grown ever more anxious to heal and be able to go where she wanted on her own.

"I can't stand this waiting," Holly told Old Calf Woman.

"The day of your freedom will come," she said. "You must be patient and work hard."

In their time together, Holly had grown close to her mentor and protector. She had always considered herself attuned to nature, but her time with Old Calf Woman had convinced her that all things were united and that the land, the people, and the animals all contained the same breath of life.

"You can't separate anything," Old Calf Woman told her. "Everything is one."

As she looked out across the distance, Holly wondered again about Justin. She had come to believe that the old woman's medicine dream had been true and that her son was being held captive in a Sioux village somewhere.

"It is a common thing," Old Calf Woman had said. "As I told you before, children are prized possessions. They grow up to become one of the tribe, and as such are helpers to all."

"But my son is not Lakota," Holly argued. "He can't change who he is."

"It's too early in his life to know who he is," Old Calf Woman said. "He must learn that with time."

"Are you saying he'll become like an Indian?"

"How is an Indian so different? If a white lives in the mountains long enough, he becomes like an Indian, as you say. But if a white lives on his own, without learning from an Indian, who does he become like?"

"I'm just saying that Justin won't forget where he came from," Holly said.

"Maybe not, but he'll learn many things with the Sioux that he couldn't have learned otherwise. And it will help him when he gets older."

Holly understood the old woman, realizing that she had already learned a number of things herself that would help with survival later. Perhaps, she thought, Justin's experiences had been similar to hers and he had been forced to enter a culture he had no understanding of, learning at the same time that his own culture might not be as broad as he had once believed.

As she gazed along the breadth of the foothills, Holly thought back to a few days before, when Old Calf Woman had spoken to her about a mystery.

"It is a strange thing," the old woman had said. "I went out to check my rabbit snares and watched a large number of Bluecoats and fort people traveling south, toward Fort Laramie. This is not the season of the year to travel, unless something very bad happened at the fort."

While listening to her, Holly's mind had raced ahead, wondering if all the forts had been abandoned for some reason. Possibly there had been a raid and everyone had decided to try and reach Fort Laramie for safety. But what did that mean for Isaac? Had he been among those who had fled or had he perished at Fort Phil Kearny?

That evening Holly had talked Old Calf Woman into another vision ceremony, to try and locate Isaac, but nothing had come of it.

"I cannot tell you anything," she had said. "I can see nothing."

"Maybe when the wagons roll through here again," Holly said, "I can ride with someone to the fort and learn what happened."

"You should wait until well into the warm moons to try and travel," Old Calf Woman suggested. "Your strength has not returned and the cold will test even the strongest of people."

Holly knew to take the old woman's advice. Her memories of traveling cross-country with the wagon train were still vivid. Even as strong as she had been then, the miles were so trying as to leave her exhausted daily.

But she would never give up her search for her son. As well, she would keep a spark of hope for finding Isaac. Her resolve to reunite her family would drive her to a faster healing.

Old Calf Woman approached from behind. "There's a rabbit roasting on the fire," she said. "You haven't eaten all day."

"I guess I should have something," Holly said.

"Yes, you can't go without eating if you intend to get better."

At the fire, Holly talked with Old Calf Woman about the time she would be leaving.

"I know I can't go as soon as I want to," she said. "But I can't wait until the warm moons, as you think I should."

"I can't stop you from going any time you wish," Old Calf Woman said. "I can only tell you that you would be foolish to go before you're ready."

"But if I listen to you, I might never be ready."

"You'll know when you're ready. And if you'll let me, I'll help you to learn something that will make you strong both in mind and body. You will be able to ask the Creator about your son, as I did."

"You would teach me your medicine?"

"I have no one to pass the ways down to, so I have chosen you as my daughter. I will teach you the medicine, if you would like."

"I'll need time to think about it," Holly said. "It's a very big step."

"You are wise to think about it," the old woman said. "Should you choose to learn my ways, it will change your life even more."

*   *   *

As the new year came, Holly's body continued to repair itself little by little. During a period when the weather broke, she climbed to the tops of hills and pulled herself up high into the cottonwoods, all to test her growing strength.

Her muscles responded well but her mending bones ached and her ankle throbbed. The break had been so severe as to leave her with a limp. She knew she would need a horse to get over the long distances she would need to travel. There would be no more leisurely walks through woods to get where she was going; she would be spending long hours in a saddle, making up for lost time.

The storms grew less intense and she became ever more anxious for spring's arrival. She continued to heal and learn from Old Calf Woman, who gave her an eagle feather and took her into sweat lodge ceremonies time and again, getting her ready for her learning of medicine ways.

But first, the old woman warned her never to misuse the powers.

"The giving of medicine is for the making of good things, and praying that good things will happen," she said. "To misuse the power will cause harm to everyone."

Old Calf Woman explained to Holly that the medicine powers did not just come automatically, but were realized over time after much praying and sacrificing. The sweat lodge ceremony was only a preliminary.

"You still have many ceremonies to complete before the Creator will send you full power," Old Calf Woman said as they sat in the darkness of the lodge. "It is a long and a very hard road. Have you decided yet that you want to turn back?"

"I don't want to turn back," Holly said, striking her back and sides with a switch made of reed grass. Holly had learned that switching opened her pores to the heat, evening out the intensity inside and outside the body.

"You may learn things you don't wish to know," the old woman said. "You may suffer more than you've ever suffered. You should know that before we continue."

"If it will help to bring my family back together," Holly said, "then I'll gladly suffer."

Old Calf Woman poured water from a buffalo horn onto the hot rocks, filling the interior with steam. Holly gasped.

"My people have always suffered," she said as she poured. "I believe that the Creator often wishes to test our faith."

"I never knew any Indian people where I came from," Holly said.

"Likely they were all driven out well before your time. That is the way of things now: All the natives are being displaced. But that's something my people knew would happen. You, too, may be given dreams of things to come, things you cannot change even though you will wish deep in your heart to change them."

"Are you saying that I will be able to see into the future?"

"I cannot say for certain, but it could be possible. Those who follow sacred pathways are given gifts they cannot give back."

"Do you know what's coming?" Holly asked. "Can you see into the future?"

"At times," she said. "But I'm not so special. We have always had Dreamers among our people who can foretell what is to come. There is a story among the Blackfeet people of such a Dreamer named Moving Another Place, who one morning called all the subchiefs of his band together. He held a blanket that he had slept on the night before and told them: 'All of you, say many prayers to the Creator, for from this time on our way of life will change forever. New and different men with light skins will come and point strange sticks that explode, killing all our game.' "

"You had men among you who saw this before it happened?" Holly asked.

"Yes, there were many. Moving Another Place became well known because he told of his vision many times. He wanted to stop what was coming, but had no power to do so."

"How could he have seen it?" Holly asked.

"Those people lived differently than we do today," the old woman replied. "They looked to the Creator for everything and the Creator gave them eyes to see and ears to hear. You see, Moving Another Place even knew that the Blackfeet people would some day be forced from their lodges into square structures made of trees.

" 'In time our thinking will become different,' he told the subchiefs that day. 'Those light-skinned men will tell us to think like them and to cut Earth into pieces for living, saying each will own the piece instead of just staying there for a time and then moving on, like we do today.' "

"Where I lived, everyone has his own piece of ground," Holly said.

"Yes, that has already happened there. In time, the same thing will take place here. That's why Red Cloud and the Sioux are fighting so hard. The Sioux are my people's enemies, but we think the same in many ways."

"It's hard to imagine how someone could see the future like that," Holly said.

"There's more to what Moving Another Place saw, and it disturbs me the most of all," Old Calf Woman said. "He told those subchiefs that day that in time there would be no more need for horses, for everyone would climb inside huge black beetles and ride around in them."

Holly shook her head. "I never heard of such a thing."

"Also," Old Calf Woman continued, "he said there would be huge geese flying through the sky, with people sitting in rows inside them."

"How could that be? Did he believe everyone would get smaller?" Holly asked. "Or that insects would get larger? What was he seeing?"

"I cannot say for sure," the old woman said, "but maybe he saw something that still hasn't come to pass."

"Are you saying things are coming that we have no control over?"

"I'm only saying what the old people saw in their visions. I believe certain things cannot be changed, while others can, depending on how a person thinks. When you think about what you're going to do with your life when you leave me, remember these stories."

Old Calf Woman poured more water on the hot stones and began a series of prayers. They were in the fourth round of the ceremony, so when the old woman had finished, Holly would follow her outside and they would roll in the snow.

As she awaited the last prayer, Holly felt the intense heat envelop her. She lay flat on her stomach, enduring, waiting for Old Calf Woman to finish and the door flap to open.

As with previous sweat ceremonies, she would leave the lodge feeling reborn. The cool air would revive her and her mind would soar like the great eagles that always circled overhead.

This time, she prayed that her mind would soar even higher and that by some chance the sacred powers that enshrouded her after each sweat would take her far out where she could see the open foothills and the snow-covered grasslands beyond, where she could find Justin sitting somewhere in a Sioux village, hopefully beside a warm fire, thinking of her, awaiting his return to her side.

Justin sat near a fire with Germain, staring into the flames. During his time with Red Cloud's people he had learned a great deal about their customs, but he still yearned for his mother and the life he had once known.

New hope had arisen within him. The weather had warmed and Red Cloud had directed the camp be moved back upriver, closer to the mountains. Scouts had discovered a large herd of elk in the lower foothills, and the villagers needed food.

"Now that we're closer to the fort," Justin said, "I'm thinking about making my break."

"You should just make your life here from now on," Germain told him. "It will do you no good to try and escape."

"But I don't belong here," Justin said. "It's not my home. It won't ever be."

"I thought you and I were friends," Germain said.

"Of course we are. It don't have anything to do with that."

"Then why leave me here? No one else wants to be friends with me."

"I didn't say I'd leave you. You're welcome to come along."

"I can't."

"Why not?"

"Because there's nothing out there for me. I don't know anything else but what's here."

"You could live with me and my family. You could learn our ways."

"No, I couldn't. Even if they are still alive, they wouldn't want me."

"They *are* still alive," Justin said. "And they would want you. If I brought you, they'd want you."

Germain smiled. "It is good to hear you say that. But what about everyone else? I know stories about how the whites feel about mixed-blood people. They hate them worse than full-blood Indians."

"Who did you hear that from?"

"I've heard it lots of times. There are trappers and traders who come to our village. A lot of them were born of trappers who came from other lands and married Indian women. When they go back to their fathers' lands, no one wants them there, so they come back to live in the mountains."

"You stay with me and my family and it won't matter."

"Your family would take me in?"

"Yes."

Germain toyed the fire with a stick. "How are you so sure we could escape?"

"I've been making a plan," Justin said. "Nobody keeps guard much anymore. We could get away in the night."

"And go where?"

"To the fort, where my pa is. I know the way."

"Could we make it through the snow? Could we stand the cold? I think we'd freeze to death out there."

"The weather's getting warmer," Justin said. "Moving the village was easy."

"You let yourself be fooled. It gets warm and then turns bitter cold. You can't depend on it staying warm, not for a long time yet."

"Back where I come from," Justin said, "people are thinking about getting ready to put crops in now."

"I don't know where you came from and I don't know what you mean by crops," Germain said, "but it stays cold here for at least another moon and most often two. It would do no good to go out into country you don't know when you don't understand the weather."

"Then you think I should just stay here and forget about my ma and pa?"

"For now. Things might change and maybe we can go without having to run."

"What do you mean?"

"I heard some talk about a messenger that came from that big fort to the south. He said the Bluecoats want peace and will bring many supplies when the green grass comes. The messenger also said that the Bluecoats want to know about captives in the villages."

"Do they know I'm here?"

"I don't know. I just heard that the Bluecoats might want to ransom for captives. Maybe give horses and guns."

"A messenger brought this news?"

"Yes, just a few days ago."

Justin thought for a moment. "Maybe I should ask Red Cloud about it."

"No. He would get very angry with you, even angrier than he is now. He knows you don't want to be his son."

"Why can't he understand that I want to be with my own parents?"

"I've told you before, his belief is that *he* is your father now. That's how it is in his mind."

"Well, it's not that way in my mind and it never will be. I would like to think that what you say about the soldiers coming to get captives back is true, but I don't want to wait for summer."

Germain continued to toy with the fire. "I wish you'd wait and maybe I could go with you. If you do go before the green grass, I'll stay here, for I don't want to test the cold. I know what it can do."

Justin thought a moment. "How long until we know if the soldiers are coming for captives?"

"There is no way to know. You have to be patient. That's all you can do."

Twelve

LIEUTENANT LANE Hodges rode his horse to a hill overlooking Fort Laramie and gazed out into the distance, the wind in his face. The sun was rising, bringing a sheen of gold to the land. To the north, thin clouds rolled over the Bozeman Road. The weather had been unusually warm and the snow had receded from the bottoms, leaving just the upper foothills and mountains still covered.

As he looked into the distance, Hodges thought about Holly Porter. He had vowed to search forever, if that's what it took to find her.

He had never stopped thinking about that disastrous day when the wagons had been attacked. He realized at the time that he should never have pursued the fleeing Sioux warriors, but his orders had been explicit: "Any hostile Indian inflicting injury or death upon an officer or enlisted man of the U.S. Army is to be caught and punished accordingly." Had he disobeyed such an order, he would have been tried for treason.

Since that day, Hodges had used every means possible to discover her whereabouts. He had questioned freighters and mountain men using the Bozeman Road but had gotten nowhere in his quest. No one had seen or heard of Holly Porter.

Still determined, Hodges had requested a search party. His request had been denied. "How can you go chasing off without knowing where to look?" his commanding officer had asked. "Besides, have you forgotten about Red Cloud? You and your men would be in considerable danger."

Then his luck had changed. A scout named Antoine Janis, whose father had been among the first trappers in the region, had been hired by the army to help negotiate a peace settlement with the Sioux. As Janis had married a Sioux woman, hopes were high that the scout could make headway with Red Cloud.

Included in the peace settlement was the ransoming of a captive white boy held in Red Cloud's village. Janis had heard from associates who had visited Red Cloud's village that the boy had become the chief's new son.

Hodges was almost certain the boy was Justin. When asked about rumors of a white woman, Janis had told Hodges that his friends talked about a white woman living on Crazy Woman Creek with an old Indian woman known to have strong medicine.

"No one goes to the little cabin where she lives," Janis told Hodges. "Everyone is afraid of her."

"Could you take me to the cabin?" Hodges asked.

"I can take you near it, but I won't go up there."

During the weeks that followed, Hodges had managed to get himself assigned to the detail working to ransom the white boy. He believed that if he could go after the boy, he would also be able to find Holly.

Now, as Hodges looked toward the north, he thought about the upcoming days. His command would be leaving in less than an hour for Fort Phil Kearny, the headquarters for the negotiation process.

Antoine Janis, who had watched Hodges ride up the hill, joined him. The two men had gotten to know each other well.

"You are worried about finding the woman?" Janis said.

"Yes, and getting the boy back as well. Do you think we can get anywhere with Red Cloud?"

"It depends on how he feels about the boy. If he wants

to keep him it will be hard; if he doesn't care, then you can trade him some horses and everyone will be happy."

"I hope I can find his mother," Hodges said.

Janis smiled. "As much as you care for her, you can't help but find her."

"How long will it take to reach the old woman's cabin?"

"Four or five days of hard travel."

Hodges looked down toward the fort. On the parade ground, soldiers were lining up with their horses.

"It's time to ride," he said. "Lead me to Crazy Woman Creek."

Holly and Old Calf Woman stood on an open ridge a distance below the cabin, one of Holly's favorite places. The rising sun had topped the horizon and the air was filled with birdsong.

"It feels so warm," Holly said. "It must be spring."

"I know what you're thinking," the old woman said. "Don't be fooled."

"I've gotten much stronger."

"Yes, but not strong enough. And certainly not strong enough to test the cold moons."

"But the snow is melting. The deer and elk are out feeding."

"Yes, but they know enough not to go on a long journey this time of year."

Holly looked out over the country, refusing to believe that the warm winds wouldn't allow her to travel down Crazy Woman Creek to the Powder River. She sat on the ridge often during open weather and stared far out into the distance. More than once she had noticed a hazy cloud hovering over the distant length of the river.

"See!" she had said. "That's smoke. I know it's smoke."

"Could be," the old woman would always say. "But it might just be frost in the air."

Holly always wondered why the old woman would never be specific and tell her if it was smoke she was seeing. Perhaps she knew better than to say it was a sure sign of a distant Sioux encampment, knowing that if Holly thought that, she would go for certain.

Again Holly pointed into the vast and distant open, toward what she believed to be rising smoke.

"There it is again," she said. "I'm sure that's smoke."

"The cold moons bring haze," Old Calf Woman said. "Sometimes smoke looks like haze; sometimes haze looks like smoke."

"I have to go and see."

"Even if it is smoke out there," Old Calf Woman said, "it's a long distance away, much farther than it appears."

"How many days?"

"Hard to say. Maybe as many as on one hand, or maybe two hands. Distance in these lands plays tricks on the eyes."

Holly was again looking out, weighing her chances of reaching the smoke, when gunfire broke out in the distance, somewhere below them on the lower Crazy Woman Creek.

"Is that near the wagon road?" Holly asked.

"Yes," Old Calf Woman said. "There is fighting going on down there. It's still the cold moons but there is no end to the fighting."

"Could there be a wagon train this time of year?"

"Not likely. It could be Bluecoat soldiers traveling through. The Sioux want their lands free of everyone."

Holly studied the distance, as if she could bring all the faraway land into focus. "So you think there are soldiers out there fighting the Sioux?"

Old Calf Woman shrugged. "Maybe. But I'm tired of hearing it. I'm going in and lay down to rest."

When she had gone, Holly made her way farther down the hill. The gunfire began to lessen until it gradually died out altogether. Then, in the still air, she could hear the sound of a running horse.

It came closer and she took cover in a grove of juniper trees. Finally, a soldier came into view, leaning over the side of his horse, barely holding on.

The pony slowed to a trot, then walked up the hill toward her. The soldier fell off and rolled over, holding his leg; the horse bolted, running over a nearby ridge.

Holly eased down toward the fallen soldier. He sat up and her eyes widened.

"Lieutenant Hodges!"

He looked up. "Holly Porter?"

"Yes, it's me."

"God in heaven!" he said. "I knew some day I'd find you." He looked closely. "You look more like an Indian than an emigrant woman."

She made her way down to him. "You've been looking for me?"

"I never thought you were dead," he said. "I saw you being dragged behind a horse, but I couldn't go after you. My horse was shot out from under me."

She sat down next to him. He was holding his right leg, blood oozing through his fingers.

"What was all the shooting down below?"

"I was leading a command to Fort Phil Kearny. We were attacked by Sioux. We drove them off but I wanted to come up here and look for you."

She studied his wound. "You're in no condition to be riding."

"I'll make it," Hodges said. "How did you survive?"

"I was saved by an old Indian woman who lives by herself not far from here."

"The one they say is crazy?"

"She's far from crazy," Holly said as she began cutting away his trouser leg with her knife.

"There's a lot of stories about her," Hodges said. "I heard about her from my scout. He said if there was a chance you were alive, you might be up here."

"It's good that you found me. Your wound needs attention."

Hodges grimaced. "How bad is it?"

"The bullet passed close to the bone but missed the major blood vessels. You'll be off your feet for a while, though."

"I can't be off my feet," he said. "I don't have the time."

"You'd better take the time." She continued to work on his leg, cleaning the wound with fresh snow. "I thought you were going to quit and become a U.S. marshal."

"I wanted to find you first. And I have another mission— to bring peace to the Bozeman Road."

Hodges explained that the army was negotiating with Red Cloud to open up the Bozeman Road to travelers, the reason he had journeyed up the trail with his command. Since the fight at the end of December that took nearly a hundred soldiers' lives—now being called the Fetterman Fight— the army decided to try and keep the bloodshed to a minimum.

"The Fetterman Fight that you talk about," Holly said. "Did a lot of soldiers go back down to Fort Laramie after that?"

"Yes, and the slain officers' wives with them. It was a hard trip for them."

"Old Calf Woman knew there was someone on the trail below," Holly said. "It must have been a bad fight."

"Something nobody ever wants to see again." He studied her. "I have a top priority. I've been given orders to ransom a captive white boy from Red Cloud."

Holly stared at him. "Justin?"

"I've wondered about that. But it's hard to say. I wouldn't get my hopes up, if I were you."

"How can I not? Wait here and I'll hurry up to the cabin. We'll get you up there with the help of my crutches."

She hurried as fast as she could, despite pains that shot through her legs.

At the cabin, Old Calf Woman met her with a stern face.

"Who's the Bluecoat?"

"His name is Lieutenant Hodges. He was in charge of the troops the day of the wagon fight. He's been shot in the leg."

"Take these cloths," she said. "Get him up here. I'll prepare a poultice."

Holly took the cloth and crutches back down. She began wrapping the lieutenant's leg.

"When are you going after Justin? I'm going along, you know."

"I don't know if the captive is actually Justin, and I have no idea when I'll go. But when I do, you will certainly not be with me."

"You can't stop me."

"You'd be better off to go down toward old Fort Collins, south of Fort Laramie, and find your husband."

Holly stared at him. "You saw Isaac?"

"Yes," Hodges said. "After the fight, we buried the dead and took the rest of the wagons on to Fort Phil Kearny. Isaac was waiting there for you and Justin."

"I knew he was alive. I just knew it."

"He had a banknote with him," the lieutenant continued. "He said he sold his claim at Last Chance Gulch. Too cold in the winter, he said. He wants to go into ranching down on the Cache la Poudre River, off the old Cherokee Trail. They're calling it the Overland Trail North now."

"What did he say about Justin and me?"

"He heard from some of the wagon people that both of

you had died. I told him there was hope you were alive. He told me he would get settled and come back to look for you."

She tightened the wrapping on his leg. "I'm glad he made good on his claim."

"He got doubly rich," Hodges said. "It seems he had a partner in the diggings, a man named Hill, who has relatives in Denver. Hill got badly burned in a cabin fire and before he died, he signed his half of the claim over to Isaac."

She helped Hodges to his feet. She couldn't count the number of times she had thought about the lieutenant. Sometimes she had missed an entire night of sleep and had felt guilty about it. Now he had risked his life to come and find her. She fought the urge to put her arms around him.

"How was Isaac's health?" she asked.

"He looked frail to me," Hodges replied. "But he was in good spirits and made the trip back down to Fort Laramie in good shape."

She helped Hodges fit the crutches under his arms. On the way back to the cabin, the lieutenant told her what had happened after his return to the wagons.

"I found a lot of the settlers had been killed or wounded," he said. "But Tillie McGivern and Burnham Hess survived. She dragged him under her wagon and they covered up with blankets."

"I saw her do it," Holly said, "just before Bad Face threw a rope over me and dragged me away. And I saw Harlan take a horse that was supposed to be for Justin and me."

"Well, he got away," Hodges said. "He showed up at Fort Laramie not long after that. Wouldn't look me in the face, though. I wanted to find a reason to string him up, but my commanding officer said to let it go. So he got his cronies together at the fort and last I heard, they were robbing stages and stealing horses down along the Cache la Poudre River.

They've caused a lot of trouble and there's not enough law down there to stop them."

"He'll meet a fine end some day," Holly said. "Where did Burnham go?"

"This will surprise you. He went down to work for Isaac. He hired on to cook during roundups."

Holly laughed. "I can't see Burnham as a cook. He's too unsettled."

"He told me he's had enough of dodging Indians. And he no longer wants any part of the gold fields. He's decided that he'll like it as a ranch cook. He and Tillie together."

"Burnham and Tillie?"

"Is that so surprising? Couldn't you see they had something for each other even before she saved his old hide?"

"She was very loyal to her husband."

"Yes, she was, up until the moment he died. But she's decided that she and Burnham are meant to be together."

Old Calf Woman watched them approach the cabin. Hodges greeted her sheepishly, wondering to himself how a woman of that age had survived for so long alone. But he thought he knew the answer: She could hunt and take care of herself, and because of her reputation for being crazy, the Sioux left her alone.

"This is my dearest friend," Holly said, helping him into the cabin, "and my adopted mother."

Hodges sat down on Holly's bed and watched as she carefully unwrapped the bandage from his leg.

Old Calf Woman squinted and worked to prepare the poultice for the wound.

"Ask him why he left you at the wagons that day," she said to Holly. "Didn't he know better than to do that?"

Holly translated for Hodges.

"He was given orders by his superiors to go after any hostile Indians. He had to do it."

"You tell him that nobody *has* to do anything. But thank

him for me, anyway. If he hadn't been so foolish I would never have been able to help you and gain a daughter."

When Holly told the lieutenant what she had said, he smiled. "It seems she's a good judge of character."

"What do you mean?"

"I think you know," he said. "I told you one night at the wagons that I thought you to be a pretty fine lady. I can see that you're a damned strong one, too."

Holly took the poultice from Old Calf Woman and applied it to his leg.

"Thank you, Lieutenant. But you must not think enough of me to let me go with you when you look for Justin."

"I told you, I don't know if it's Justin."

"I think you know that it is."

"Even so, I can't allow you along. Army regulations."

"Fine. I'll look for Justin myself just as soon as I can. Then we'll go down and find Isaac."

"That's not a good idea, Holly. It's my job to find him."

"Where is Red Cloud?"

Hodges pointed. "We've gotten word he's camped on Powder River, near the mouth of Bitter Creek."

"Is that where you were going?"

"No, just to Fort Phil Kearny, to start the whole process."

"When do you plan to go after the boy?"

"As soon as the orders come through."

"And how long will that be?"

"Probably spring."

Holly shook her head. "You expect me to wait until spring to find my son?"

"You don't have a choice."

"Oh, yes, I do have a choice, Lieutenant."

"You can't go after him alone," Hodges said. "There's a plan to all this. It's a delicate matter."

"What's so 'delicate' about it?"

"I shouldn't have told you," he said. "I knew better."

"You listen to me, Lieutenant. I don't care about your damned orders. He's my son and his safety's at stake. I can't wait until the army thinks the time is right."

From down the hill came the sound of horses. Hodges pushed himself to his feet on the crutches Holly had given him and made his way outside. She followed and Old Calf Woman stayed inside.

Hodges hurried as best he could, with Holly beside him.

"Lieutenant," she said, "surely you understand."

"I've got orders and I have to follow them. Don't you see how all this can fly apart at any time?"

"And don't you see that without my son I have nothing?"

Antoine Janis and five soldiers rode up to the cabin. A sergeant named Culwain arranged the men in formation.

Janis held the reins to Hodges's horse.

"We tracked your pony here, Lieutenant. We thought maybe you'd been killed."

Hodges took the reins. "Thank you. I'm lucky. My wound's not serious and it's been taken care of."

Janis and the soldiers were all staring.

"This is Holly Porter," Hodges said. "She was with the wagons last fall—the woman who was dragged away."

They all looked at Holly with wonder, Janis especially. He hadn't actually believed she was alive.

Hodges introduced Janis and the other soldiers in turn. Holly smiled half-heartedly.

He struggled onto his horse. "That old Indian woman that lives up here saved her. I guess I should be grateful to her myself, as she put a poultice on my leg."

"Is she as crazy as they say?" Janis asked.

"She didn't seem crazy to me." He turned to Sergeant Culwain. "What happened at the fight? What about the others?"

"We lost two, and four wounded," Culwain said. "But we put the run on the renegades."

Hodges sat silent a moment, pained by the loss of his men,

reminded again of the death of the wagon people caused by Bad Face and his renegades.

"Could you see who was leading these Sioux?" Hodges asked Janis.

"It was Bad Face."

"I guess he wants to kill everybody on this road," Hodges said. He turned to the sergeant. "You take the men on below. I'll join you soon."

The soldiers tipped their hats and Culwain led them away in formation.

Janis remained behind. "Should I stay with you?"

"Thank you, Antoine, but I'll be fine," Hodges said. "Go with the others. I'll catch up."

When Janis had left, Holly said, "Is he going to help you find Justin?"

"He'll be with me," Hodges said. "He's a good man." He leaned over the saddle. "You don't really intend to go after your son, do you?"

"I told you, I want to reunite my family. We had a lot of dreams on the way out here, and I intend to see that they come true."

"I wish you'd think about it. I'm glad you're alive and I'd hate to see something happen to you."

Holly watched him ride away and join the others. Old Calf Woman ambled down to her side.

"You like him, don't you?"

Holly turned to her. "What are you talking about?"

"You know what I'm talking about. You like him. You have feelings for him. You can't hide it." She started back up toward the cabin. "And he's right, you know. It would be sad if something happened to you."

Thirteen

LATE THAT afternoon, Holly looked across the country from the ridge and noticed a stray horse. She worked her way over to where it was pawing for grass under the snow, thinking the animal must have belonged to one of the fallen soldiers.

She caught the horse and discovered a pistol and a pouch of bullets in a saddlebag. The weapon felt cold and heavy in her hand.

She mounted the horse and rode back toward the cabin, pausing where she had met Hodges earlier. His blood soaked the snow and she wondered if his leg wound would worsen. Old Calf Woman had said that if he kept the poultice in place, nothing bad would happen. When he reached Fort Phil Kearny, the post surgeon would take care of him.

At the cabin, Old Calf Woman stood in the doorway.

"Ah! You found a horse. We may have to eat it when the weather changes for the worse again."

Holly walked past her into the cabin. "No, we won't eat that horse. I'm going to ride it to Red Cloud's village." She tossed the pistol onto her bed.

"And that pistol? Are you going to take it too?"

"I'll shoot rabbits for food."

"Do you know how to shoot it?"

"I've fired Isaac's before. I can get used to this one just fine."

"Will you get used to it quick enough to save your life?"

"If I have to."

"If you don't go, you won't have to."

"I appreciate all you've done for me," Holly said, "but you can't keep me from seeking out my son."

"Did I say I wanted to do that?" She picked up a moccasin and began mending a tear in the sole.

"You keep telling me that I'll fail."

"It's not that you'll fail, not if you do it right and at the right time."

"I can't wait until the grass is up."

"What about Bad Face and his renegades?"

"I'll use the pistol against him."

The old woman continued to sew the moccasin. "You must have decided against learning the medicine from me."

"You've stopped teaching me," Holly said.

"The time to continue is not here yet," Old Calf Woman said. "I told you that. We can't go on until the weather is warm."

"Then maybe I can't finish," Holly said. "I want to look for Justin now, before another storm comes. Then I want to go and find my husband and start our life over again."

Old Calf Woman laid the moccasin down. "First I gain a daughter, and then she takes herself away from me."

"Did you think I'd be here with you for the rest of my life?"

"I'm trying to tell you that you'll shorten your life if you don't wait to go after your son. Even if you don't run into Bad Face, there's the cold. Do you remember the cold?"

"I'll find Justin before the cold returns."

"Do you know what it's like to die in the snow? They say it's like laying on feathers." She stared hard at Holly. "They say that at the end, when you are nearly frozen, the snow is like feathers. Do you want to lay down in feathers?"

"I'll come right back up here as soon as I get Justin back,"

Holly said. "If it's cold, we'll stay on until it gets warm again. But we'll both come visit you."

"Yes, I believe you'll come back," Old Calf Woman said. "I just hope it's you and not your spirit."

She left with first light, a thin pink band across the eastern sky. She stuffed a bag with pemmican and tied it to the horse, then strapped the pistol around her waist and took the wolfskin coat and two heavy blankets to keep her warm during the night.

As the sun rose, Old Calf Woman remained in her bed, sound asleep, or maybe pretending to be. She had said that she wouldn't be witness to such a foolish thing.

Holly's surprising discovery of the lieutenant and the news he had given her had invigorated her. Now she felt she had the opportunity to reunite her family, and she intended to make the best of it.

With the Bighorn Mountains at her back, their jagged peaks mantled with white, she set off toward the lower reaches of Powder River. Her course took her down Crazy Woman Creek to where it flowed into the main channel. The bottom provided adequate food for the horse: Slivers of willow and dried salt grass would give him enough energy to travel the distance.

She made camp the first evening, just before nightfall, in a grove of cottonwoods. Flocks of sharp-tailed grouse flew into the top branches to roost while a pair of chickadees flitted through the low limbs of a nearby juniper tree, darting to the ground for small morsels of pemmican that Holly left for them. Though they flew away at dusk, she saw and heard them in her dreams that night.

She rose early the following morning, peering into the distance for signs of smoke rising. Still too far away, she told herself, and mounted the horse.

By late afternoon she still hadn't seen any smoke and began to worry. Yet she realized the land was vast and the river long. She still had a lot of territory to cover.

Then, just before nightfall, Holly stopped to look far downriver. The sun was dropping below the western horizon and the late light shown across a cloudless sky. She was certain that she could see smoke drifting in the hazy distance. It had to be the village.

She thought seriously about traveling on, but realized it was a foolish thought. Better to wait for the warmth of the day and not take chances with the winter night.

The darkness settled in with a slight breeze and the sounds of elk and deer combing the bottoms for food. Then the herds disappeared and only the sounds of an owl came from the heavy tree cover.

She fell asleep near a small fire, huddled in her wolfskin coat. Visions of her son flooded her mind; she saw him running to her, grinning and shouting as he greeted her. All around them the Sioux people stood clapping, glad to see that she had braved the winter for her son.

Then she saw Isaac, greeting them with a large bag of gold, pointing to a map of the land he had settled on for the ranch. "Lots of cattle coming in," he said. "Up from Texas. We'll build there, by those aspen trees."

The dream changed suddenly. In her deep sleep Holly heard the horse snorting and a loud, piercing scream that chilled her blood. She flew awake to find her pony squealing in terror, pulling at his rope, while something lurched from the shadows.

In the moonlight she could see the silhouette of a mountain lion leaping upon the horse's back. The pony jerked its head, snapping the rope, and rushed past Holly, kicking ashes from the fire, the huge cat clinging to its back.

She searched frantically for her pistol. Out from camp, the

pony crashed into the river, thrashing through the soft ice. The cat jumped free, splashing back to shore, while the pony continued into the current. Midway across, it became trapped in soft mud and she knew from the sounds that the pony was drowning.

After finding her pistol, Holly scrambled through the willows and wild rose at the shoreline. She saw the cat, a black shadow along the river. She fired and it bounded away into the darkness.

Her horse, too exhausted to reach the opposite shore, now struggled feebly for its last few breaths. Tears filled her eyes. Her pony was lost, and with it, her hopes of reaching Justin.

Holly stood at the river's edge. The early sun shone on the river. The pony lay partially submerged, its head underwater. The back and shoulders were layered with dried blood, where the cat's claws had torn through to the bone.

She turned to gaze downriver. In the far distance, a mantle of heavy white clouds was making its way down from the north. Holly realized a storm was coming; but if she turned back, she might forever lose her chance to find Justin.

She knew the storm would not just come and go, leaving a little snow that would melt, as it had during the past several days. No, it would be much worse, as a large, thin ring had formed around the sun: a "sun dog," a sure sign that a heavy invasion of winter weather would arrive soon.

She knew this to be true, for Old Calf Woman had talked about sun dogs, showing her the same kind of ring that had formed around the sun just before the strong cold at Christmas.

Holly vowed to continue on, hoping that the Sioux winter camp lay lost in the oncoming ice clouds, in the direction of the rising smoke she had seen the day before.

She would hurry and she would reach the village in time. It would be a race to beat the storm, and it was a race she couldn't afford to lose.

She trudged through the day, past herds of deer browsing shrubs, and roaming bands of elk that sought out dried grass on the hillsides. The warm air of the past week had opened up the foothills, softening snow and melting it completely in places.

Yet she knew the storm was moving fast, for a biting north wind had already begun to blow.

Though her legs ached, she sought the top of a nearby hill and searched for signs of rising smoke in the distance. She saw nothing but the oncoming storm.

Snow began falling, lightly at first, and then heavier as the wind increased. She drew the wolfskin coat around her face and walked backward into the blowing snow, falling often, rising against the pain each time.

Now the deer and elk were huddled together in groves of trees along the bottom, standing or lying still while the snow piled onto their backs.

Holly continued downriver, staying in the trees as much as possible, fighting the drifting snow. Fear gripped her with each step, for without adequate shelter, she wouldn't last the night. She said a prayer that Old Calf Woman had taught her, used by her people in times of crisis:

Creator, guide my way, show me the trail.
Let me hear the trees talk and the voice of the wind.
Let the rocks tell me how to go and the spirits of my
grandfathers will be glad.

Old Calf Woman had told her that it wasn't a prayer for survival but a request to the Creator for a good trip, whether it be to death or continued life. "Whether or not your body dies at such a time," the old woman had said, "after such an experience you are reborn."

Tonight, Holly knew, would certainly be a night for rebirth.

With the storm worsening and darkness near, she discovered four small tepees made of heavy tree limbs and branches, layered with mud, standing against a cliff along the river. She knew they were war lodges, used by Sioux enemies traveling through, as Old Calf Woman had told her stories of warring tribes and their habits while on horse raids.

Upon closer inspection, she discovered that two of the lodges had fallen in and a third was filled with firewood. She took an armload and entered the fourth lodge.

At the doorway, she dropped the wood, and stood rooted with shock. Sitting upright in the back of the lodge were three frozen bodies—a man, a woman, and a small child in the woman's arms.

Holly knew they hadn't died recently, but likely during the previous cold that had come at Christmas. Their faces, dull and dark, looked contented, though, and she realized she would have to endure their company throughout the night.

She lit a fire and tried to eat. Hungry as she was, she had to give it up for a time, until she could get used to their dull, staring eyes.

Then tears came and she thought of how they must have had their own hopes and dreams. She wondered what had brought them here and how they had become trapped.

It seemed that the man had been mixed-blood, for a wispy beard clung to his chin. Possibly a trader passing through with his family, trying to avoid the Sioux village. Had they been sick when they had stopped, or without food for a long time? Why had they died here? Questions, Holly knew, that would never be answered.

Though very tired, Holly found it difficult to sleep. She awoke repeatedly, sitting upright, staring at the frozen bodies. Each time she awoke she stoked the fire, placing more wood on it than she had the time before. She couldn't get warm enough.

Finally, near dawn, she fell into a deep sleep. In her dream she saw the woman pointing toward a soiled and tattered blanket. She pointed once, twice, three, and then four times. Then she resumed the position of holding her child in death.

Holly suddenly awoke and sat up. She stared at the frozen bodies, fragments of the strange dream lingering in her mind. Unnerved, she stepped outside.

Though the air was bitter cold, the skies were clear. She climbed a nearby hill and searched longingly for signs of smoke in the distance, but saw none.

She returned to the lodge and pondered going farther downriver but decided against it. Should she be caught in the open in another snowstorm, she might not survive again. She would wait a few days and see if the weather changed once more.

That night she ate sparingly of her pemmican. She had but a day's supply left. She might possibly shoot small game with the pistol, but she had seen only one rabbit her entire journey, and birds were nearly impossible to hit, even when they were sitting still.

No matter which direction she took, Holly realized she would face starvation. She thought about Old Calf Woman's warning and realized how foolish she had been. If Justin were alive and living in a Sioux village, he would be well cared for throughout the winter. What good would she be to him dead? And how would she get him away from them once she reached the village?

She knew she must go back. She knew nothing of the landscape that lay ahead. She could take the trail back and possibly carve some meat from her dead horse. Possibly she would be able to shoot one of the grouse from the trees. But with cold hands, her aim would certainly be less than sure. She stared continuously at the frozen bodies and thought about death. Had theirs been easy, like drifting off to sleep? Or had they suffered immeasurably before losing consciousness?

They say it's like laying on feathers. She remembered Old Calf Woman's words. *They say that at the end, when you are nearly frozen, the snow is like feathers. Do you want to lay down in feathers?*

She stoked the fire throughout the night and decided at first light, storm or not, she would have to turn back. She took a few bites of pemmican and lay down for rest.

Deep in sleep, she again saw the woman point four times to the blankets. One, two, three, four, her face earnest. Neither the man nor the boy moved. Just the woman, pointing her bony, frozen fingers.

Holly tried to speak, to ask her what she was doing, but no words would come. The woman pointed four times and turned back to her frozen death.

Holly bolted awake. She sat up and stared at the woman. The fire had dwindled to coals, so she stoked it and placed more wood on the faltering flames.

Holly spoke to the frozen woman. "You look as though you want to say something."

She reached forward and touched the dead woman's face. It felt rubbery, thawed from the warmth of the fire. She drew her hand back. She then turned her attention to where the woman had pointed.

Gingerly, she touched the blanket. Something about it intrigued her. She felt it, discovering that beneath the worn fabric lay something formed of wood and steel.

She peeled away the shredded blanket and pulled a rifle free, a Henry repeater filled with cartridges. Next to the rifle lay a half-filled box, its top open.

Holly stared at the woman, certain she saw a faint smile on her lips.

That morning the weather cleared once again. Though sorely tempted, Holly resisted the urge to travel farther downriver in search of the village. Instead, blinded by tears and guilt for having to forsake her mission to find Justin, she turned and made her way back along the river.

The snowy footing was treacherous and she fell frequently. Her body ached and though she brought down a rabbit with the rifle, it wasn't enough; hunger gnawed at her, drawing from her reserve of strength.

Distressed by weakness and the failed attempt to find her son, Holly's anger rose and she marched forward, swearing bitterly that she would try again just as soon as the first wisps of grass appeared.

Late that afternoon, she saw five riders coming down the river toward her. They saw her at the same time and the two in front rode forward, screaming war cries.

She leveled the rifle. Flame burst from the barrel and the lead warrior fell backward off his pony. The second pulled up.

She levered another round into the barrel, aware that the second rider's pony was a mousy-gray color.

Bad Face! Now is my time to settle things with you!

The rider turned the horse and it reared in the snow. Instead of hitting the rider, her bullet struck the pony in the neck, splintering the spine, killing it instantly. The rider pitched backward onto the snowy ground.

The other three warriors ran their ponies to the top of a nearby hill and watched while Holly rushed up to the fallen one, jamming the rifle barrel into his face.

But it wasn't Bad Face.

The warrior lay with his eyes wide, waiting for Holly

to fire. He began singing a death song and she backed away.

She laid the rifle across the sagebrush plant and quickly made sign.

"I don't intend to kill you, not unless I have to. I want to know who you are and what you're doing here."

She picked up the rifle and leveled it while the warrior answered her in sign.

"I and the others are out hunting. We thought you were an enemy."

She pointed at the fallen horse. "Is that your pony, or does it belong to Bad Face?"

"The pony once belonged to Bad Face, but I won it from him in a race. How do you know him?"

"He tried to kill me one time by dragging me behind that pony. I was hoping that I had found him, to make things even."

The warrior's eyes grew wider. "I was there that day of the wagon fight. I saw him drag you. How could you be alive? Are you a spirit?"

She reached toward him and the warrior shrank back.

"Let me touch you," she said. "Then you can see if I'm a spirit or not."

The warrior started to rise and Holly put the rifle in his face once more.

"I have more questions. Is there a white boy in your village, one who is now Red Cloud's son?"

"Yes."

"I want you to take a message to Red Cloud. I want my son back. If I don't get him back soon, I will make trouble for all of you."

"If I tell him that," the warrior said, "he might kill your son."

"He won't kill my son," Holly said. "If he does, many of his people will die as a result. And maybe him too."

The warrior stared at her. "You couldn't kill Red Cloud."

"A spirit can do anything." She watched his eyes widen. "Want me to show you?"

She reached for the warrior and he lurched to his feet. He ran madly up the hill. When he reached the other three, he climbed behind one of the riders and they kicked their ponies into a run, disappearing into the dusk.

Holly caught the loose pony and tied it to a cottonwood. She started a fire, then cut a branch and sharpened the end. Returning to the dead horse, she cut a chunk of meat from the hind quarters and skewered it on the stick.

She sat near the fire, huddled in her wolfskin coat, eating the meat half raw. She thought about how she had treated the warrior and the look on his face. It made her laugh. She knew why this place was called Crazy Woman Fork.

Fourteen

JUSTIN RODE his pony through the snow, following the course of the river back toward the mountains. It had begun to storm and he knew that if he didn't find shelter soon, his escape attempt would lead to disaster.

Germain had told him not to go, pointing to the sky and saying, "It will get very cold soon. That ring around the sun is a sign."

Justin had argued that the recent warm spell had brought wisps of green along the riverbank and on the south slopes of the hills.

"It can't stay cold. Look at the changes," he had said.

"Maybe spring is almost here," Germain had said, "but Old Man Winter doesn't know it yet."

He hadn't listened to Germain but had planned his escape instead. He waited until late in the night and snuck to the horse herd. It had been easy, as no one was on watch and no one saw him leave.

Justin had left dressed in deerskin, carrying a pouch of pemmican. He couldn't have asked for a better night, as the temperature was moderate and a light snow was falling, which covered his tracks.

Then at dawn bitter cold had set in. He wondered if he had been all that wise. Well into the following day, the snow fell even heavier. A wind began to whip the snow into flurries that stung his face like sharp sand.

His hands and feet were already cold and tingling. He dismounted and stomped his feet to keep the dull pain from getting worse. More than once he had thought about turning around, but each time the fear of what Red Cloud might do kept him moving away from the village.

As the storm worsened, Justin realized he couldn't see in any direction. He knew that he was still on the river bottom, as the trees and brush loomed through the snow. Still, they provided no shelter or security.

It wasn't until he reached four wooden lodges that he felt any hope. War lodges, he thought, remembering stories told by the old men in Red Cloud's camp and translated by Germain. He didn't know why they were there along the river but he gave thanks for having found them.

Two of the lodges had fallen down and a third was filled with wood. He took an armful and retreated into the fourth.

He didn't see the frozen corpses until he had seated himself. The first thing he noticed was that a fresh fire had been built not long before, and it intrigued him. Only then had he looked up to see the three—a man, woman, and a child.

He sat petrified, looking into the faces of the three. He thought of leaving but the howling wind outside told him that would be foolish. Instead, he piled fresh wood over the ashes and realized to his horror that he had nothing with which to light a fire.

Of all the things to forget, a piece of flint was the last thing he could afford to be without.

The snow continued and a cold wind crept into the lodge. He sat back, huddled in his deerskin coat.

I guess I'll be joining you three before long, he thought as he studied the corpses.

He thought about trying his luck in finding his way back, but the wind howled even louder and he wondered if his death wouldn't be less painful where he sat. He concluded it would and lay down to await the end.

He closed his eyes but jerked awake when he heard a voice at the doorway of the lodge.

"You thought you could run away?" Bad Face said.

He jerked Justin from the blanket and dragged him outside, slapped him twice across the face.

"If you were my son, I would teach you to stay at home. Now, get on your pony. We have to get back before the deep cold hits."

Bad Face said nothing during the ride back. He led Justin's pony so there was no way he could attempt escape.

In the village, everyone watched while Bad Face led Justin in a circle around camp, showing them that he had caught the white boy.

"I brought this boy to Red Cloud in the beginning," Bad Face announced, "and I will see to it that our chief has this boy always."

At Red Cloud's lodge, the chief stepped out and said to Bad Face, "Why did you go after him?"

"Because he's your son. Because I brought him to you in the first place."

"Better to let the cold have him," Red Cloud said, "if he doesn't wish to be here. Besides, there's a spirit who wants him to be released. A Wolf Woman spirit."

"What?" Bad Face asked.

The chief explained how a party of hunters had just returned after having lost one of their number to a woman dressed in a wolf skin.

"I was told that the being was either a woman, or a woman's spirit, dressed in wolf skin," Red Cloud told Bad Face. "She knows who you are because she shot your horse. She thought you were riding it."

Stunned, Bad Face released Justin's pony and rode to another part of camp, where the returned hunters had gathered some of the warriors together to tell them what had happened.

Red Cloud took the pony's reins and spoke to Justin.

"So, you do not wish to be my son? Maybe I should send you back out in the storm."

"You would do that?"

"You have shamed me in front of my people," Red Cloud said. "Certainly I have other sons, but you filled a special place. Or I thought you did."

"I'll stay," Justin said. "I won't run off again."

"Why did you run?"

"I miss my ma and pa."

"You could never accept me as a father?"

"Maybe, if I knew my pa was dead."

"Get down off your pony and come inside," Red Cloud said. "When the warm moons come we'll decide what to do with you."

The trees were filled with birds singing nesting songs and the slopes of the foothills were covered with wildflowers, their red and yellow and blue colors blending with the deep green of the tall grasses.

Holly had come to believe Old Calf Woman, who had said that she needed to have her own medicine, her own special powers if she were to be successful in finding her son. After her ordeal in the cold, she knew this to be true.

Old Calf Woman was now preparing her for a special part of her learning. Holly already knew what to expect, for she had been told it would involve dreams and pain, similar to when she nearly died from being dragged behind Bad Face's horse.

Holly had often told Old Calf Woman the story about her meeting her deceased brother behind the door of their cabin. "This will be the same in some ways," the old woman had said. "But the beings you will meet will not be like your brother."

The vision quest would take place high on a mountain above the cabin. For two days Old Calf Woman fasted and prayed, gathering the right materials for the ceremony, foremost of which was a sufficient quantity of sage, plus a buffalo robe and some rocks that had been used in her sweat lodge.

Old Calf Woman also ripped pieces of yellow cloth into strips, as well as others of white, black, and red. "It's the right medicine for you," she told Holly. "It will give you the strength you need in your life."

The climb to the mountain, which lay at the base of Cloud Peak, began on the fourth day. The eastern sky was streaked with scarlet as they took a trail that led through the foothills and then up into the heavy timber of the mountains.

Despite her age, Old Calf Woman moved remarkably well. "I'm helped by the spirits," she said.

They journeyed farther upward, through meadows bursting with color. The high-country snows had given way to warm sunshine and evening thunderstorms, bringing life back to the land.

Birdsong drifted everywhere, from every bush and tree, and herds of elk wandered the meadows, browsing for food, their calves bouncing along behind them.

Other animals appeared, including the mountain sheep. Holly marveled at their enormous curled horns.

A short distance farther, along a densely wooded trail, Old Calf Woman pointed out a bush in full bloom.

"These flowers will become berries later on in the warm moons," she said. "They're good to make pemmican with."

"What's that strong odor?" Holly said.

Old Calf Woman, whose senses were failing her, asked Holly about the smell.

"Very strong. And musky."

The old woman's eyes grew large and she told Holly to sit down with her and remain still.

"What is it?"

"Be very still and don't speak."

Holly looked to the hillside above the trail. An enormous grizzly bear stared down at them, her two cubs at her side. Holly held her breath. Based on Old Calf Woman's stories, she knew how unpredictable these animals were and how much damage they could cause if angered. The reality made her dizzy. Still, the animal's majesty captivated her. The two cubs, little more than round balls of fur, squalled and cuffed each other in play. As soon as they discovered Holly and Old Calf Woman, they started down the hill toward them.

"What do we do now?" Holly whispered.

"Pray," the old woman said. "Pray just as hard as you can."

The mother grizzly grunted and the two cubs returned to her side. The three of them soon disappeared into the brush.

Holly breathed a sigh of relief.

"You must have prayed pretty hard," the old woman said. "We'll wait a little while. We want a clear trail from now on."

As they sat, Old Calf Woman spoke of life and death and the thin veil separating the two worlds.

"You have no way of knowing when it will come, unless someone with the gift of knowing tells you," she said. "But I've never known someone with that gift to speak of someone's death to their face. It's forbidden."

"Will I be able to see that when I complete my medicine studies?"

"I can't say, because I don't know," the old woman replied. "Whatever comes to you is a gift from the Creator. I can only guide you in learning, then you must go from there and use the powers with wisdom."

"What I really need the power for is to bring my family back together."

"As I said, the Creator will decide your gifts."

Holly helped Old Calf Woman to her feet and they continued up the mountain. As they neared their destination, Holly's fear grew. Old Calf Woman tried to calm her.

"You've come this far," Old Calf Woman said. "It would be foolish to give up now.'

Holly watched the old woman amble up the trail. Here was a woman more than three times her age who could face anything.

She caught up with her and apologized.

"You have nothing to be sorry for," the old woman said. "If you had shown no fear, *then* I would be worried."

A short distance farther, Old Calf Woman stopped at the base of an old pine tree whose branches were naked and gnarled.

"This tree has been dead longer than I've been alive," she said. She pointed midway up. "You see that platform built in there? That's mine."

Holly noted a platform made of pine branches tied together and fitted to lie flat in the tree. She had been told about such platforms by the old woman, who said they were used for burials.

Old Calf Woman climbed to the platform and placed her hand upon it. "When the time is right, I will come up here and meet the Creator," she said. She pointed into the sky, where an eagle soared. "I will give my body to my brothers and sisters of the wind. Then I will be free to go where I must."

From the ground, Holly watched while the old woman lay sage on the platform and raised her head to the heavens. When her prayers were finished, she started back down the tree.

At the bottom, the old woman again looked to the platform and to the sky, then started up the trail.

"How much farther?" Holly asked.

Old Calf Woman pointed. "Not far ahead the trail will come to a small lake. Just above these waters is where you will seek your vision. We must hurry and reach the spot. We've a lot to do before the sun falls to let the darkness come."

*   *   *

That night, by the light of a small fire, Holly took dried buffalo meat from Old Calf Woman and mixed it with roots the
old woman had dug earlier in the day. She placed it in a small
iron kettle over the fire.

"This will be your last meal before you fast," the old
woman said. "Eat slowly and pray when you swallow."

"What should I pray for?"

"The Creator knows what you need, but you could ask
for health and, when you find your son, happiness after
that."

Holly looked into the old woman's eyes. "Surely I would
be selfish to think only of Justin and myself. I thought you
once told me that prayers should be for one and all, for the
benefit of everyone."

Old Calf Woman smiled. "That is what good prayers are
for, yes."

Holly ate slowly, asking for a good vision quest and for
blessings on herself and her family. She also asked for blessings on Old Calf Woman, without whom her life could never
have gone on.

After the meal, Old Calf Woman let the fire die down and
covered the coals with sage. A strong aroma filled the air and
Holly turned her face to the sky.

The heavens were shot full of stars, seemingly so close she
could reach out and touch them. Old Calf Woman pointed to
a group of stars in the vast distance.

"The Bunched Stars," she said. "Some call them the Seven
Sisters in the Sky, or maybe the Seven Dancers. There are
many names for them but I prefer to think of them as sisters."

Holly stared, hypnotized by the vastness.

"My people have a story about those stars," the old woman
said. "It has to do with dogs and how my people have always
loved them, especially before the coming of the horse."

Holly remembered Old Calf Woman talking about how dogs carried the heavy loads from camp to camp before the horse.

"I want you to listen carefully," the old woman continued, "and think of this story when you are fasting and looking into the sky."

She began her story by telling of the Seven Sisters, born to a very poor family. As their wealth was measured mainly by horses and clothing, the girls' father was considered very poor, as he had no buffalo ponies for hunting and depended upon handouts to feed his family. In the same fashion, the girls had very poor clothing and had to depend on castoffs to keep themselves warm.

"Among the people," Old Calf Woman said, "it was considered a great honor to have your children dressed in red robes. The buffalo calves in the spring bore the finest of red color in their coats, and after the hunting, young boys and girls were used to wearing red robes, to show their prowess in the village.

"Year after year the Seven Sisters went without a single red robe between them, and though there were extras among the other villagers, no one would give any of them up. They were teased by the other children and made to feel shameful.

" 'I'm tired of being without a red robe,' one sister said to the others after a spring hunt. 'I say that we should leave the village and go into the sky to live.' They discussed it and vowed that should there be no red robes for them the following spring, they would make their home in the sky."

Holly watched a blaze of light trail across the heavens.

"When they fall, it means a campfire of long ago has gone out," Old Calf Woman said. "It means some of the Sky People are no longer camped out there."

"What happened to the Seven Sisters?" Holly asked.

"Yes, I was telling you that story, wasn't I? Well, the following spring the Seven Sisters again went without a single red robe among them and were again teased and called names by the other children. So the eldest sister gathered some medicine and the sisters traveled to a place outside of camp.

"Using weasel hair, the eldest sister rubbed the backs of the other sisters and said, 'Close your eyes.' She then blew the weasel hair into the night sky and they suddenly found themselves among the Sky People, in the house of Sun, and his wife, Moon.

" 'Why are you here?' Sun asked the Seven Sisters.

" 'Because we are without red robes,' the eldest sister replied. 'We've come to ask your help.'

" 'What do you want me to do for you?' Sun asked.

" 'Take the water away from the people for seven days and nights,' the fourth sister said.

"To this Moon said, 'It shall be done, but you must all stay here in the sky.' She turned to Sun, but he said nothing. She asked him seven times to help her make the Earth hot and he finally agreed.

"The next day it was so hot on Earth that it boiled the water from the streams and lakes. That night was also hot and Moon shone down on the people. They chose two dogs to help them the following day.

"The next day, Sun shone hot again and the people took the two dogs where the river once ran with cool water. The people dug holes in the bank to get in out of the heat and the dogs dug far into the riverbanks until water poured out. These were the first springs.

"The dogs continued to dig and on the sixth night, they began to howl at Moon. 'Take pity on the dogs of Earth,' one of them sang. 'Take pity!'

"On the seventh day Sun and Moon sent a big rain that lasted a long time. Ever since that time there has been great respect for dogs, especially when they howl at night."

"And so the Seven Sisters had to remain in the sky and live there to this day?" Holly asked.

"That's right," Old Calf Woman said. "Remember that story when you are fasting and praying. You will understand what I mean when the days become hot and there is no water to drink."

Fifteen

AS THE sun rose, Holly sat with Old Calf Woman while she prayed over a sage fire. Then, filled with fear, she followed the old woman to a long ridge below the base of Cloud Peak.

There, Old Calf Woman selected an area the size of a large bedroom among the rocks and timber where Holly would seek her vision. She prayed most of the day, moving the colored cloth around, tying it to various bushes and trees, positioning it just right.

"I'm doing it the way the spirits tell me," she told Holly. "It has to be right."

Holly waited patiently. Late in the afternoon, Old Calf Woman gathered her things and Holly's stomach churned even more.

"Give your fear to the Creator," the old woman said.

"*Must* you leave?"

"I'll return when the time is right. Now is your time to fast and pray. Whatever you do, don't leave this spot. Do you understand?"

"I'll stay here," Holly promised.

She watched the old woman move slowly out of sight, down off the trail toward the bottom. She felt vulnerable and fought the urge to leave her spot and run after her friend. But the time had come to face her test.

Remaining on the ridge was a far harder task than she had expected. That first night, as the sun went down, she felt so alone that she desperately wanted to get up and run.

But where would she go? She had no idea where Old Calf Woman had gone and she certainly didn't know her way through the forest in the dark. Besides, after all this preparation, it was time to finish what she had started.

She wrapped herself tightly in her blankets and lay down to watch the stars. The vast heavens were aglow with sparkles of light. She wondered if the Seven Sisters might be watching her.

Once asleep, she drifted into a realm without dreams, without boundaries. It was an open black void without feeling or understanding, an absence of experience or memory.

Something awakened her as the sun rose, and she sat up. In a nearby pine, chickadees jumped from limb to limb, their gleeful voices filling the air. Overhead, a raven flapped lazily, cawing in its raucous voice.

The sun began to warm the ridge. The chickadees left and silence followed.

Holly looked around her. "Old Calf Woman? Are you here?"

The silence was broken by a stirring in the trees, a wisp of wind that traveled through the branches like a song.

"Old Calf Woman?"

Again silence.

Holly's stomach tightened. She wanted to get up and find the old woman but remembered her instructions to remain on the ridge and told herself again that she must finish what she started, no matter the fear.

She could move about the area laid out by Old Calf Woman if she wished. But Holly felt more secure sitting in the spot where she had slept. It felt familiar on this mountain ridge that seemed isolated from every other place on earth.

The air remained cool, and after a deep breath, she lay back down in her blankets. Overhead, a swirl of clouds slipped off the peaks and flittered out over the foothills. From a nearby cliff two eagles took flight and circled.

She closed her eyes. A pleasant breeze kissed her cheeks and the chickadees returned, singing *dee-dee-dee* as they hopped on the ground beside her, each of them so small as to fit into the palm of her hand.

"What do you want?" she asked, as if they could answer.

The tiny birds cocked their heads and picked through the pine needles, then flitted off into the tree cover, their song trailing behind them.

A small wind touched the trees and suddenly vanished. Again Holly heard the silence and turned inward. She lay back down and tried to sleep, but felt too energized.

Her mind raced with images; names and faces and places from throughout her life rolled by endlessly. She found herself filled with the feelings of those moments, good and bad. She found she couldn't stop their coming and lay back, her eyes shut, while the pictures in her mind progressed endlessly.

Then her mind quieted and sleep again found her.

Late that afternoon Holly felt her first pangs of hunger, slight yet still obvious. Her mouth had gotten dry and she knew her thirst would worsen as the day turned into night.

As the sun fell, she reviewed the thoughts that had filled her day. Her life had passed before her eyes, the good and the bad, and she knew that everything from this time forward would change.

That night her thirst worsened. She fought anxiety and fear, and the desire to rise and run off into the night.

Once she had settled herself, she realized her hunger had grown. She envisioned tasty meals of meat and potatoes, and the fruit pies her mother used to make.

Holly worked to get her thoughts off food and drink. She made her mind blank, as black as the night around her.

"When you get past your cravings, then you will begin to learn," Old Calf Woman had told her. "But first you must allow yourself to suffer."

Holly hadn't realized the depth of the suffering needed to remove herself from her desires. She thought of the fresh mountain water in the streams and how wonderful it would taste in her mouth, flowing down inside of her, making her whole once more.

Though her craving for food was great, she realized that it was water that called to her, pure and simple water, the substance that binds all things together.

The third day the weather warmed. The heat sapped her strength. She paced the ridge, her head spinning, the sun unrelenting. She fought the impulse to run, anywhere, just to get off the ridge. She looked to the sky for relief, but no clouds appeared, no rain that she could turn her face to for moisture.

She began to dance, a soft movement that Old Calf Woman had taught her, one foot before the other, bouncing slightly. Old Calf Woman had pounded a small drum for rhythm and then had taught her the steps.

Now, in Holly's mind, the drum sounded and she followed it with her footsteps. Late in the afternoon she stopped to rest, but something inside her said to continue. She rose to her feet, the sun falling, and continued to dance.

She called out to the Creator and, her strength renewed, danced past midnight and into the early morning hours of her fourth day. Finally, exhaustion overcame her and she lay down on her back to face the deep well within herself, feeling herself falling down into a whirlpool of darkness, into a place she had never been before.

She cried out, time and again, and shivered uncontrollably, not from cold but from the intense feeling of desolation. Then her mind opened and another world appeared.

She began to drift and found she could move anywhere with but a mere thought.

She noticed a door, similar to the one she had seen with her brother behind it. Before she could will herself there a strange man appeared before her. His face was colored half red and half white, with one blue eye and one black; his hair was half blond and half black, hanging long and loose behind him, and he had an eagle on his shoulder.

"Who are you?" she asked.

"I came from inside you," he said. "There are others also, but maybe you will not meet them. I cannot say."

He beckoned her to follow him. His world was green and lush, the skies a deeper blue than she had ever known.

Holly thought she should be afraid. Instead, she felt a surge of confidence and a thirst to learn more.

"I am your past," the man said, "and your future."

"Why are you here?"

"I come to show you things for you to remember. You may not understand what you see to begin with, but the images will stay with you and sooner or later you will see. What you do with the knowledge is up to you."

"That door back there, the wooden one," she said. "Where does it lead?"

"We will not go through any doors," he said. "We are to stay out in the open." The eagle on his shoulder flapped its wings.

"When will I learn how I can find my son and my husband?"

"It is better that you watch and listen and ask few questions."

"I don't understand."

"If you learn, then you will know how to use the knowledge, for whatever purpose."

"But I'm here to learn a way to find my son and my husband."

"You are here to learn how to do things, and you will see that you never do anything on your own. There are always others involved. So do not think you can learn to do something by yourself."

She realized the man was looking right through her, past any defenses she might throw up against him.

"Do you understand?" he asked.

"Yes, but it will be hard for me. I've always felt I had to do things myself. Nobody else cares for my son or my husband but me. How can anyone else help?"

"That is for you to learn. Once you understand to call on others for help, it will be easier for you to get things done, no matter what it is."

The man turned and suddenly Holly found herself being swept behind him.

"Where are we going?" she asked.

"I will show you some things and then leave you," he said.

"Please don't leave me. I'll be alone here."

He turned to her. "Realize you are never alone. The Creator sends help for you, always, whether times are good or bad. Ask for help when you need it and give thanks always."

He turned and started off again, Holly behind him. She realized they were traveling high above the land, through a heavy, swirling mist. They rose above the mist into pure blue. In the distance hovered a heavy mantle of roiling white.

"It is the storm that brings change," the man said.

The eagle flapped its wings and soared off into a cloud filled with lightning. The man turned a circle and changed into a wolf, then tumbled downward below the clouds.

Holly felt herself being dragged behind the wolf, falling, rolling over and over. She had no control over her movements. She finally came to rest in a cottonwood, the wolf beside her, a storm building around them.

"Where are we?" she asked.

"Hold on," the wolf said.

The air, filled with lightning and clogged with dust, contained a herd of buffalo that surged past on both sides, some running in the air and some on the ground. They bellowed with tremendous force.

Suddenly, mixed with the buffalo were Indian lodges. They came apart and came back together again while horses and buffalo ran among them.

Holly clung to the cottonwood. The wolf, drifting among the branches beside her, raised his voice to the sky. He rose up and out of sight.

The lightning increased and the dust thickened. Holly remained in the cottonwood, drifting through open space, past buffalo and horses and Indian lodges, all mixed together.

She drifted on past soldiers sitting in a circle. In their midst was a boy whose arms were outstretched to her, a smile on his face.

She circled the soldiers time and again, but the tree never drifted down to the boy. Instead, the boy began to rise toward the tree.

She suddenly awakened to the morning light and sat up, her mind still spinning. The chickadees were beside her, hopping and chittering, picking at seeds among the pine needles. She heard a voice beside her.

"You've done very well, my daughter. Very well."

Holly took four days to recover, pondering her experience throughout each day. Old Calf Woman gave her broth and herbs and nodded when Holly told her of the things she had seen.

"I can't say what they mean," Old Calf Woman said. "That is something you will have to learn for yourself."

"How long will it take?"

"Who can say? Time means nothing where visions are concerned."

On the fifth day, with her strength back, Holly prepared to begin her search for Justin. Much of her vision remained a jumbled heap of images, and as the guide had told her, she would recover the memories later when she could make sense of them.

Putting her vision behind her, she concentrated on her mission. She knew the village had surely moved from winter camp and could be anywhere now. But she had to begin her search.

She stood on the hill above the cabin, holding the reins of the pony she had taken from the fallen hunter during the cold weather, taking a last look at the country and the cabin where she had recovered her life.

Old Calf Woman stood behind her. "Are you certain you are ready for it?"

"Yes," Holly said. "You know I've been living for this day. And I'm grateful that you prepared me."

"You did all the work, my daughter. I merely pushed you in the right direction." She blinked back a tear. "Will I ever see you again?"

"When I find Justin, the first thing we'll do is come back up here."

"Do not wait too long," the old woman said. "I'm ancient, you know, and the Creator could take me at any time."

Holly hugged Old Calf Woman once again, as she had done many times during the past few days. Her decision to leave hadn't been easy, as living with the old woman had become second nature to her.

Her horse packed, Holly mounted and waved good-bye to Old Calf Woman, riding off through the foothills, searching out the trail that would take her down the Crazy Woman Fork to the Powder River.

She knew it would not be an easy journey. The days since her vision had been unsettled, the weather unpredictable. Heat and clear skies had mixed with sudden cool spells and heavy rain. A few days before, the skies had thundered and the clouds had opened up to drop heavy hail.

The first night she spent huddled in her blanket while a cool breeze swept down off the peaks. She remembered her time on the ridge below Cloud Peak, when she had sought her vision and had fought the temptation to work her way back to Old Calf Woman, the dearest friend she had ever known. But she had remained on the slope and had learned from her ordeal.

This night she felt whole and on her way to fulfillment. Loneliness had left her and the feeling had given way to a form of contentment.

Just before dawn, she heard shooting in the near distance, followed by barely audible shouting. She awakened and sat up, wondering if she had been dreaming.

Her drowsiness was further interrupted by a heavy rumbling.

A pink light broke across the eastern horizon and she knew that a buffalo herd was nearing. Their musky smell came strongly on the morning wind and they arrived so quickly as to catch her still sitting up in her blankets.

They passed as a brown-black sea, so close to her that she could hear their grunting and snorting. Petrified, she climbed the slope to take refuge among the rocks. They surged below her, their dust blurring the rising sun.

But for the time of day, it reminded her of when she had sat on the wagon with Justin, watching a different herd pass by, and it made her miss her son even more.

She remembered seeing the buffalo in her vision and realized this was not a dream. But what did it mean? She knew there had to be a connection.

The buffalo finally passed by, engulfed in a cloud of dust, flowing out from the foothills and onto the rolling prairie below. Holly rose and looked for her pony, which she found a short distance up the slope, grazing peacefully.

She mounted and watched the herd turn northward, still running, toward the distant Powder River, their heavy hoofbeats still shaking the morning calm.

Riding down the foothills, Holly turned her attention to her quest for Justin. With her mind on watching the far distance for smoke, she rode right into a troop of crazed cavalrymen, all of them afoot.

Some of them spotted her and began yelling. Two of them fired upon her before she could say a word. One bullet whanged off a rock to her right and another whizzed over her head.

More of the soldiers began shooting as she kicked her pony into a full run, losing herself over a nearby ridge while the entire company loaded and fired. She could understand them mistaking her for an Indian at first, especially since she was wearing the wolfskin coat, but she could not understand them shooting at her without reason.

As she rode well out of rifle range, she concluded that the soldiers had been involved in the shooting she had heard just before dawn. Likely they had been raided by the Sioux, perhaps the same renegades that had attacked Lieutenant Hodges and his command.

As Holly wound back to the trail that would lead to Powder River, she concluded that Bad Face and his renegades had struck again. She thought no more about it as she urged her pony faster toward the distant cloud of dust that marked the moving herd of buffalo.

Sixteen

THE TROOPERS mounted their horses and formed a double line, awaiting orders from Lieutenant Hodges to march out of their camp along the Powder River.

The weather had been unusually hot and humid, with numerous evening rainstorms. Though the day had opened with a cloudless sky, the boom of thunder already loomed over the mountains.

Hodges stood at his horse's side, peering toward the south. A second command from Fort Laramie was to have arrived the night before, bringing fifty good horses for Red Cloud. They had gotten a late start after twenty horses had accidentally been sent along with yet another command going toward Denver. The second command had been sent to retrieve them and hurry along to catch up with Hodges.

Hodges had decided to take most of the command ahead, along with the trade supplies. They would be traveling slowly anyway. It wouldn't be that hard for the second command to catch up, driving fifty horses and having no mules and packs to hinder them.

But now he had begun to fear the worst. There had been no sign of the command and time was running out. He had sent Antoine Janis to the top of a hill to watch for them while the company prepared to march.

He rode to the top of the hill and asked Janis, "Any sign of them?"

"None. Are we going ahead?"

"We have to. You wait here for a while longer. I'll go down and start ahead with the men. If you don't see the other command in an hour, catch up to us."

Hodges rode back down to the column and Sergeant Culwain asked, "Did Janis see them?"

"No, not yet. I'm leaving him here for an hour."

"Do you think they'll show, sir?"

"They have to."

"Maybe they don't know the way."

"Of course they do. They've all been up this way before at one time or another." He dismounted and tightened the cinch on his saddle.

"Do you think all these provisions might be enough to make Red Cloud release the boy?"

"Nothing's going to make him happy," Hodges said, remounting. "Whether he gets a thousand tons of food and clothing and a thousand horses, he won't be happy. And certainly without the horses we haven't got a chance of getting that boy back."

"Then maybe we should stay here in camp until they arrive," Culwain suggested.

"We can't afford to wait for them any longer," Hodges said. "Red Cloud is set to break camp any time now to take his people to the Sun Dance grounds. We've got to get there first."

"We can't just forget about them."

"Send five men and Janis back to try and locate them," Hodges said. "We'll go on ahead."

"Five men won't be enough."

Hodges thought a moment. Despite the fact that Red Cloud had declared a temporary cease-fire, the renegades could be active.

"You're right," Hodges said. "We can't go back and we can't wait here either. Order the men to march."

Hodges hoped to reach Red Cloud's village by midafternoon. Since his meeting with Holly, he had learned there had been some peace talks with the chief regarding wagons along the Bozeman Road. These had been organized by other officers at forts north along the trail. Gifts of food, clothing, and tobacco had been presented and accepted by some of the Sioux leaders.

But no one knew for certain if Red Cloud had accepted any peace proposals or offerings. Hodges knew only that the chief wanted to end the costly war for the Bozeman Road.

Red Cloud had said many times that while he hated seeing his warriors killed, he had to think of all his people. He worried about the hunting grounds along the Tongue and Powder rivers. Until there were no more wagons, there would be fighting.

Within the past month, messengers had reached Fort Laramie, announcing that Red Cloud wanted to discuss peace. Now included as part of the peace process was the ransoming of the white boy Red Cloud had been keeping as a son. Still, no one had seen the boy yet, and there was speculation that perhaps no such boy existed.

Hodges felt otherwise. He knew the chief to be a man of his word. If he wanted no more wagons along the Bozeman Road, he wouldn't lie about something as important as a white captive.

And though Hodges had no way of knowing, he suspected the captive to be Justin Porter. He had said as much to Holly and he knew from discussions with friendly Indians that Justin was the only captive white boy in Red Cloud's village.

Since the attack on the wagons under his command late the previous fall, there had been no reports of missing children, but there had been very few wagons through this direction, either, as most parties were following the Bridger cutoff, which took them along the other side of the Bighorn mountains.

The day wore on and as they traveled, Hodges stopped on occasion to view their backtrail, hoping that the lost command would be arriving with the missing horses. Red Cloud's messengers had made it clear: No horses, no captive white boy.

Antoine Janis rejoined them, saying he had seen no sign of the column or the horses. Once, at the request of Culwain, Hodges held his command up for over an hour. One of the junior officers had spotted dust in the distance. The officer and three troopers rode to check it out, only to discover a herd of buffalo pounding over the hills.

"We can't stop again," Hodges told the sergeant. "We've got to reach the village and make sure the white boy is alive and well."

"Do you think they'll attack us?"

"The messengers said they wouldn't, not if we held four flags of different colors. I've got red, yellow, blue, and green. That's what the messengers said."

"Be sure and keep the colors in the open," Janis said. "If the warriors can see them, we will not be attacked."

Justin sat beside Red Cloud, awaiting the soldiers' arrival. The meeting and the exchange had been set for the first day of the new moon.

He knew why they were coming, for it had been the talk of the village for many days: horses to ransom the new white son of Red Cloud.

Red Cloud himself had sent messengers to Fort Laramie. He believed that the boy could no longer be his son and that there would be benefit toward a peace proposal if an arrangement could be made for his release.

The messengers had reached the fort with the demand of fifty ponies for his freedom. Many in the village had voiced their opinion that the boy should be killed, or at least driven out to find his way across the open land. He knew little of hunting and would surely die of hunger eventually.

Everyone knew that it was a long way to any *Wasichu* settlements and that it would be no use for him to try and reach the fort called Phil Kearny. It was too far to go with no food. Red Cloud had voiced his disagreement in council, telling the people that the feared Wolf Woman might be a real woman rather than a spirit, and might well be the boy's mother. Even though the chief held great authority and was known to be a very wise man, many scoffed at his idea that Wolf Woman even existed.

"It is not a wolf woman, but the Crazy Old One that lives by herself," a warrior said in council. "She has medicine and she is crazy. She could change into a wolf."

"Yes, but a wolf does not seek out warriors to warn and send back to the village."

"We all know that Bad Face is losing his mind," the warrior argued. "He has been ever since his medicine went bad."

"Yes, Bad Face is losing his mind," Red Cloud said, "but it was another warrior, Long Bull, who saw Wolf Woman. He is a very sane man and I believe him."

"Do you think Wolf Woman will come for you, since you have the boy?" someone asked the chief.

"I refuse to worry about such things," Red Cloud said. "I have taken good care of the boy, so there are no spirits who would be angry with me."

After the council, the people began to wonder. Mothers kept their children close, even during daylight hours. More sentries were posted each night. Maybe Red Cloud's words held true meaning and Wolf Woman was real.

In addition to ridding himself and his people of the Wolf Woman fear, Red Cloud saw an opportunity to earn some wealth for himself, while at the same time negotiating a peace process. Though wagons still used the Bozeman Road, their numbers had declined. Maybe, Red Cloud thought, he could negotiate a way to keep all wagons off the road.

Justin only wanted the entire thing to happen very quickly. He wasn't certain if Wolf Woman was his mother or not. He knew his captors to have fears about many things and wondered if the warrior in the council hadn't been right, that Wolf Woman might actually be a real wolf rather than a real woman.

No matter, he wished only to be free and to find his way to Fort Phil Kearny, despite the distance he would need to travel across a land of sparse food and water. His father might still be there, waiting for him and his mother. He had to think that, for there was no other future for him.

As the council awaited the soldiers, the skies to the west filled with low-hanging clouds and the heavens took on a greenish tint. Justin sat beside Red Cloud, wondering at the strange weather.

"There is an omen in the sky," Red Cloud told the council. "I cannot understand what it is and I do not like it."

Out a distance from camp, a great cloud of dust rose in the air. Red Cloud sent a party of warriors to investigate.

Bad Face suddenly arrived and asked to join the council. The chief invited him in.

"I have not seen you for a few days," Red Cloud said. "You and the warriors that follow you have been gone from the village. You did not say where you were going."

"Hunting," Bad Face said. "We were scouting for buffalo. There is supposed to be a herd near here."

Red Cloud pointed to where the dust cloud rose. "I just sent some warriors out to look at that. If that is a herd, it's a big one."

"I have other news," Bad Face said. "The Bluecoats are not far away and they are without your ponies."

Red Cloud frowned. "They have no extra ponies?"

"None."

"Maybe more Bluecoats are coming and bringing the ponies with them," another warrior suggested.

"We saw no other Bluecoats anywhere near," Bad Face said. "Other than what the Bluecoats are riding, there are no other horses. They don't want peace; they want war. I think we should give it to them."

"Why would they go to all the trouble of coming out here with presents and horses if they refuse to bargain in good faith?" Red Cloud asked.

"They will say or do anything to get what they want," Bad Face said.

Though Justin believed that it was Bad Face who wanted war, he sat silent. Since his attempt to escape, he had been beaten for speaking out of turn. Red Cloud had never laid a hand on him, but some of the older women had taken willow whips to him and no one had intervened.

He believed that if he spoke his mind regarding Bad Face, it could mean trouble for him. He didn't want to take that chance, so he said nothing.

"I will take a war party and meet those Bluecoats," Bad Face said. "They deserve that."

"No, you will wait," Red Cloud said. "I gave my word. I see no reason yet to go back on it."

"But the Bluecoats have broken their word," Bad Face argued.

"I will admit, this is all very strange," Red Cloud said. "But I will give no permission to attack, not until I learn some things from the Bluecoat leader."

Justin remained still and silent. The soldiers had appeared, proceeding in single file down the twisting trail through the rough country to the camp on the valley floor, thunder booming in the skies behind them. They were still too far away for him to make out their leader.

"As you can see, there are no extra horses with them," Bad Face said.

"We will wait awhile," the chief said. "Maybe that dust cloud is a horse herd."

Bad Face shook his head. "That is too much dust for just fifty horses. Maybe they think you have ten white boys to ransom."

Red Cloud frowned. "I believe you talk too much."

"And I say that the Bluecoats want to trick us," Bad Face said. "Do you want me to bring the Bluecoat leader to you?"

"No. I will tell you when to get him." He turned to Justin. "Are you anxious to go with the Bluecoats?"

"Yes, I want to go back to my own people," Justin said.

"If they have no horses for me, then you cannot go."

Justin fought back tears. He watched while the soldiers rode to the edge of camp, leading a long procession of mules packed with supplies. They halted and waited in formation for their invitation to join Red Cloud.

Their leader, a tall man with sandy hair, looked very familiar to Justin. He wanted to get up and run to him, for he was certain it was Lieutenant Hodges.

"You act as if you know the Bluecoat leader," Red Cloud said.

Bad Face spoke up. "He does know the Bluecoat leader. It was that one who led them at the wagons."

The chief looked sternly at Bad Face. "Then why is he not dead? You should have killed him."

Bad Face looked away.

"Because you were too busy trying to kill a white woman?"

Bad Face continued to look away.

"Speak to me!" Red Cloud said.

"Yes, I was trying to kill a white woman," Bad Face said.

"And when the Bluecoats came after you, you ran instead of fighting?"

"I brought you this boy!" Bad Face said. "That's all I cared about!"

"Little good it did you or me to bring this boy," Red Cloud said.

Both men looked at Justin. There was nothing he could say. He had proved he didn't want to live with Red Cloud.

"Maybe," Bad Face said, "since they have no ponies to trade, you should tell them they can have the boy. But without his head."

Justin felt his stomach tighten. Red Cloud frowned. "What good would that do?"

"The Bluecoats would know that you don't like being cheated."

"How have I been cheated?" the chief said. "I have not yet spoken to the Bluecoat leader. He has not yet said that he wants the boy for no ponies. Is it that you want to see misfortune befall the boy, and the peace process?"

"I am only trying to show you the truth," Bad Face said.

Red Cloud studied him. "Are you? Maybe you believe you have to exact vengeance against the boy and his mother."

"What do you mean?"

"I heard the story that he handled your medicine bundle down at the Bluecoat fort called Laramie. Is that true?"

"It is true," Bad Face said sheepishly.

"How did that happen?"

"He took it and spilled my medicine on the ground."

"Oh? I understood that you had filled yourself with the strong drink and lost your bundle, and this boy found it."

"Still, he shouldn't have touched it," Bad Face said. "And his mother should have left it alone as well."

"Ah, and she was the woman you were dragging behind your horse. Is that true?"

"Yes."

"And you left her dead?"

"Yes. After we saw the soldiers were coming back, I shot an arrow into her back. I would have shot more but I saw the

Old Crazy One standing on the hillside. She appeared out of nowhere."

Red Cloud thought a moment. "Did the Old Crazy One find the boy's mother?"

"I do not know," Bad Face replied. "We left."

"So how can you be certain the woman was dead?"

"There is no way she could have lived," Bad Face said. "Even if the Old Crazy One found her, she would have died."

"You know nothing, really, do you?" Red Cloud said. He turned to Justin. "Is that why you have resisted becoming my son? Do you believe that your mother still lives?"

"Yes," Justin said. "In my heart, I believe she's still alive."

"Do you believe that she is the one called Wolf Woman?"

"I can't say. I only feel that she's alive. And I want to be with her, like any boy would want to be with his mother."

Justin knew the chief would understand. The villagers thought it very important that children be nurtured by their mother for at least the first ten years. After that, the boys became ready for the road to a warrior's life.

"That answers many of my questions," Red Cloud said. "Do you think, if she is still alive and she is not Wolf Woman, she would want to live in this village?"

"I think she'd want to look for my pa," Justin said. "He's waiting for us, to take us to the gold fields."

"Yes, the gold fields," Red Cloud said. "I have never understood why your people cared anything about that soft metal. You cannot make knives or tools from it."

"It's not for that," Justin said. "Gold is for buying things, like a big ranch, where a person can live free."

"Why do you need a ranch to live free? My people care little about the slow buffalo, the cattle, as you call them. We live and hunt free with the buffalo."

"I might be young," Justin said, "but I've come to know that your life won't be so free if all the people back home come out here."

"You are a wise boy," Red Cloud said. "Now maybe you can understand why I wanted you to become my adopted son. You think clearly and you are not afraid to speak your heart."

"I'm sorry that I can't be your son," Justin said. "Like I said, I have a pa of my own who's waiting for us to find him. I wish you and your people the best, but I would be better off with my own kind."

Red Cloud pointed to the soldiers. "I will have their leader come speak with me. But while I do that, I want you to wait in the lodge."

"Why can't I be here?" Justin asked.

"I want to learn some things from the Bluecoat leader first. You go and I will soon know if the Bluecoats can tell us about the ponies. Maybe you will have a chance to find your mother and your father."

Seventeen

HODGES SAT with Culwain and Antoine Janis. Red Cloud and his council members sat opposite. Through sign and speech, Janis interpreted for Hodges.

"Red Cloud wants to know if the rising dust is horses being brought for him."

"No," Hodges said. "I don't know what is causing the dust, maybe wind, but we don't have that many horses coming."

Janis looked to Red Cloud and back. "He wants to know how many are coming."

"Fifty, like we bargained for."

"He wants to know where the horses are."

"Tell him I want to see the boy."

Janis said, "He insists that there be ponies before he shows the boy."

"Tell him again that the ponies are coming, that another group of soldiers have them," Hodges said. "They'll be along very soon."

"He says," Janis told Hodges, "that many of the horses you and your Bluecoats are riding will do him well. He'll settle for them."

"No, we have to ride them ourselves. His will arrive soon."

"He says that he expects you to keep your end of the bargain."

"Tell him I'm telling the truth; they're coming," Hodges said.

"He says he believes you. Still, he wants to wait to show the boy."

Culwain leaned over to Janis. "He doesn't seem to trust us."

"He doesn't trust anyone with a blue coat on," Janis said.

Red Cloud made sign to Janis, who then said to Hodges, "He wants to know about a spirit woman, the one they call Wolf Woman, who lives with the Old Crazy One. He believes the Wolf Woman is the boy's mother."

"Tell him that it's true, and that she wants her son back."

Janis spoke to Red Cloud and turned to Hodges. "The chief says the Wolf Woman can have the boy when he gets his horses."

"How do we know if he even has the boy?" Hodges asked.

"Red Cloud says we have to trust each other," Janis said.

"Does he trust that his horses are coming?"

Janis nodded.

Hodges turned to Sergeant Culwain. "Have the men distribute some of the supplies."

They watched while Culwain supervised the distribution of presents and provisions to the people.

"Red Cloud says that he is impressed with the quality of goods we have brought," Janis said.

"Tell Red Cloud," Hodges said, "that I have shown trust, that I've given gifts to his people in good faith, and that he should show the same to me by bringing the boy forward."

Janis translated for Red Cloud and the chief nodded, motioning for the boy to be brought to the council.

Justin arrived in his buckskins, his long hair untrimmed. Hodges stared at him and smiled. Justin grinned and sat down.

"You look pretty good," Hodges said. "Have they been treating you well?"

"I've done fine here," he said. "Do you know anything about my ma and pa?"

"As a matter of fact I do," Hodges said. "I talked with your pa at Fort Phil Kearny after you were captured from the wagons. He was set to go south and start a ranch. You can join him soon."

"What about Ma?"

"I met her not long ago, living up in a cabin at the base of the mountains, along the Crazy Woman Fork of the Powder River. She was hurt badly after being dragged by a horse. She's recovered and is looking forward to seeing you."

"These people here say she's a spirit or something. They call her Wolf Woman."

"Well, she wears a wolfskin coat and I believe she scared some of the warriors, so they all see her as a ghost."

"She didn't just scare them. She killed one of them deader than stone."

"You know that for a fact?"

"I saw him. They brought him in draped over a horse. A white woman here in the village speaks Sioux real well and she tells me they believe she will bring death to the Sioux people because Bad Face killed her."

"Well, he didn't kill her. You'll soon see for yourself."

Justin could hardly sit still. "When are we leaving?"

"Just as soon as another group of soldiers bring the horses for Red Cloud."

Justin looked into the sky. "I hope they hurry. A bad storm is coming."

Janis said to Hodges, "Red Cloud wants to send the boy back to his lodge now. He says that you've seen him and know that he's well. It's time for him to go until the other Bluecoats come with the horses."

"Ask him for a little more time," Hodges said. "I need to learn some more things from the boy."

"Red Cloud says no," Janis said. "He says he will release the boy when the horses come to him."

At first, Justin refused to go, but Hodges assured him that he should be patient.

"You've been here this long," he said. "A few more hours won't matter now."

A warrior escorted Justin back to Red Cloud's lodge. On the way, Bad Face stopped him and stepped in front of the boy.

"So, do you think you are going back with the Bluecoats?"

"Yes, as soon as the trade horses get here," Justin said.

"How can you be so sure the horses will ever come?"

"Lieutenant Hodges said they would."

Bad Face laughed. "Your Bluecoat friend is a liar. There will be no horses. The day you and your mother touched my medicine I vowed that I would destroy you both. Now that will happen. Very soon."

With thunder rolling above her, Holly rode her pony onto a hill above the village. A cool wind began to blow and she threw her wolfskin coat over her shoulders.

Below stood a village filled with Sioux, many of them receiving supplies that blue-coated soldiers pulled from the backs of mules. Still others were gathered at the center, in a large circle.

Within this large circle sat a smaller circle of men, many of them in blue uniforms. She remembered how Old Calf Woman had told her about councils and the way tribes made important decisions.

"Whenever you see a big circle of men," she had said, "you know something important is being discussed."

Holly realized that a peace conference was taking place

and longed for the sight of her son. But there were too many people below, mingling and moving about, to identify any one of them.

As the wind blew and the sky roiled above, she drew her wolfskin coat tighter. From the beginning, the day had been strange and it appeared to be getting stranger.

She turned behind her to judge the coming dust cloud. She knew it to be filled with the buffalo she had seen that morning, for she had passed to one side of the herd on the way to the village.

Ever since they had run past her camp at dawn, they had acted strangely. Throughout the day the large herd had moved one way and then another, frantically, as if trying to run from something they knew they could not escape.

She looked overhead and saw lightning flash. Scattered rain began to fall. The sky was growing ever darker and she knew that soon there would be a huge storm.

Below, the people began to run about. Some of them had spotted her and were pointing up at her, their hands over their mouths. A group of warriors rode up toward her, but kept their distance, yelling chants, riding back and forth.

From among the warriors emerged a soldier on horseback, who rode toward her, winding his way up a trail that led to the top of the hill.

"Holly," Hodges said, "I expected to see you."

"Have you got Justin? Where is he?"

"He's fine. Please leave, so I can conclude this business and bring him to you."

"You've been in council for quite a while. Why don't you have him by now?"

"It takes time."

"There's something you're not telling me, Lieutenant," she said. "What are you leaving out?"

"I'm telling you, this is all going to take time."

"There isn't much time," she said. "There's a bad storm

overhead and I want my son before it and the buffalo herd get here at the same time."

"Buffalo?"

Holly pointed. "That wall of dust coming. It's a huge herd and they'll be here very soon."

He looked into the sky and out toward the oncoming dust cloud. He pointed into the village.

"You see that large tepee in the center of everything, the one with all the red markings?"

"I see it."

"That's Red Cloud's lodge," Hodges said. "That's all I'm going to tell you. Now, I have to get back to the council."

He turned and rode back down the hill. The young warriors, still riding back and forth, moved to allow him through, wondering at his power to be able to talk with an angry spirit and survive.

After Hodges rode away, Holly looked up into the sky, where the roiling storm had grown denser and darker. She fought to hold her pony steady, as something was happening in the clouds.

She turned and saw that the buffalo herd had reached a nearby hill and was churning its way toward the village. She kicked her pony into a dead run, down the hill toward Red Cloud's tepee, through bolts of lightning that began to flash all around her.

Hodges reached the council circle and dismounted. Everyone was on his feet, pointing, and Hodges turned to see the huge cloud of dust approaching. The ground trembled as a massive herd of buffalo appeared, headed directly for the village.

"What are we going to do?" Janis said.

"Ride out of here!" Hodges said. "Save yourself!"

The buffalo rumbled toward the village, bobbing brown shapes clothed in a wall of dust.

Janis turned and joined the fleeing soldiers. Red Cloud pointed to the hill and yelled, "The Wolf Woman! She caused this!"

Villagers scattered in every direction; mothers screamed for their children, dodging horses that had run into the village ahead of the oncoming herd.

Red Cloud pointed. "Look! The Wolf Woman is coming! Bring the boy from my lodge!"

Hodges hurried toward Red Cloud's lodge. Justin had already emerged and stood watching the turmoil going on around him.

Suddenly Holly was there, holding her hand out.

"Climb on behind!" she yelled. "Hurry!"

Justin was so surprised he just stared. His mother looked like a cross between an Indian and a wolf.

"Justin!" she screamed.

With Hodges's help, the boy scrambled up behind his mother and held on as they rode toward the edge of camp, past screaming villagers, just ahead of the oncoming herd.

Justin looked back to find Hodges but he was lost in the chaos.

"You worried at all about the lieutenant?"

"He can take care of himself," Holly said.

"But what if he gets caught by the stampede?"

"We've got ourselves to worry about. You hold on and don't let go for anything."

She urged her pony ahead as hard as she could, looking back to see the destruction behind her. Buffalo had already entered the village, trampling lodges, and thunder crashed in the sky overhead.

Holly saw her vision unfolding before her. Lightning popped all around them as she urged her pony faster, just ahead of the stampeding herd.

The sky opened up and a torrent of rain fell. Holly shouted for Justin to hold on as the pony began to slip on the muddy ground. If they fell, the herd would sweep over them in a matter of seconds.

Just ahead a small boy ran out from behind a lodge. Holly turned the pony to avoid hitting the child. Suddenly the pony lost its footing and Holly and Justin tumbled off.

They ran behind a lodge. But the herd also had trouble with the footing and a number of the lead animals fell, those behind tumbling over them, creating a huge pileup. The herd behind them turned and ran in a new direction.

Animals staggered past Holly as she caught the pony. She mounted and pulled Justin on behind her, urging the pony ahead.

They rode for what seemed like an eternity before the storm let up and the sun appeared. From atop a hill they looked out onto the flats beyond the river, where the herd had scattered over the open plains.

Justin took a deep breath. "Ma, I never thought I'd see you again."

"You don't know how hard I prayed for this day," Holly said. "I only knew it would some day come to pass and that our life would get back to normal."

"I'm glad we found each other," Justin said, "but I don't think our lives will ever get back to normal."

"Why do you say that?"

"Because I don't feel normal anymore and you sure don't look normal. Not the way I remember."

"But I'm still your ma."

"Yeah, that part's normal," he said, smiling.

They walked for a distance, to let the pony rest. Their talk centered around their experiences—he with Red Cloud and she with Old Calf Woman. That they had both gone looking for each other was of no surprise, but having both been inside the lodge with the three frozen people made them wonder what might have happened had they been there at the same time.

"We can't say how things would be different now," Holly said. "Let's just thank God we're back together now."

Holly's momentary joy ended when she looked behind them, seeing figures on horseback coming up the river.

"We've got trouble," she said. "Bad Face and his renegades."

"Can we outrun them?"

"Not with all this mud, and two of us on one horse. But we'll be fine." She mounted and pulled Justin up behind her. "You stay low, you hear?"

The pony surged forward, grunting against the weight on its back. Holly realized that to stay along the ridges would do them no good. In fact, no matter what she did, they would be in dire peril.

She decided to head toward a thick grove of cottonwoods along the river. There wasn't much time, but she could make it before Bad Face reached them. Being in cover would save them from an open attack and it would give her time to enact a plan.

Bad Face and his renegades, seeing her intent, turned their horses to cut her off. But they were too far away.

Holly wondered if she was making the right decision. Once in the cottonwoods, Bad Face and his warriors could surround them. With no place to go, they would be done for in no time.

There was one other option. She kicked the pony into a run, entering the cottonwoods well ahead of Bad Face's arrival. She helped Justin down and told him to stay put.

"Where you going, Ma?" he asked.

"I'm going to do my best to save us," she said. "If I don't come back, you hightail it back to the village. You'll be safe with Red Cloud."

Justin had never doubted his mother and wouldn't start

now. Still, his stomach was in a knot as he climbed into a cottonwood to watch.

Holly fitted herself into her wolfskin coat and made certain the rifle was loaded. She levered a round into the chamber and rode out to meet Bad Face and his warriors. As they approached, she raised her rifle and began to ride back and forth, screaming loudly.

Bad Face came ahead but halted his pony when he realized that his warriors were not behind him.

"What are you doing?" he asked them. "We have her."

"I don't think so," one of them said. "She is calling on her medicine and it's too strong."

"Follow me!" Bad Face said.

They reluctantly rode behind Bad Face. He reined his pony a long stone's throw from Holly and made sign to her.

"If you give up your son to me, I will not harm you."

"You cannot harm me, nor can any of your warriors," she said. "The spirits are with me this day."

"I told you," the warrior said. "Her medicine is strong."

One of the others agreed. "You told us she was not the Wolf Woman. You lied."

"I told you she had no special medicine," Bad Face said. "I told you my medicine was stronger than hers."

"You could not kill me before," Holly said. "Why do you think you can now?"

"I would have killed you before," Bad Face said, "but for the Old Crazy One."

"No, you tried to kill me anyway, and couldn't. Now I'm going to kill you and your warriors as well."

Holly raised her rifle and, screaming loudly, rushed Bad Face and his renegades.

As her pony pounded toward them, she worried about the footing. Already two of the renegades had turned back, one of them falling under his pony as it slipped in the mud. The warrior struggled to his feet, limping, and jumped back on his horse. Then, the others turned back as well, leaving Bad Face to do the fighting on his own.

But Bad Face turned his horse and hurried after his comrades. He stopped a distance away and raised his fist in the air. Soon they were all lost in the distance, headed back toward the village.

Holly smiled. She turned her pony and rode back to Justin, who awaited her, grinning broadly.

"I knew he'd run. He's a coward. Maybe he'll leave us alone from now on and we can find Pa in peace."

"I hope so," Holly said, "but I wouldn't bet any money on it."

Eighteen

THEY RODE well into the evening without incident, relaxing, talking at length about Red Cloud and Old Calf Woman. Justin was anxious to meet the old woman and thank her for saving his mother's life.

"It seems she did some kind of miracle," he said. "From the sounds of it you should've died."

"The good Lord has His ways," Holly said. "Old Calf Woman taught me how to pray. I don't know how to explain it, but some day you'll understand."

They followed the Powder River up toward the mountains, watching the sunlight reflect off the rippling water before leaving its course to journey along the Crazy Woman Fork. She knew the trail well and they rode in the light of the half moon, making good time, drawing farther and farther away from Red Cloud's village, closer and closer to Old Calf Woman.

Past midnight, Holly found a good spot in a patch of quaking aspens to camp. She picketed the pony nearby and opened a pouch of pemmican for herself and Justin.

"No fire tonight," she said.

When they had finished eating she sat with Justin against a fallen log. A cool breeze nipped at the night air and she wrapped the boy and herself in blankets and shared her wolfskin coat.

"This is the real thing, ain't it?" Justin said with pride. "A real wolfskin coat that makes you look ferocious."

"It served to keep me warm. Whatever else is what people made of it."

"All the Indians are afraid of you."

"Well, there's at least one who wants badly to cause me misery," she said.

"Don't you think he's given up?"

"I doubt it. Maybe we can just keep moving out of his territory and he'll finally give up chasing us."

"You really think so?"

"They turned back awfully fast back there when I charged them," she said. "I guess they don't want to take any chances fighting me. They probably all went back."

"But not Bad Face. He wants you too badly."

"Old Calf Woman told me that crazy men like Bad Face are more dangerous than a fearsome warrior, because they come at you at any time of the day or night and from the back, not the front."

"What did she say you could do about it?"

"Just be watchful, very watchful, and use your senses to help you."

"She must have taught you a lot."

Holly smiled. "It appears you learned a great deal yourself."

She was amazed to hear how much her son had learned about Indian life and surviving against great odds. He had to have learned well or he would have perished when he had gone searching for her in the storm.

"I figure I would have learned a lot more had I wanted to stay and be Red Cloud's son," he said. "But I'm your son. I belong to you and Pa."

"I'm glad you feel that way," Holly said. She peered into the overhead sky, black and vast and filled with light. "Let's look at the stars and talk," she said, "just like we used to when you were little."

"I remember those times," he said. "And before the stars

came out we used to go out and watch the sunlight on the river as it went down, and we used to talk about all kinds of stuff. Mainly Pa and if he was happy."

"Your pa's always been a restless man," she said. "You shouldn't blame him for it, as it's always been his nature."

"He could've stayed around more. He never made much for us, wandering around, doing odd jobs. He should have stayed and plowed the fields and not let you do it."

"Your pa was never a farmer, Justin."

"Well, if he'd farmed instead of going off to fight, we'd be better off now."

"Don't hold his soldiering against him, Justin. He did what he thought was right."

"Yeah, and got himself shot up."

Holly knew her son had been holding in a great deal of anger about his father. He had to express his feelings, somehow. He believed all would be well now if only his father hadn't gone to war.

"At least he came back," Holly said. "A lot of boys lost their pas, you know. At least he came back."

The boy was silent a moment. Then he said, "Do you suppose we can find him down on the Overland Trail?"

"Sure we can, Justin. You have to have faith that we will."

He pointed his finger at a star, as if shooting at it. "Where do you suppose Uncle Harlan is now?"

"Lieutenant Hodges told me he's turned outlaw."

"Sounds right to me."

"Yes, he's with an outlaw gang stealing horses and mules along the front range of the mountains north of Denver, along the Overland Trail."

"He'll get himself hanged, sure enough."

"Enough talk for now," Holly said. "We need rest for tomorrow, and the long trip ahead of us."

* * *

Near daybreak the pony snorted. Holly awakened to see it, ears up, looking hard into the nearby brush. She grabbed the rifle.

Justin rolled from his blanket. "What is it, Ma?"

"You stay put, you hear?" she said in a whisper. "No matter what, you don't move."

"But what if somebody comes? Or what if it's a bear?"

She thought a moment, then slid the rifle close to him.

"Don't shoot unless you know full well what you're shooting at. You hear?"

She eased out toward the horse, thinking about bears and also remembering the mountain lion that had taken her pony during the winter, nearly costing her her life. It could be another lion, or possibly a bear, or—and the thought struck her soundly—possibly Bad Face.

She eased toward the brush, searching the shadows, her pistol cocked. Though the sun would soon rise, the shadows were thick and deep. Anything could be hiding anywhere.

Whatever made the noise, she decided, it couldn't be Bad Face. It would have been easy enough to track her and Justin in the daylight, but after the sunlight was gone he wouldn't have been able to pick his way through the hills and find her.

But he had to know she was headed for Old Calf Woman. His fear of the old woman would keep him at a distance, but his desire to kill her would push him to catch her before she reached the cabin.

She eased closer to the pony, her pistol cocked, her heart pounding wildly. The horse danced at the end of the rope, tugging and snorting, looking wildly behind her.

Then she realized her mistake: She shouldn't have left Justin alone.

She hurried back to find Bad Face holding the boy fast, a knife at his throat. Holly tried to make a sign, but it was too dark.

Justin had learned enough Lakota to translate.

"He wants you to drop the pistol."

Holly complied. "Ask him to let you go."

"He says he won't let me go until you come over here."

Holly could scarcely breathe. She knew he wanted her to witness him killing her son.

"He says for you to hurry," Justin said, "or he'll use the knife quickly."

"Tell him that he can have me, but to let you go. He can do anything he wants with me."

"He says he already knows that. He wants you to build a fire. Quickly."

Holly worked feverishly, gathering dried limbs from the aspen grove, barely able to control her shaking. Bad Face watched, keeping the knife against Justin's throat. When the fire was kindled and small flames began to erupt into larger ones, Bad Face again spoke through Justin.

"He says you were smart to scare his warriors away yesterday, but not so smart to think he wouldn't follow. After all, he must make amends to his medicine."

Holly knew he was referring to the incident with his medicine bundle at Fort Laramie.

"Ask him what he intends to do with us," she said.

"He wants you to think about it for a while. First, he wants you to see me burn in the fire. After that he'll decide what else to do."

Holly started for Bad Face, but he drew the knife tighter across Justin's throat. She backed away, angry and desperate, while the renegade laughed.

She waited for him to push Justin into the flames, but it never happened. She realized he had no intention of killing her son but wanted only to see her anguish.

"Do you think Bad Face wants to take you back to Red Cloud?" she asked.

"I thought of that. It would give him something to brag about again."

Bad Face growled in Lakota, pulling Justin's head back by the hair.

"Don't!" Holly screamed.

The renegade loosened his grip. Justin said, "He don't want us talking back and forth."

"Ask him what he wants of us."

When Justin spoke Bad Face said nothing. He tied the boy to a tree with a rope and turned to Holly.

"You ain't going to go anywhere with him, are you?" Justin said.

"I'll make it just fine. I lived through this once. I'll do it again."

Bad Face was smiling again, knowing Justin's anguish. He motioned for Holly to come over to where he waited. He bound her hands in front of her with a long length of rope and placed the knife at her throat, directing her ahead of him toward his pony, hidden in the trees nearby.

"Ma, be careful!" Justin called out from behind her.

At the pony, the renegade turned his attention toward tying the rope to his saddle. Holly knew his intent was to drag her again, this time until he was certain she was dead.

As he finished tying the knot, she dropped to her knees in front of him and clutched a large rock between her tied hands. When he turned to see what she was doing, she rose and with all her might slammed the rock into his face.

Bad Face stumbled backward, clutching his shattered nose. Holly followed and brought her knee up into his groin.

The renegade doubled over on the ground and she slammed the rock into the side of his head. While he groaned she took his knife and cut her bonds, then wrapped the end of the rope around his neck. His pony, now becoming nervous, began to pull at its picket.

The rope tied securely around Bad Face's neck, Holly cut the pony loose and slapped it across the rump. She watched while the animal raced over the rocks and brush, headed back toward the Sioux village, the renegade warrior bouncing along behind.

She hurried back to Justin and untied him. They watched together as the pony ran over the hills through the dawn and out of sight, dragging Bad Face's limp body along behind.

At midmorning, Holly turned the pony off Crazy Woman Creek and up the hill toward the cabin. Since their ordeal with Bad Face, she had said little to Justin and he little to her. The shock of narrowly escaping death at the hands of Bad Face had yet to wear off.

They were so grateful that they knelt and prayed for a considerable time, hugging each other often. Holly felt that at last she was free of some kind of curse and that the rest of their journey would bring them happiness.

"Can't get no worse," Justin said, "unless we find that Pa's dead."

"We don't want to think that way," she said. "I prefer to believe he's alive and well, and that we'll have a big spread of cattle to help him take care of."

"That would be something," he said.

At the cabin, Holly called for Old Calf Woman. She was surprised that the old lady hadn't already come out, as she always knew instinctively when someone approached long before they got there.

They dismounted and found, inside the cabin, signs of a ceremony. Holly realized the old woman had gone up on the mountain for some reason.

"Let's go find her," Holly said. "I promised her she would meet you."

The ride took most of the afternoon. They stopped along the way to drink fresh water and watch chickadees flit among the trees.

"They came to me all the time while I was with Old Calf Woman," she said. "They're my special friends."

"You make it sound like they're human or something," Justin said.

"They may not be human, but they're special. You'll learn as you grow older that all life is special. Being human doesn't make us more or less in the eyes of the Creator."

"The Creator?"

"God."

"I've never heard you call God by any other name before."

"I've become aware," she said, "that different people have different names for God. It all means the same thing, so we have to learn to open our minds a little."

"You wouldn't have stood for such talk before we came out here," he said.

"I know, but I've changed. What's happened to me has made me different."

"You're still my ma, though," Justin said. "You still tell me what to do. That ain't changed."

"I doubt that ever will," Holly said.

"When I get bigger it will," he said. "I'll have to help Pa with the cattle regular and you can't always be there a-telling me what to do."

"Maybe you're right," she said. "I'm going to have to face the time when you grow up, that's a fact."

They journeyed on and found the ridge where the old dead pine stood reaching into the heavens. A thin line of smoke filtered skyward and the sounds of singing carried downslope.

"She's up there," Holly said. "Maybe we should wait a little while, until she's through."

"What's she doing?" Justin asked. "That sounds like a death song to me."

Holly realized her son had been exposed to every part of Sioux life, including various worship ceremonies. He had heard death songs before and was likely correct in assuming the old woman was talking to the Creator for the last time in an earthly voice.

Saddened, Holly looked up the hill and saw the old woman, her hands raised to the heavens.

"Maybe we shouldn't be here," Justin said.

Old Calf Woman struggled to her feet and beckoned them up.

"What do you want to do, Ma?" Justin asked.

"She wants to meet you," Holly said. "Let's go talk to her."

They climbed the hill and stood at the base of the tree next to a fire, where sage burned. The old woman's eyes, the flicker in them dying, brightened when Holly hugged her tightly.

"You have survived a great ordeal to find your son and bring him back," she said. "Did your vision help you?"

"I owe you more than I can say," Holly said. "Without your help, and the vision, I couldn't have done it."

Old Calf Woman studied Justin. "A strong one—oh, such a strong one."

The boy tried not to stare. He had never seen anyone so old.

"I'm glad to meet you," he said. "I'd like to give you something, but I don't have anything."

"Why would you give me something?"

" 'Cause you saved Ma's life. I want to thank you somehow, but I don't know how."

"Just coming to see me is thanks enough," she said. "It has been many, many winters since I've seen a young person. I consider it a gift from the Creator to see you now, when I'm so close to going over to Him."

Justin didn't know what to say. He felt special by her words.

"You take good care of him," Old Calf Woman told Holly. "He has learned much already. Maybe in time he will become a great leader of your people."

"For certain he'll own a ranch someday," Holly said. "We wanted you to come with us down there to live. I think you'd like it."

The old woman smiled. "You are very kind. But as you can see, I will do no more traveling on these old feet. That is the way it must be."

Holly blinked back tears. "I'm glad we got here in time."

"I am glad you did, too," she said, pointing into the tree. "Now I must get up to my bed before the sage burns out."

As she started up, Holly offered to help, realizing the last time she did, the old woman had refused her. This time it was different.

"You can help, as I am weaker than I thought," she said. "But feel good that I waited."

Holly helped her into the branches and, after climbing up after her, helped her onto the scaffold. It seemed to Holly a very courageous thing, lying down in the open of the forest to await death.

It was something she could never do. What if it took longer than you thought? What if it took days? But Old Calf Woman had to know the end was very near.

The old woman covered herself in a buffalo robe. "Thank you for coming. You have brought me great joy and taught me many things. And your return with your son has gladdened me again. I must go now. I hope the Creator sends you many blessings."

Holly hugged her tightly, not wanting to let go. But the smoke was dwindling and it was time to leave.

After descending the tree, she stood back near the small fire and watched the sage smoke rise. Justin stood beside her.

"The smoke's getting less and less," he said.

"I know," she said.

The late-day sun hovered over the jagged mountains, coloring the forest in gold. Birds sang evening songs and the wind whispered through the leaves. The fire eased itself into a thin wisp and finally died. Then the breeze stopped and the birds were still, and the forest rested in silence.

Nineteen

THEY RODE past timbered buttes and through rocks flaring red in the sun, through passes once used only by horses but which now were rutted by the wheels of wagons and stages. The old Cherokee Trail, now the Overland Trail North, a stage line and wagon road that had sprung up to serve northern Colorado Territory, was as busy as any part of Tennessee.

"You'd think all the folks from back home were coming out here," Holly said to Antoine Janis, who had offered to lead them down from Fort Laramie to the Cache la Poudre River.

"I don't like it, no, not at all," Janis told her, "but where would I move to?"

Janis, as he led the way, told them that he didn't care for the changes. He had seen the land before the gold rush and the stampede for land.

"It's not like when my father came for the furs," he said. "To the south where we go, the Cache la Poudre, my home, she was a virgin then. She ran deep and cool and on forever without a soul along her banks. Now there's a bridge across her and the wagons pass by the hundreds. The buffalo are leaving and the cattle are coming. The days of my father and the fur men have passed forever."

Holly would as soon have taken herself and Justin south without Janis's help. But he had offered to lead her down, and maybe it had been the best thing. Had she not encountered him by accident at Fort Laramie, the trip would have been much more difficult.

The men at the stage stops along the way all knew him and they were fed a free meal at the Little Laramie and again at Virginia Dale, just for sharing news of the Sioux and the Bozeman Road. As they had traveled a hard day, Virginia Dale had been their stop for the night.

"It's no more dangerous up there than down here," a wrangler had told them during the meal. "And I don't mean just the Indians."

He went on to describe how a band of outlaws led by a man named Musgrove regularly stole horses and mules, killing stage drivers and wranglers at the stops.

"They blame it on the Indians, but it ain't them," the wrangler said. "That was last year. The Indians are up north now but still we've got to keep four to five men at each stop. We don't aim to lose no more stock to them thieves."

Janis wondered why there had been no organization against them and had learned that the stock detectives and U.S. marshals out of Denver were spread far too thinly.

"Too much thieving and killing all over," the wrangler had said. "We've got to do it ourselves if we want to put a stop to it."

Holly had heard the warning about outlaws as soon as she and Justin had reached Fort Laramie. They had stopped for provisions and the sutler said to her, "It appears you're traveling alone, you and the boy."

"We are," Holly said. "We're headed toward the Cache la Poudre. My husband has a ranch near there."

"You won't make it, not by yourselves. You look to be of a tough nature, ma'am, but take it from me, you won't get down there."

The sutler detailed some stories he had heard of travelers losing their belongings and their lives. He suggested waiting until a party of wagon people started down.

Holly's argument had been that most wagon people were headed north, not south.

"By the time anyone going south comes along, it'll be fall."

Then Antoine Janis entered the store. He recognized Holly and had at first backed away.

"The Wolf Woman," he said. "What are you doing here?"

Holly insisted to him that her days of seeking out Justin by any means possible were over and that she was starting her life over again as an emigrant woman and rancher's wife.

"That is very good," Janis said. "The Sioux will feel much better for it. And what of Bad Face?"

"He won't be bothering anyone again."

Janis smiled. "And that is good also."

She asked about the events after the storm at Red Cloud's village.

"We all got out alive, but I don't know how," Janis said. "The lieutenant is up at Fort Phil Kearny now. He is on report for his actions at the village. I don't think the army likes him anymore."

"What did he do wrong?"

Holly hadn't gotten a satisfactory explanation, just that after she left with Justin during the storm, the soldiers all scattered and came together far above the village.

They traveled on to Fort Phil Kearny, where Lieutenant Hodges was detained for questioning, while the rest of the command traveled back down to Fort Laramie. There, Janis had been asked a lot of questions about why the peace commission had failed and then dismissed from his position.

Holly had quickly tired of talking about it, knowing no good would come of it for Lieutenant Hodges. For a time she blamed herself, believing that she had caused the problem. But Janis had told her that the problem had been entirely with the second command of soldiers coming up from Fort Laramie, who had failed to bring the fifty head of horses.

"They never came," Janis said. "Those horses and those

soldiers never came to the village. Bad Face and his renegades stole them."

Holly informed Janis that she had passed a number of soldiers on foot that morning. "They shot at me," she said. "They must have thought I was one of the Indians who stole their horses."

"Bad Face wanted no peace and he wanted the boy to stay with Red Cloud," Janis said.

"He always thought," Holly said, "that he could gain Red Cloud's favor through Justin."

"Because of Bad Face there is still war along the Bozeman, and I don't know if the lieutenant will be an officer much longer," Janis now said as they rode. "I believe they will blame him for everything going wrong. Too bad. He's a decent man."

"But how could anyone be blamed for what happened?" Holly asked. "I mean, besides losing the horses to Bad Face, the storm and the stampede were to blame for most of it."

"And you," Janis said. "But I'm saying that because that's what I told the army, so that the lieutenant wouldn't be blamed."

"I don't care if anyone blames me," she said. "I would do it all over again."

"Yes, I'm sure you would. If I had a son taken captive, I would also."

"Lieutenant Hodges told me that you helped to settle the problems with the Sioux near Fort Collins and that because of your efforts toward peace, they shut the fort down. They didn't need a fort any longer because they had you to keep the Sioux from warring against the emigrants."

Janis laughed. "The lieutenant makes it sound like I stopped the fighting and killing by myself. Yes, I helped, but it took a lot of soldiers and their guns to drive the warriors north."

"A lasting peace is what counts," she said. "Too bad that can't happen on the Bozeman Road."

"Yes, I wish for peace there as well," Janis said. "But now it matters not to me. I tried my best to help them but it all went bad. I'll go back down to my home and my life will go on."

Holly pondered Lieutenant Hodges and wondered what the future held for him. Maybe, she thought, he would pursue his ambitions toward law enforcement. She hoped his life brought him happiness and fulfillment, knowing that even when she found Isaac, she wouldn't stop wondering about him.

They traveled on through the morning and into the afternoon, along the edge of the great Rocky Mountains, passing wagon trains and stagecoaches along the way. Janis said little. He was a quiet man, which suited Holly, as it gave her ample time to discuss the upcoming reunion with Isaac.

Justin wanted things to return to how they had been before the war and before the fight at the wagons. But he realized there could never be another time like they had had before the war. It had been a peaceful time, hunting and roaming the woods with his pa, learning the land and watching each day pass with an eagerness for the next dawn.

Then the war had come and his father had come home torn apart. Things must have happened to him, but Justin knew his father would never talk about them.

Justin saw things differently as well. Now, after his time with the Sioux, he had come to understand how things can change.

"I wonder what Pa will think of us now," he said.

"Why would he think any different of us?"

" 'Cause we both spent time with Indians. You remember how those wagon people at Fort Laramie stared at us? Especially after they heard we lived with the Indians for a spell."

"Your father won't be bothered by that."

"But how could things ever be the same?"

"He's your pa, your own flesh and blood," Holly said. "That's how it is. We've been through some things and we've spent time apart, yes. It will take some getting used to, is all. Everything will get back to normal. You'll see."

They stopped to rest at the Cherokee-Stonewall Stage Station. The Stage Station help met them with shotguns and rifles, wanting to be sure they weren't the Musgrove Gang coming after fresh horses.

The station master recognized Janis and said, "My apologies. Can't be too careful these days, you know."

"We won't be long," Janis said.

"Take your time," the man said. "Make yourself at home."

After a cool drink of water, Janis led Holly and Justin on down the trail to a spot he said had been used by ancient Indians, a place called Grayback Ridge.

"They would make their spears and arrows here," he said. "They would run buffalo over that cliff over there."

Justin stared into the distance to where a red cliff shone in the sun, dropping off abruptly into a cool flow of water.

"That's the North Fork of the Poudre," Janis said. "A lot of buffalo went over that cliff. I heard tell they'll bring cattle onto this land before long. It will be a good country for them."

The boy was interested in the history but he was still startled by the greeting they had gotten down below at the stage station.

"Will somebody steal the cattle?"

"Maybe. Who can say?"

"Are the outlaws around here that bad?" he asked Janis.

The Frenchman smiled and patted his knife. "Not bad enough for me."

They walked a short distance along the bluff where it flattened off and the ground was better for sitting. Justin plopped down and suddenly jumped up quickly.

"There's something in that hole right there," he said, pointing.

"Move away," Janis said. "Rattlers are everywhere here."

Justin stepped back and stared at the hole. Momentarily a half-grown cottontail rabbit poked its head out.

"I jumped for nothing," he said.

"Ah, but maybe not," Janis said with a laugh. "Those fuzzy bunnies have a terrible bite. They are bad scoundrels."

They sat back down and the Frenchman went to his saddlebag.

"I see you don't have a knife," he said to Justin. "A man has to have a knife."

"I left it in the village," Justin said.

"Well, I'll give you this one and you can keep the outlaws away." He smiled. "The first deer you skin, you give me the hide. Fair?"

"That's more than fair," Justin said. "That's an awful big knife."

"Yes, it's called a Green River knife. Back when the beaver were everywhere, the trappers would skin them with a knife like that."

Justin smiled and slipped the knife into his belt, knowing he had gained a new friend.

As they neared the Cache la Poudre, Holly became more anxious to find Isaac and the ranch. It seemed years, rather than months, since the last time she had seen him. She began to wonder, as Justin had, if he might see them differently now.

They reached LaPorte, a log town that served as the commerce center for northern Colorado. A number of dry-goods and mercantile stores stood next to blacksmith shops and saloons, all teeming with travelers. Under a knob hill in one part of town stood a little church. She had lost track of the days but it must be Sunday, she thought, as a throng of people milled about in front.

During her time with Old Calf Woman, Holly had lost her

concern about time. In the mountains all seemed to revolve around the seasons and nothing much important happened but life itself, and then death, and a return to life again.

But she realized that as a rancher's wife, she would be required to return to the ways she had always known. She would need to fit into the community as a woman who stood beside her husband, not a woman who had learned Indian ways.

As she studied the town, Holly yearned to find herself a new dress, and a shirt and new pair of pants for Justin, to surprise Isaac. She wanted to appear respectable when she set foot on the ranch for the first time, reuniting with her husband. But her pockets were empty and she would have to greet them in buckskins.

Nearby, a bridge over the Cache la Poudre rattled as a train of wagons passed over.

Janis looked around, frowning. "Too many people. They come too quickly."

"In all this commotion, there's got to be somebody who knows Isaac," Holly said.

Janis directed her to a saloon near the center of town, the oldest in the area, where everyone gathered to learn the news.

"Someone in there will know of him," he said. "I wish you good luck."

"I want to repay you," Holly told him. "I will bring a side of beef down to you and your family."

"Thank you, but I prefer the buffalo and the elk. I have to go out to hunt them, but their meat is better for my middle. But come visit us any time you like."

Holly thanked him again and Justin held up the Green River knife Janis had given him.

"Every time I skin a coon or a deer, I'll remember you," he said.

At the saloon, Holly left Justin mounted outside. "I'll be out soon," she said. "We'll get to the ranch by nightfall."

"Are you sure anyone in there knows Pa?"

"You heard Janis. He said this is where to go if you're looking for someone."

"Just be careful, Ma," Justin said. "That's all."

The saloon was dank and smelled of chewing tobacco and stale liquor. Men drank in the front, or played cards, while others occupied a section that had been added on to serve as a billiards hall.

She crowded her way to the bar, where a bartender was cleaning glasses.

"We don't serve Injuns," he said.

"Look closer," Holly told him.

He squinted. "Well, I'll be damned." He studied her. "You don't look to be the drinking type."

"I came in for some information," Holly said. "I'm looking for Isaac Porter's ranch."

"Isaac Porter?" He turned to a group of men drinking nearby. "Any of you know Isaac Porter?"

One of them said, "Yeah, he's the one who's sick, who owns half of the Diamond Rock Ranch. Word is he's not long for this world."

"How do I find him?"

"Just ride upriver. You aim to help him get better?"

The others laughed. Another one said, "How much you want to help me get better?" More laughing.

Holly turned away from the bar and right into a man who had been standing behind her.

"Long time, Holly," Harlan Porter said.

The other men at the bar moved away.

"You two know one another?" the bartender asked.

"We sure do," Harlan said. "But I thought maybe she'd died or something."

"She don't look dead to me," the bartender said. "You want another drink?"

"Yeah, pour me one." He turned to Holly. "How in hell did you escape those Sioux?"

"I didn't yellow-belly my way out of it like you did," Holly said.

Harlan laughed and downed the drink. "So, you've come looking for Isaac. I guess you heard. He's not doing any better."

"He must be doing some better, to have a ranch and all."

"It's his partner, Clyde Watson, who's doing all the work." Harlan laughed. "Isaac spends most of his time in bed coughing. Oh, he gets up once in a while, but it don't amount to much."

"At least you didn't get his gold," Holly said.

Harlan studied her. "Maybe not, but there's other ways of getting my share from him. You can tell him that I'm coming for a visit real soon."

He disappeared into the shadows, melting into a group of men heavily armed with pistols and knives, who stared at her before leaving.

"You don't seem none too afraid of him," the bartender said. "You ought to."

"Why?"

"He runs with a bunch of horse thieves that hide out at Bonner Spring, west of Owl Canyon. Their leader's a man named Musgrove, who used to steal from Fort Collins when they had horses and mules there. Now they've took to stealing from the ranchers. But that won't last long, to my way of thinking."

"Why do you allow them in here?" Holly asked.

"I know better than to get shot," he said. "Besides, their money spends good."

Holly left the saloon and met Justin standing outside.

"What are you doing? I thought I told you to stay on your pony," she said.

Justin pointed down the street. "Uncle Harlan came out of the saloon and took him, and yours too. See them?"

Holly watched Harlan and the others ride down the middle of the street, leading their horses along behind as if they owned them.

She ran down the street, with Justin yelling after her, "Wait, Ma, it ain't worth it!"

Holly reached Harlan and he leisurely dropped the reins in the street.

"Don't ever do anything like that again," Holly said, picking up the reins.

"You going to stop me?" His expression was cold. "You can have them horses back this time. But next time don't expect me to be so nice. Say hello to Isaac for me."

Twenty

THE DIAMOND Rock headquarters lay just north of the Cache la Poudre River, below a rock formation from which the ranch had taken its name. Pleasant Valley and Bingham Hill were two locations well known in the area, and Holly took her bearings from them. She had no trouble finding the place, riding past pine-studded foothills that lay on both sides of the river, giving way farther up the canyon to high mountains still streaked with snow.

A new two-story frame house, complete with porch and railing, sat on a bench above the river. Two log cabins, one considerably larger than the other, stood nestled among some cottonwoods behind the house. A small tack shed sat close to the largest cabin.

Nearby was a large, oblong corral with a double gate that faced the river. A few horses paced anxiously inside. Adjacent was a smaller, round corral with a hitching post in the middle.

Holly and Justin rode to the front door. Justin remained in the saddle while she dismounted and knocked.

A dark-haired woman dressed in a lavender dress came to the door.

"Can I help you?" she asked.

"This is the Diamond Rock Ranch, isn't it?" Holly said.

"Yes. Who are you looking for?"

"My name is Holly Porter. I'm looking for my husband, Isaac. Is he here?"

The woman's mouth dropped. "I beg your pardon?"

"My husband, Isaac," Holly said. "I was told he owns this ranch. Is that true?"

"Well, he is a partner," the lady said. "He's also my fiancé."

Dumbfounded, Holly said, "No, I'm his wife. You can't be getting married to him."

"I can be and I am," she said. "My name is Eva Watson, sister to Clyde, who shares ownership here with Isaac."

"I'd like to know more about this," Holly said.

"Maybe you should step inside," the lady said. "Is that your son outside?"

"It is."

"Have him get down from his horse and join us."

Still reeling, Holly called for Justin and he entered the house with his mother. They followed Eva Watson, who walked casually ahead of them as if nothing in the world bothered her.

"Would you care for some tea?" she asked Holly.

"I suppose so," Holly said. "Could you please explain all this to me?"

Justin, who had heard the conversation while sitting his pony, decided he would say nothing. Too much was happening too fast for his blood and he wished it would all be over and the woman would just disappear.

As they took their place on a sofa, and Eva Watson in a chair opposite, a Hispanic woman with child appeared, holding folded laundry.

"Rosa, we would like some tea," the lady told her. She turned to Holly. "How about the boy? I believe we have some milk."

Justin shook his head no.

The maid left and Eva said, "She works for me and her husband for Clyde. They're not so bad, I suppose, but I'm not anxious to have a little one running around. You understand, it will take away from her service time."

"I need to understand what you said about being Isaac's fiancée," Holly said.

"Well, I'm terribly sorry about the mix-up," she said. "I became engaged to Isaac two weeks ago last Saturday. We plan to marry down in Old St. Louis. It will be a grand affair."

"I'm certain it *would* have been," Holly said. "But what you've got to understand is that it won't happen. You see, I'm still married to him."

"It was Isaac's understanding that his wife and son had been killed by Indians."

"As you can see, that's not the case," Holly said.

"But how can I be certain you're who you say you are?" Eva asked. "You understand, there's a good deal to be gained by saying you're Isaac's long-lost wife."

"Yes, and there's equally as much for you to gain by marrying him, I would imagine," Holly said. "Where is Isaac now?"

"He's in bed, resting."

Holly looked around the house, searching for bedrooms on the main floor.

"May I see him, please?"

"Oh, he's not in the house. He's in the larger cabin out back. This house belongs to my brother, Clyde, and me."

"All this for just two of you?"

"Yes, we wanted it that way."

Holly studied the woman. "Isaac is half owner here and he lives in a little cabin?"

"He prefers it," she said.

Rosa brought the tea and placed the tray on a table. After pouring the cups and distributing them, she left.

"She's so small to be so pregnant," Eva said.

"I don't know why Isaac wouldn't be where it's more comfortable," Holly said.

Eva smiled thinly. "If you were actually ever married to Isaac, you would know him well enough to realize that he doesn't like to have someone fuss over him."

"Fuss is one thing," Holly said. "Comfort for a sick man is another. There's certainly enough room for him here."

"Actually there isn't," Eva said. "Not if we intend to entertain guests."

"So why didn't Isaac build his own house?" Holly asked.

"I told you, he likes the cabin." She sipped her tea. "Naturally, I must stay here in the house until we're married. You can understand that, I would think."

Holly said, "I guess you weren't listening. There'll be no more marriages for Isaac. His union with me is certainly enough for him."

"Perhaps it is you who is not listening. As I said, how do I know who you are? Aren't you part Indian?"

The door opened and a man's voice said, "Eva, whose horses are tied out front?"

The man stepped into the living room, his hat still on. He was of medium size and exceptionally lean of build. His eyes were dark and small, and darted everywhere.

"Clyde, this woman says she's married to Isaac," Eva said.

"Isaac's wife was killed by Indians," the man said.

"I wasn't killed, a point that seems hard for me to make," Holly said. "I'm Isaac's wife and I'd like to know why he's in a cabin and you two have this house."

Justin, who had sat silent the entire time, leaned over to Holly. "Can I go back out?"

"I need you here, to hear what's said."

"I'm Clyde Watson," the man said. "I'm sure you know by now that I'm Isaac's partner here at Diamond Rock. Eva is my sister. I suppose she told you already how she and Isaac came to fall in love."

"Fall in love?"

"Eva caught his eye from the beginning. You see, Isaac figured you for dead. He asked at Fort Phil Kearny, up north, and no one could say for sure about you. A lieutenant named Hodges said he'd go looking for you, but Isaac never put much stock in it."

Holly studied Clyde Watson. "Did Isaac tell you all this?"

Watson went on talking. "You see, Isaac was a lonely man and when he met up with Eva down in Denver, we all figured it was a good match. Simple as that."

"Yes, but it's not so simple," Holly said. "I'm still married to Isaac. You don't seem to be understanding that fact."

"More tea?" Eva asked.

"No, thank you," Holly said. "I believe I'll go out back and find that cabin Isaac's in."

"It would be best not to disturb him," Eva said. "He's awfully weak and needs his rest."

"I believe," Holly said, "that he'll perk up considerably when he sees me. I'm willing to take that chance. Thanks for the tea."

Holly found Isaac resting in the larger cabin on a feather tick. She and Justin eased up to the bed.

"Isaac," she said. "How are you feeling?"

He lifted his head. "Holly, is that you? Justin?"

He rose from bed, obviously in pain, and hugged them both, his face wet with tears. It was the first time Justin had ever seen him cry.

Holly noticed a collection of small bottles on a stand next to the bed.

"Is that laudanum?" Holly asked.

"It's something the doctor gave me for pain," he said.

Holly inspected a bottle. "It's laudanum. He gave you a lot of it."

Justin frowned, seeing the bottles on the stand and scattered on the floor beside the bed.

"I figured you both for dead," Isaac said. "The good Lord sure has blessed me today."

"It's good to be back together," Holly said. "But I've learned we have a problem."

"A problem?" he said.

"Eva Watson. She says she's going to marry you."

Isaac laughed. "She wants to marry me. That don't mean I want to marry her. Holly, you know I'd never settle for anyone else after you."

"She and Clyde said you were lonely."

"Maybe, but I never told them any such thing. It was the two of them who put the pressure on."

"You mean," Justin said, "she would have married you without even knowing for sure if Ma had died?"

"That's about the size of it, son."

"I'll put a stop to that right away," Holly said.

"I'd like that," Isaac said. "And you can help me work to keep Emilio on. He's the wrangler. He and his wife, Rosa, do a lot of good here."

"Why would they be leaving?" Holly asked.

"Emilio's the best you ever saw with horses, but Clyde thinks he's better and wants to let him go," Isaac said. "Let Emilio go and keep Rosa on, can you figure that kind of thinking?"

"It doesn't surprise me," Holly said, "I don't understand any of their thinking. Where's Burnham and Tillie? I heard they came down to work for you."

"Clyde made it so hard on them they left," Isaac said. "I told them that sooner or later I'd either buy Clyde out or we'd split the operation. One or the other. As you can surely tell, things ain't working out."

"Do you know where Burnham and Tillie went off to?"

"I heard they work in a dry-goods store in LaPorte. I ain't been down to see, though, as I've been feeling poorly of late."

"Let's get you out of this cabin for a little while," Holly said. "It would be good for you."

"I don't feel much like traveling, Holly."

"I didn't say we'd travel," she said. "Let's go sit down by the river and talk. We've got a lot of catching up to do."

At the water's edge, Isaac threw pebbles in the current, listening intently to Holly and Justin's stories. He found it difficult to believe they had found him and were anxious to renew their lives together.

"I heard so many stories about that attack on the wagons," he said. "Each one worse than the one before. I don't know how any of you made it."

"Lieutenant Hodges got his soldiers back to the wagons in time to save a lot of people," Holly said. "Otherwise, no one would have lived."

Isaac looked at Holly and back to the river. "To hear Hodges talk about you, you'd think he was sweet on you."

"He's a nice man," she said.

"He said I was a lucky man to have such a good woman."

Holly blushed. "I guess he thought I made a lot of sacrifices for you."

"Well, you did, coming out with Justin and all, fighting the weather and the country in a wagon. It's a brave woman who'd do that."

"Uncle Harlan never made it any easier," Justin put in.

"I reckon he didn't at that," Isaac said. "But you've got to understand, the war did him a lot of harm."

"It did us all a lot of harm," Holly said, "but it didn't make you a thief."

Isaac was silent.

Holly continued. "I went into a saloon in LaPorte to find out where this ranch was and Harlan walked up, bold as you please, and said he was coming out to pay you a visit someday. I don't want him out here."

"Maybe he means it for a friendly visit, to patch up our past."

"If he was friendly, why hasn't he come out yet?"

"Oh, you know Harlan. He doesn't get around to doing things very fast."

"Well, he made Justin get off his horse and then took mine and his, both. I had to run down the street to get them back."

"Maybe he was just funning you a little bit."

"I don't like his idea of fun."

Justin never liked hearing the two of them argue, and he blamed himself for bringing Uncle Harlan's name up in the first place. He considered getting up and roaming the river, like he had when he was small, but he hadn't seen his pa in so long that he didn't want to leave.

"You know Harlan likes to tease," Isaac said.

"It wasn't teasing, I know it wasn't," Holly said. "And I think you should know that the bartender told me that he rides with an outlaw named Musgrove, and that they've got the local ranchers in a stir."

"I've heard about Musgrove," Isaac said. "There's been talk of having a meeting and deciding what to do about that bunch. They've been stealing a lot of horses lately."

"You ready to see Harlan hang?"

"No," he said, finally admitting that Harlan might be involved with horse thieving. "You know I never could talk sense into him. Our ma always hated that we fought, and she blamed me 'cause I was the oldest."

"We've been over this before," Holly said. "None of it was your fault."

Isaac continued to reflect. "Maybe, when I've got my own spread, I'll cut Harlan in on part of it."

"How could you even think of such a thing?"

"I told you, Holly, he pulled me out of the river when we were young. I've always felt I owed him for that."

"You've done enough for him over the years to have set-tled."

"Still, I want to give him something. I figure part of the ranch would be fair."

"Isaac, you know that would be a mistake," Holly said. "Besides, he won't settle for part. He wants the whole thing."

"I still wish we could get along," Isaac said. He began coughing. "I can't seem to get rid of this derndable hack. I need to have some more medicine."

He sent Justin for one of the bottles, coughing uncontrollably.

"Who is this doctor that gave you all that laudanum?"

"Eva brought one out when I was in a poor way," he said. "I don't remember his name. He filled me with the painkiller and I've been using it ever since."

"You need a doctor who'll do more than just give you laudanum."

"They come and go in these parts."

"We'll go to Denver, where the good ones are. Lord knows with the gold you found, you could afford to have a good doctor treat you."

Justin returned and the two of them watched Isaac tip the bottle and drain a third of it.

He took a deep breath. "That's better."

Holly changed the subject. "We need a house, Isaac. We'll build one like the one Clyde and Eva Watson have, only bigger and better. There's no call for you to live in a little cabin, unless you prefer it."

"I don't prefer it," he said. "I've lived in enough of them."

"Eva said that you preferred the cabin to the house."

Isaac didn't answer. It had always been hard for him to realize that someone wanted to take advantage of him. He had always wanted to see the best in human nature, even after the war, when he learned that humanity didn't apply to everyone.

"She doesn't really want you for a husband, does she?" Holly said. "She and Clyde figured on having the whole ranch once you passed on. Isn't that it?"

Isaac found a large rock and chucked it angrily into the water. "You said it all. They want this place and they're hanging in a tree like a couple of vultures."

"They won't have your half, ever," Holly said. "I'm going to town and find Burnham and Tillie. They can come back to work first thing tomorrow."

"It might be hard to convince Tillie. She's taken to making dresses, real pretty ones, that she sells to the wagon folk passing through. She might not want to stop that, being it's been going good for her."

"Maybe she can divide her time," Holly said. "Or she can make the dresses up here."

"I hope you can get her to do it."

"She'll listen to me," Holly said.

She helped Isaac to his feet. Justin stood close by.

"I know it ain't Tennessee," he said, "but can you be happy here?"

"I can be very happy here." She looked over the country. "We'll have the best ranch in the Cache la Poudre valley."

Twenty-One

BURNHAM HESS looked odd in an apron, sweeping dust from a hardwood floor. It didn't flatter him, and Holly wondered why a man who had spent so much time in the mountains would ever handle a broom.

"First time I ever did this and you catch me at it," he said with a laugh. "It's good to see you didn't become wolf food."

"I nearly did," Holly said. "One of these times I'll tell you about it."

"I'll hold you to that," he said. "I reckon you've already been to the ranch and heard what's going on, otherwise you wouldn't have found us."

She then told him that he and Tillie were due back at the ranch the following day, to begin work for her and Isaac.

"I wouldn't have left but for Clyde and Eva Watson," he said. "I was afraid I'd do something I'd regret later, so it was easier to just leave. And Isaac can't do nothing. He's taking too much of that laudanum. It's working on his brain."

Holly had already begun to worry that Isaac's addiction to the medicine was affecting his decision-making process, not only with Clyde and Eva Watson, but with his brother, Harlan, as well.

"But I figured all that was Isaac's business," Burnham continued. "Tillie and I decided to just go off on our own. That's when Tillie took a job across the street, selling dresses. Maybe Isaac told you, she's gone to making them herself, the old Irish style from the old country, and sells them faster than she can make 'em."

"Maybe she likes what she's doing," Holly said, "but I wouldn't say you're all that happy."

"I help a young know-it-all tend this store. I ain't cut out for it, though. With you and the boy back, maybe I'd do best back helping Isaac however I could."

"You've got to help me get his share of the ranch back," Holly said. "Clyde and Eva are slowly taking it away from him."

"They're taking it, is right," Burnham said, "and none too slowly, for my money."

"What about Emilio and Rosa?"

"I like those two, but sooner or later Clyde's bound to run them off as well."

"Some things are going to change out there," Holly said, "and real soon."

"I figured you'd say that," Burnham said. "I'll finish up here and give notice, then meet you across the street."

Holly had no sooner gotten inside the door of the dress shop than Tillie was in her arms, hugging her tightly.

"Why, lass, how in God's name did you ever survive out there?"

"I told Burnham that you and he would hear the whole story out at the ranch, where you both belong."

"So you've already been out there to see things for yourself, have you?"

"And I don't like what I saw, not one bit. I won't stand for some hussy trying to take my man away."

"She knows better than to tangle with you," Tillie said. "She's as good as gone, I'd say."

Tillie told Holly about their ordeal after surviving the attack and how good things had been with Isaac, until Eva had showed up and begun working on him to marry her.

"I thought if I stayed out there any longer I just might wring her neck. But I found my calling here, making dresses." She held one up for Holly to admire.

"That's about the prettiest dress I ever saw," Holly said, feeling the blue fabric lined with lace trimming.

"It's yours, if it fits," Tillie said. "I insist."

Holly held the dress in front of her and stepped over to a mirror. She twirled around and around.

"It suits you, lass," Tillie said. "It suits you plumb fine."

"Do you think I can fit in with the ranch wives here?"

"You can fit in with anyone, lass. Anywhere. Before long you'll be the talk of the town."

Holly discussed her plans for a new house, and flowers in a large garden near the river, along with some squash and pumpkins and melons.

"I want to make things like they were back home," she said. "As soon as Isaac recovers, things will get to be like they were before the war."

"Yes," Tillie said, "a nice house and garden should be a good start."

Holly continued to stand before the mirror. Tillie showed her a number of different dresses. Holly held each one in front of her, settling on a blue one and a pink one to begin with.

"I'll have to have more," she said, "once I get into society around here."

Back at the ranch, Holly tidied up the cabin while Isaac and Justin walked the river. She wondered if her husband would ever get back to normal. He had been sick for so long that his lungs might be permanently damaged. She worried that tuberculosis had set in. But maybe it was just the high air—they were nearly a mile in altitude—that made it harder for him to breathe.

But there would be enough time for him to heal, she reasoned, and she would help him rid himself of the laudanum. In the meantime she would make the cabin a home. She had already located a good spot for the new house, near a creek that fed into the river, close to a grove of aspens always filled with chickadees.

There were plenty of wildflowers around and she thought about finding some tulip bulbs in town come fall, when she could plant the bulbs and look forward to their color popping up after the snow left in the spring.

She had gotten used to the mountain country, the snow and the high peaks that always stayed white. This country was nothing like Tennessee but it had grown on her almost from the beginning. She knew that she would never want to leave it now.

As soon as the problems were cleared up, this would be a grand place to raise Justin to manhood. He was nearly there already, and in many ways thought like a grown-up.

She thought about what Old Calf Woman had said, that Justin would become a great leader some day. He already showed signs of wanting to learn steadily. He had found himself some books to read and was searching for more.

LaPorte had an adequate school system for those who cared just to learn some reading and writing skills and a little math; but it wouldn't do for Justin, who would soon be thirsting for knowledge that only a bigger community like Denver could offer.

With the cabin cleaned, she slipped into the blue dress and knocked on the door of the main house. The maid came to the door this time and told Holly that Miss Eva was asleep.

"Please wake her up," Holly said. "I've got some words for her."

Rosa leaned over. "It will make her very unhappy if she's awakened."

"Then when she gets up, please tell her I'm interested in speaking to her as soon as possible."

"That will not be necessary," Eva said, adjusting her hair in her bedroom doorway. "Rosa, you may go."

Holly remained on the step, waiting to be invited inside. But this time there was no feigned politeness.

Eva stepped to the doorway.

"I don't appreciate your attitude, Mrs. Porter, if that's indeed who you are," she said. "And the dress doesn't become you. You still look like an Indian."

"Indian or whatever, I'm married to Isaac," Holly said. "You never will be and you can count on that. We'll soon be building a new house and getting settled here."

"You'd better talk to Clyde about that. He's in town right now."

"He can stay in town until he's an old man for all I care," Holly said. "He doesn't have a say in where or when we build our house. Or maybe you've forgotten that Isaac owns half of this operation."

"Yes, I suppose he does," she said. "But I'm through with this conversation. Now if you'll excuse me, I haven't finished my nap."

"Let me give you something to think about while you're resting," Holly said. "You ever come near Isaac again and I'll scalp you."

Eva's eyes widened. "I beg your pardon."

"Your place is not with Isaac. It never was and it never will be. You remember that or you'll see just how much Indian I can be."

Eva hid herself in the bedroom and Holly left, noticing that Rosa had been eavesdropping from the kitchen. Rosa came out the back door and met her.

"Please, Miss Holly, don't make Miss Eva angry. She will send me away."

Holly said, "She can't send you away. You work for me now, not her."

Rosa looked puzzled. "I work for you?"

"That's right. Move your things into the bunkhouse with your husband."

"That's how they wanted it, Mr. Clyde and Miss Eva," Rosa said, tears brimming in her eyes. "I do what they say and no question them about it."

"Well, it's not that way now," Holly said. "Get your things and move them. If Eva says anything, have her talk to me about it."

"I will," Rosa said. "But who will tell Emilio?"

"I'll go tell him now," Holly said. "I've not met him yet, anyway."

Holly made her way to the round corral, where Emilio stood leaning against a pole, watching a roan bronc pull against a rope that held it to the center pole.

"He's a wild one, that one," Emilio said. "But he'll be a very good horse, once he knows who the boss is."

He was small and well built, with a thin film of beard and smiling dark eyes. His sombrero had seen a lot of exposure to wind and dust, likely from the trip up the trail with cattle.

Holly had never spoken with a Mexican vaquero before but felt at ease since he had opened the conversation.

"You seem to enjoy your work," she said. "My husband says you're good at it."

"Your husband's a good man," he said. "And it's good that you've not been killed by Indians. That will do him good and it will be bad for Eva and Clyde."

"I only want what's fair," she said.

"Take more, if you'd like," Emilio said. "It would go good with me and Rosa. I'm close to leaving here and taking her with me because of those two."

Holly sensed no love lost for Clyde or Eva, and wasn't surprised. In fact, she felt drawn to him because of it.

"I hope you don't leave," Holly said. "I just told Rosa that she's working for me now, not Eva. She'll be staying in the bunkhouse with you from now on."

"What did Eva say?"

"There's nothing she will be able to say, when I decide to tell her."

He studied Holly. "You're a strong woman. That's good. I'll get this horse finished now."

She stood back while Emilio entered the round corral. She had never seen anything like it before and watched with fascination as the small vaquero did his special work.

He moved in on the bronc with a long rope. It stood with its feet spread, still pulling back against the rope that held it fast to the center pole. He came in slowly, talking low, but stepped back quickly as a flailing forehoof narrowly missed his face.

Holly heard him say something to the horse in Spanish, laughing good-naturedly. With his rope, Emilio formed a noose and started back in, dodging strikes and kicks, awaiting his chance. The bronc reared, angered by the vaquero's darting movements, squealing as the noose flew under and wrapped tightly around its front legs.

The bronc snorted and lunged forward, then back and sideways, still squealing, working to loosen the noose around its front legs. But the rope held and Emilio deftly doubled the loose end over into a coil and slipped it handily under the hind feet.

The vaquero stepped behind the horse, pulling both sets of legs together. He jerked sideways and the animal toppled onto its side with a heavy grunt.

He hurried, while the bronc lay dazed, and swiftly ran the loose end of the rope between both sets of legs, tying half-hitches faster than Holly could see the knots formed.

He came out of the corral, wiping sweat from his forehead.

"We'll let him think about it a little."

"Do you have to ride him?"

"Soon, after he thinks about all those ropes holding him."

"He's a good-looking horse," she said. "I assume he belongs to Isaac."

"Yes, Isaac is the only one who allows me to work his horses," Emilio said. "Clyde thinks I'm not needed here and that's why he won't pay me his share of my wages."

"Can Clyde break horses?"

"Clyde's not good at much of anything, except being mean. He must have taken lessons at it."

"Why do you think Isaac became partners with him?"

"Clyde's a big talker and since his brother mined gold with Isaac, he believed Isaac would trust him," Emilio said. "I guess at first he did."

"So it was Isaac who hired you?"

"Yes. Isaac told Clyde he needed a horse breaker and wrangler. Clyde didn't like me working but he knew Eva wanted Rosa to cook and wash clothes." He kicked his boot through the dirt and added, "Clyde has a big white stallion that needs to be broke, but he believes he can do it better than me. He'll learn one of these days, when that big white kicks him between the eyeballs."

"He should know better than to try and break horses when he doesn't know how," Holly said.

"There's a lot of things Clyde thinks he can do but can't," Emilio said. "He says he can shoot and that he'll keep the outlaws away from here. I don't believe it."

"I hear they've become a serious problem."

He looked at Holly. "I know you're tough, but what are you going to do about Isaac's brother?"

"I understand there's a stockgrowers' group organizing," she said. "They'll do something about Musgrove and Harlan, plus any others."

"I hope so," he said. "I'd hate to break all these horses just to see them get stolen."

He lifted a saddle and a hackamore from the ground near the gate and walked in. Holly closed the gate behind him. She watched while he approached the bronc, still trapped on its side, showing a row of teeth to Emilio as he closed in with the hackamore.

Dodging the snapping mouth, Emilio pulled the hackamore up over the horse's nose and into place. He draped the saddle over his shoulder and loosened the ropes holding the roan to the center pole.

The bronc lifted its head, rolled wide eyes, and surged to its knees. Emilio slipped the saddle on its back and, after loosening the knots, tightened the cinch as the bronc struggled to its feet, kicking at the ropes around its legs.

Quick as a cat, Emilio was in the saddle, holding the bridle tightly as the bronc exploded skyward, arching, wrenching to one side and then the other. Emilio remained tight in the saddle, knees locked, one arm flying wildly.

Holly watched while the bronc twisted its way around the corral, unable to shake the small vaquero who stuck like a burr to its back. Each time the animal stopped for breath, Emilio raked his Spanish-style spurs along the horse's flanks. Jumping and jolting, twisting and crow-hopping, the bronc could do nothing but tire itself out repeatedly.

Finally, the horse stood still, its sides heaving, sweat matted into a lather under the saddle and along its forelegs. Strong as rock, the bronc had been reduced to a staggering wreck, working hard to keep from falling down.

Emilio stepped down. The bronc stood still as he placed the loop over its neck and nose, and tied the end off on the center post.

He walked over to Holly, smiling. "We'll let him think about it."

The bronc needed no time to think about it. Its days of bucking and crow-hopping were over. Holly had to smile. Emilio Vasquez could work for her anytime.

Twenty-Two

LATE THAT evening Isaac and Justin returned from their walk, both silent. Holly wondered if something had happened between them, and Justin informed her that his pa was just tired.

"We walked too far," he said. "We should've turned back sooner."

That night Holly lay in the dark next to Isaac. It had been so long since they had last made love that he seemed like a stranger to her.

He had wanted her badly, and she him, but it had been very awkward and his abilities had failed him. She wondered what contribution the laudanum had made to his problem. His poor physical health would have been enough, but adding the medicine had made things impossible.

He slammed a fist into his pillow. "This ain't the way a man should be."

"You needn't worry about it, Isaac. It's not the end of the world."

"That's how it feels to me."

"No, things will get better when your health returns. You'll see."

Isaac said nothing for several minutes, then asked, "Holly, you ever sleep with anyone else while we were apart?"

"No. I'd never think of it."

"But you missed me, didn't you?"

"Of course I missed you. But what does that have to do with sleeping with another man?"

"It's been a long time, is what I meant. I mean, you must have had notions."

"Notions are one thing, acting on them is another."

She lay wondering: Had he acted on his own notions? She knew what soldiers often did when they came upon women. She couldn't envision Isaac doing that, though, and dismissed the thought.

She had been taught by her mother that men had needs and women had to bear them. It had never been that way for Holly. She hadn't found closeness and intimacy a duty. Yet it had always been difficult for Isaac to open up.

She reached over and lay her hand on his shoulder. She began to rub his chest, but felt tension building within him.

"You can relax, Isaac. We have all the time in the world together."

His voice cracked. "I don't feel much like a man."

"Of course you are, Isaac. You don't have to concern yourself about it."

"But of late, I've not been the same."

"It's understandable."

"Not to me, it ain't."

"It's not your fault. You got shot. You need time to heal up."

"I don't have any time," he said. "I don't want you feeling the need and wanting someone else—someone like that lieutenant."

"What does he have to do with this?"

"Justin likes him. He talked about him all during our walk."

"Justin likes men in uniform. He liked you in your uniform. Remember?"

"I'm talking about something else. I talked to that lieutenant. I tell you, Holly, he's sweet on you."

"What does it matter if he is? I don't want anyone but you," Holly said. "How many times do I have to tell you?"

"I guess I shouldn't have said it."

"No, you shouldn't have. It was always some other man when we were younger, and now it's the lieutenant. I wonder if you trust me."

As long as she could remember, Isaac had felt unworthy of her love and inadequate with himself. She had endured it when they had first married, because she thought it would make him feel worse to argue. Then had come the war and all its hardships, along with the lung wound, and it had certainly deepened his self-doubt. Now he seemed to believe that he wasn't even worthy of life, much less a happy one.

His gloom affected everyone. Justin had mentioned his concerns, saying, "It ain't like Pa. He seems to want to die. I don't understand it."

"He hurts something terrible inside," Holly had said. "There's nothing that can stop his pain."

"What about the medicine he takes?" Justin asked. "He sleeps good when he takes it."

"But then he wakes up and needs more. He's not healing inside, he's just existing."

But there was little choice in the matter. He either took the laudanum or spent his nights gasping in pain. She didn't totally understand addictions but she knew them to be real and had heard numerous soldiers screaming for painkillers, then screaming again once they wore off.

She blamed Clyde and Eva Watson. They had made no secret of keeping several bottles on hand and even force-feeding him at times to keep him calm.

Yet it would do no good to confront them about it. They would either deny it or insist it was done in Isaac's best interests.

Holly now considered insisting that he go to Denver and see a specialist. Surely a physician who knew about lung problems had made his way to that city, with its high altitude and the many settlers pouring in. It would be well worth a try.

Until then, Holly would have to get used to seeing Isaac pour himself full of laudanum. She was going to have many long nights, she knew, staring into the darkness and wondering why their future couldn't be as bright as she had once dreamed.

Over the days, Isaac maintained a fair humor, as long as he remained supplied with laudanum. The only thing he took special comfort in was his time with Justin. They had become ever closer over the days and the bonding did in fact help Isaac learn to cope with his lack of strength. Justin never questioned him about his lungs or the medicine or anything other than when they would go riding together. "Soon," Isaac would tell him. "One of these days soon."

While Isaac rested, which was often, Justin amused himself with one of the neighbors, a boy his own age named Nathan Rains. The two met while exploring the river separately and became immediate friends. Nathan's younger brother had a bloodhound who was soon to whelp. Justin had been offered the pick of the litter.

Holly had mixed feelings over Justin's new friend. He was a pleasant boy and thoughtful, but took up a lot of Justin's time. When Justin wasn't with Isaac, he was with Nathan, and that left little time with him for herself.

She felt she had only herself to blame, as she had forbidden him from helping Emilio with the broncs. He had been thrown once, the fall knocking the air from him. It might have been worse, and after that she had made him promise to leave the horse breaking to Emilio.

Though he had discovered a new friend, Justin never wanted his mother to feel left out.

One evening he brought her a bouquet of flowers for the table.

"Nathan's a good friend, but I don't want you to ever think

that you're not a special ma," he said. "I wouldn't be here now if it wasn't for you, and I won't forget that."

Holly hugged him tightly. "Things will get better, you wait and see."

"I know they will. Soon we'll have our own house and there'll be more room for us."

"We'll get Emilio to help us," she said.

Emilio, with help from some cowhands from neighboring ranches, had built another small cabin for himself and Rosa. He laughed about how cowboys hated that kind of work but that they gladly helped him in return for his services breaking their hard-case broncs.

Holly and Isaac had no problem with Emilio breaking broncs for other ranches, as he had no trouble keeping the Diamond Rock horses ready to ride. But Clyde and Eva complained constantly, insisting that their hand, even though they weren't paying him, stay at home.

"I'm not *your* hand," Emilio told Clyde one day. "Isaac and Holly pay my wages."

"You're not worth a dime," Clyde said.

"You'll wish you'd paid me something when you try and break your white stallion," Emilio said. "You wait and see."

True to Emilio's prophecy, Clyde got kicked by the prize horse. He had been lucky! He had ducked in time for the hoof to miss his head, but hadn't moved sideways fast enough and had been clipped on the shoulder. Luckily it had been a glancing blow or his shoulder would have shattered under the force.

Still, as fortunate as he had been, his temper had grown worse. His arm now out of the sling, he worked as if he had never been injured, the soreness contributing to his ugliness.

Burnham and Tillie spent a lot of their time in town because of him. Burnham complained to Isaac that he had better break his ties with Watson soon, for the longer he waited the harder it would be to end the partnership, which had already fallen to ruin.

"I'll come back here for good once that happens," he told Isaac. "Until then I prefer town to looking at Clyde's sorry skunk face."

"You'll come out to cook for the roundup, won't you?" Isaac asked.

"I'll cook for Emilio and the cowhands you hire," Burnham said, "but I won't touch neither a pot nor pan for Clyde Watson."

Tillie also mostly remained in town, making more clothes all the time. She often journeyed to the ranch in a small buggy to teach Holly some of the basics of dressmaking. Holly welcomed the new knowledge, as sewing in her girlhood had been a relaxing pastime.

"One day you'll be as good as me, lass," Tillie told her one evening as they worked by lantern light. "You could easily sell your own dresses right now, if that's what you wanted."

Tillie was forever trying to get Holly out of the country and down to Denver. Holly had thought about it often, especially when considering Justin's education. But that would come in time.

Holly saw Denver as barely a civilized community. Someday, when the droves of people coming in got settled, new and diverse businesses would flourish. More schools and churches would arise, including schools for advanced education. But for now the city was little more than a large boomtown.

"When you think the time's right, we'll put a business together down there," Tillie said. "I know how you love this ranch right now, but there's no future for you here, lass. Can you see that?"

"Are you talking about Isaac?"

"Do you figure he'll recover?"

"No, I don't think he ever will," Holly admitted. "I'm worried about him making it through the winter."

"Why, lass, you've not told me this."

"I'm sure the lung wound from the war is killing him," she said. "And the laudanum is making him worse. He won't go to Denver to see a specialist. He's giving up and I can't seem to do anything about it."

"Then can you see what I'm saying? Your future is not here."

"I want to stay here, Tillie. I'll just take over for Isaac."

"Women don't run ranches, lass. Men do."

"I can do as well as anyone. I've got Justin, who's near to a man already. Emilio and Rosa can help."

"Don't you see, lass, none of them will be here forever. Justin won't stay here all his life, much as he loves you. And Emilio and Rosa will have their own family soon and be looking for a place of their own."

"Maybe I can cut them in on the ranch."

"Maybe," Tillie said, "but you've got Clyde and Eva to get rid of first."

Holly spent the rest of the evening thinking about that problem. Even after Burnham came and picked Tillie up to take her back to town, she reflected on it. Clyde and Eva stayed in their house, a separate life apart from Holly and her family. They might as well have been located miles away, for they rarely spoke and never spent any time together. Holly knew that Tillie's advice about ending the partnership soon was well founded. How to go about it was another matter.

The day before the fall roundup was set to start, Holly decided to get it all out in the open. She would make it plain to Eva that there could be no more coexistence, even if no words were ever spoken between them.

She would suggest to Eva that after the roundup, she and Clyde relocate to a new ranch with half the cattle and horses, and take several hundred dollars in gold dust to compensate for the inconvenience. "We want to buy you out," Holly would tell them. "It's better for all of us."

Holly had recently learned from Isaac that he had a number of pokes stashed in various places around the ranch grounds. "I was going to tell you and even show you where I put them," he said. "But I keep forgetting." He didn't trust banks and didn't even know how much he had. But he was certainly willing to part with some of it to rid them of Clyde and Eva Watson.

She made her way to the house, passing the little garden that Rosa tended. She had filled it with tomatoes, corn, and potatoes, together with jalapeño and green peppers. As a peace offering, she had brought some of her produce to Eva, hoping to make the living situation better. But she had been refused. "Keep your poor people's food," Eva had said.

So Rosa had made herself content to do for those who appreciated it. Holly and Justin both grew to love her corn tortillas and her fine blendings of peppers, tomatoes, and beefsteak. They had tasted nothing like it in Tennessee.

But Isaac wouldn't try the food; he was content to live with steak and potatoes, fried in the ordinary manner. He wanted only to be left alone.

The only thing that brought him up from the bed or chair was the mention of Clyde and Eva cheating the cowhands. Emilio said often that Clyde never paid his fair share of the wages, and they stayed on only because they knew Isaac would make it right.

Holly had now dedicated herself to making it right by everyone. This would be the day everything got straightened out.

On the porch, she heard Eva and Clyde arguing inside. They were talking about moving, Clyde wanting nothing to do with it, while Eva, missing the finer comforts of life, wanted to go back to Denver.

"He'll never marry me anyway," she was saying. "We've got to find another way."

"Now's not the time to discuss it," he said.

Holly knocked and Watson answered the door, looking sheepish.

"It's a rare thing to see you here," he said. "You been eavesdropping?"

"I just got here," Holly said. "Was there something that you didn't want me to hear?"

"Speak your piece. I ain't got all day."

"It's a matter concerning the partnership in the ranch. Isaac and I don't think it's working."

"Why didn't he come with you to discuss it?"

"Justin took him to town for medicine."

"That's about all he's good for, I'd say—just laying around pumped up with medicine."

"I came mainly to make you a proposition," Holly said. "We're prepared to buy out your interest in the ranch."

He leaned against the door frame. "Really? And what if I don't want to sell?"

"It would be best for all of us, don't you think?"

"How much you offering?"

"I can't say offhand. Isaac would have to give you the figures. I just thought I'd throw it out as food for thought."

"Food for thought. That's a fancy way of putting it, I'd say."

"I just want our troubles resolved and I don't see any other way."

"Well, you listen to me. If anyone around here's going to be eaten up, it will be you and Isaac and all your lowly workers, not Eva or me. You understand?"

"I don't think *you* understand," Holly said. "Isaac is the one financing this operation right now. Not you or Eva."

"You don't know anything about it."

"I know all about it. Maybe I should have waited for Isaac. I think maybe he wants to move his headquarters and take all the hands with him. You and Eva could stay here, if that's what you want. What do you think about that? You'd get to pay all the bills yourselves."

Watson stared hard at her. "You've got a lot of gall."

"Just something for you to think about."

"Clyde, what does she want?" Eva yelled from the background.

"I'll tell you later," Watson said.

"Why don't you tell her now?" Holly said. "Maybe she'd like to give her opinion."

"Her opinion is the same as mine."

"I'd like to hear her say that."

He glared and said, "Tell you what. Eva and I will get back to you on this. Have Isaac with you next time you come, 'cause I don't like uppity women." He turned and slammed the door.

Holly started back for the cabin, muttering to herself. From up the valley rose a dust cloud that made its way to the ranch. Emilio quickly dismounted.

"What's the matter?" she asked.

"I came back to check on the new horses in the corral," he said. "Thieves robbed a rancher north of here."

"Was anyone hurt?"

"There was shooting but no one was hit. I want to take Rosa to town, just until this horse thief thing is over."

"She can stay with Tillie," Holly said.

"*Gracias,*" Emilio said. "I want her safe. Maybe it will be over soon, since the ranchers are calling a stockgrowers' meeting in two days. I could go, if you'd like, since Isaac's not up to it."

"That's kind of you, Emilio," Holly said. "I'll go with you. I want to make certain that someone is planning to put an end to this."

Twenty-Three

THE STOCKGROWERS' meeting was held just downriver from LaPorte, at the old officers' building at Fort Collins. Holly entered, wearing her new blue dress, and met the stares of nearly twenty men, established ranchers who had come together to discuss the outlaw problem.

She knew immediately that she had ventured into their domain, their realm, where women were the exception rather than the norm. She did not see them as bad men, just used to their routine, of which women played little or no role. Though no one said as much, Holly realized they believed that she should be home sweeping the floor. She was glad she had left Rosa in the store with Tillie.

Emilio stood beside her, gathering nearly as many stares. He was good with horses, everyone knew that, but he wasn't considered an owner.

"He may become a partner with Isaac and me, in time," she told the gathering.

No one there knew Isaac that well, either, only that he was sick and bedridden a good deal of the time. They knew Holly only by reputation and expected her to be dressed in buckskins with a feather in her hair.

She wanted them to know that she had not come necessarily to direct the conversation. Isaac deserved a representative, though, and he would have one. She had no illusions about her stature among the men, but had told herself she wouldn't forfeit Isaac's voice in the outlaw matter over a little discomfort on their part.

Isaac might have come, as he was feeling better again. Up one day and down the next—there was no telling how he would feel from day to day. Instead of sitting in a smoky room, as most of the ranchers were puffing on cigars, he had decided to take his first horseback ride upriver with Justin, something he had been promising for a long time. So Holly and Emilio, the ever-faithful wrangler, had come to see what was to be done about the thieves.

Clyde Watson was conspicuously absent. Holly wasn't surprised, as he was too full of himself to ever make a meeting. Any decisions made about anything would be made by him alone; he didn't trust committees.

As the meeting came to order, the stares continued. Everyone was uncomfortable. The men talked among themselves but none would make the move to try and remove her and Emilio. A good thing, for she might have had to make a scene after all.

Finally, a slender, middle-aged rancher named Abner Loomis introduced himself and asked her if she was liking the Diamond Rock Ranch and getting used to the valley.

"I find it very pleasant here, thank you," she said. "I only wish that my husband was in better health."

"I'm concerned that your husband's partner, Clyde Watson, isn't here," he said.

"I can't speak for him," Holly said. "I only know that Isaac and I have a great interest in the proceedings today."

"There may be some unpleasant subjects discussed," Loomis said. "I do hope you can understand that what we say here stays here."

"I have no problem with that."

Another rancher spoke to her. "We've heard you lived with the Indians. So you'd likely know something about horse thieving."

"Probably no more than you do, sir," Holly said flatly.

The meeting got underway and the outlaw matter was discussed at length. It wasn't the first time that trouble had broken out in the valley. An employee of the stage line, one Jack Slade, had turned murderer and made his escape to Virginia City, Montana, where he was promptly hanged by a lynch mob.

"He deserved it," one man said. "Before he left, he killed a man here. He cut his ears off and kept them till they rotted away."

"I heard his wife, Virginia Dale, got to the hanging a little late," another said. "She screamed at the hangman for not shooting her husband so he'd go quick. They say he hung for half an hour before he died."

"We've got some similar business to discuss today, gentlemen," Loomis said. "We all know how the Bonner Spring Gang is causing trouble throughout the valley, stealing horses and mules, and now cattle as well. It's got to end."

Loomis mentioned that Musgrove, the leader, had come to his place some months before and had shot a prized mule.

"I even invited him in for breakfast," Loomis said. "I wanted to see if he'd tell me that he was stealing stock—if he was brazen enough to do so."

"I guess he showed you he was," a rancher commented, "if he just up and shot your mule."

"He told me it was an accident," Loomis said. "He was getting off his horse and his shotgun went off. I don't believe he's that careless ordinarily."

Since the incident, Loomis attested, he had been trying to get help from the U.S. Marshal's Office in Denver.

"I agree with you. I'd prefer it was handled by them," one of the men said. "It gets sticky when you go to carrying a lynch rope around."

Some of the men agreed, while a large man named Davis

said, "I don't cater to losing any more of my stock. I see them anywhere near my place and I'll draw a bead on them, legal or not."

"That don't make you look any better," another rancher spoke up.

"Well, if we would all stick together and get them once and for all," Davis said, "the law wouldn't come after any of us."

"I suggest," Loomis said, "that we at least give the marshal's office a chance. They're supposed to send a man, or maybe two, up here soon."

"How soon?" Davis asked.

Loomis shrugged. "I can't say."

There was talk back and forth, divided evenly between waiting or going after Musgrove and his men. Holly knew that going after Musgrove meant going after Harlan as well. She thought it a good idea, except for how Isaac would feel when he heard the news.

Holly's anger had been building over Isaac's feelings of guilt regarding Harlan's behavior. To hear Isaac talk, you would think he was solely responsible for what his brother said and did, and how he treated others. Holly had told her husband far too many times that Harlan was a grown man and able to sort things out for himself.

After so many discussions, she stopped trying. If Isaac insisted on brooding over his brother, then he could do it as much and as often as he liked. But he would have to do it alone. She only hoped that he would someday come to his senses.

The discussion over what to do continued. "We can't wait for the law," Davis said. "There's not enough marshals and they're spread too thin. By the time they get up here, all our stock will be gone."

One stockman suggested hiring gunmen from outside the

area. " 'Regulators' is the term I've heard used for them," he said. "They could be of use to us, and we won't actually get involved."

"Oh, we'd be involved," another rancher said. "Whether or not we hold the noose, we'd be involved."

"Not that anyone could prove," the first rancher said.

Still another stockman, obviously very young, said, "How can you be sure that men of that sort won't go over to Musgrove's side?"

" 'Cause we'll pay them more money, that's why," the first rancher replied.

"You can call them regulators, but they're plain gunhawks," the young rancher said. "They'll do what they want once they get here."

In the end it was decided that the young rancher was right: Hiring shooters by any name was little different than taking a few of Musgrove's men aside and asking them if they'd care to make some extra money in their spare time. It didn't suit the problem to create more trouble by bringing in men who would turn on one another for a quick dollar.

After a vote by hands, Loomis said, "We're all in agreement, then, that we should allow the U.S. Marshal's Office to handle this. Is there anyone who is greatly opposed to this measure?"

A few in the room grumbled, but no one stood and spoke. Loomis turned to Holly.

"In all fairness, we should hear what your husband would think on the matter. Surely you discussed it before you came to attend."

"We discussed it," Holly said. "Our feeling is that the majority should decide."

"Do you have an opinion of your own?"

"Like someone here said, I know about Indians," Holly replied. "When they have horses stolen from their villages, they solve the problem by going out and stealing them back.

They don't necessarily try to kill the thieves, they just prove they are better at keeping horses than their enemies."

"Hey, that little lady's onto something," Davis said amid laughter.

"Maybe she's not so far off," another rancher said. "I'd follow her."

More laughter rose from the group. Holly sat silent while Loomis regained order, and the vote was retaken on going after Musgrove or waiting for a U.S. marshal. Waiting again won out by a slim margin.

After the meeting, Emilio left to water the horses before the ride back to the ranch. Loomis took Holly aside.

"I hope you don't judge us too harshly. We're not used to having women involved in making decisions of this kind."

"Maybe there should be more women involved," she said. "I feel we would bring a broader perspective to many matters that directly affect us."

"A point well taken," Loomis said. "Maybe in time, considerations for women in this organization will be allowed."

"In an organization such as this, time is not a woman's ally," Holly said. "It never has been."

Loomis studied her. "We've been gathering names. Musgrove has a number of men following him. One of them carries the name Porter. Harlan Porter, I believe."

"I'm afraid he's my husband's younger brother."

"Oh?"

"Yes, Harlan wanted Isaac's benefits from the gold fields. When he couldn't get them, he took to thieving."

"I'm sure this must be hard for Isaac."

"Terribly. But what can he do?"

"Let's hope the marshals come and take Musgrove away," Loomis said. "Then the rest of the bunch might see the light and disband."

"Yes," Holly said. "Let's hope so."

*　*　*

Clyde Watson rested his rifle against the gatepost of the round corral. The main corral was filled with horses and a few mules. It was better to keep them close until this thing with the horse thieves got cleared up.

Besides the thieves, whom he really did not fear, he had other things to think about. The arrival of Holly Porter and her son cramped a lot of plans he and Eva had put together. It would have been so easy had the woman and the boy actually been killed by Indians.

He reached the tack shed, thinking about the ranch and about his prized stallion, standing in the round corral. It occurred to him that Isaac Porter was about as stubborn as the stallion when it came to being broken. That man just wouldn't die. Before Holly and the boy, there had been nights when it seemed he wouldn't make it to dawn, but he always woke up.

Pushing the laudanum on him had been Eva's idea. "Get him to needing it and maybe he'll take too much," she had said. Since his family's arrival, that wouldn't happen.

He went inside the tack shed and selected a good rope. He would show that Mexican wrangler that he could break horses as well as any man alive. That stallion was going to learn a few things today, and Emilio would have to find another job.

"Clyde?" Eva yelled from the door. "Clyde, you'd better hurry up and get down to LaPorte."

He looked to the house. She shouldn't be bothering him. She knew perfectly well he had no intention of going into La-Porte for the stockgrowers' meeting, or for anything else.

"Clyde, can you hear me?"

"Woman, would you stop your wailing at me?" he yelled back. He strode angrily to the door. "What's all the fuss?"

"That meeting's today," she said. "There's no need to get angry with me."

"Did I ask you to remind me about the meeting?"

"Well . . . no."

"So why are you reminding me, then?"

"I thought you'd forgotten. I was certain you'd want to attend, being it has to do with those outlaws."

"I don't need anyone to help me with outlaws." He pointed to the round corral, where a rifle was leaning against the gatepost. "Me and that Henry repeater can talk louder than those pussyfooters in that stockgrowers' group."

"Maybe you should go in anyway, just to see what they've got planned."

"You haven't been listening, Eva. I don't care what they've got planned. I've got plans of my own. Such a group as that don't care about what's important. They just want to get together and talk about nothing while the rest of us with sense go on about doing our work."

"That other woman went in."

"Holly?"

"Holly, or whoever she is."

"Eva, she's Isaac's wife. No matter how much we don't like it, she's legal."

"So where does that leave me? How does that leave us with getting the ranch after he dies?"

"I don't know. There are things we have to figure out."

"So go into town, before it's too late, and speak up about this place and how we want protection. Who knows what she'll say."

"They won't listen to her," he said. "They won't give a whit about her. They'll likely have her in tears."

"Not her."

"Eva, they won't take her seriously. We'll deal with her in time ourselves."

"What about the boy? He'll fall heir as soon as Isaac and her are gone."

"One at a time, Eva. One at a time. Now get back in there

and cook that steak and don't bother me no more about the stockgrowers. Understand?"

On his way back to the corral, he kicked the dirt several times. He had been to one of the first stockgrowers' meetings, to discuss the roundups and how they would be held. At that time no one wanted to listen to him or make him their leader. Some of them disregarded his suggestions entirely.

He couldn't see how things would have changed, or that any of them would have learned by now to listen to him. Such men were not worth fretting over. He had better things to do with his time, and threw a lariat over his prize stallion's neck.

He jerked hard. "Get over here to me. Hurry up, now."

The stallion fought him and Watson considered taking the end of the rope to him. Instead, he looped the rope around a corral pole and tied it off.

While the horse fought the rope, Watson went to the creek bank and cut a large willow. He returned to the round corral and slipped through the gate.

"I'll teach you some manners, I will," he said.

Before he could swing the first lick a voice came from behind: "That's no way to treat a horse."

Watson had been so intent on his business that he hadn't seen the riders come into the yard. To his horror, there were four of them, all heavily armed.

"You hear me?" Harlan Porter smiled as he spoke. "How am I going to sell that stallion for good money with whip marks on him? Now, you drop that willow, you hear?"

Watson contemplated going for the rifle. There was no chance. It rested near the gate as if a thousand miles out of reach, much closer to the outlaws than to him.

"Well, ain't you going to say something?" Harlan asked. He threw an empty whiskey bottle on the ground near the corral.

"You caught me off guard," Clyde said.

Harlan laughed. "You got that right. How about if you

untie that stallion and let him out the gate? We'll drive him in that big corral with the others."

One of the outlaws, whom Harlan referred to as Bat, opened the gate and rode in. "Loosen that rope around his neck so that he can run free," he said.

"Listen, you don't want to do this," Clyde said. "The stockgrowers are meeting right now and they'll come after you."

Harlan looked to the others. "Any you boys see a stockgrower around here?" They laughed.

"Hurry with that noose," Bat said, watching the stallion prance and pull at the rope.

Clyde tried to pull the stallion to him. The horse fought all the harder.

"You don't know a lot about horses, do you?" Harlan said. "Just come out of the corral. We'll handle him."

Watson stood his ground. "I'll stay in here and do it. I know about horses." He looked over to the house, where Eva had appeared in the doorway.

"Clyde, do we have company for dinner?"

His face whitened.

"Bat, come on out of there," Harlan said. "We'll tend to that stallion later."

"Just take the horses and go," Clyde said.

"Tell her we'd be proud to have dinner with her."

"Go back inside, Eva," Clyde yelled.

"Clyde, I can't hear you."

"I said, go back inside!"

Harlan motioned to Bat. "Go and help her with dinner. And behave yourself."

Bat turned his horse and Harlan told another one of the group—the youngest one, a kid named Lick, to reach over and pick up Clyde's rifle.

"I saw you looking at it earlier," Harlan said. He took it from Lick. "Here, you can have it."

He flung the rifle over the corral toward Watson, who instinctively raised his hands to catch it. Harlan quickly drew his pistol and fired twice. The bullets thumped into Clyde's stomach.

Watson grunted and grabbed his middle. The rifle bounced off his shoulder and fell to the ground.

"What's the matter?" Harlan said with a laugh. "Can't you catch?"

Clyde slumped to his knees. His face took on a distorted frown and he fell forward, groaning loudly.

"He don't feel good, does he?" Lick said to Harlan. " 'Spose I ought to pop him a couple of times?"

The fourth outlaw, a tall man named Garrett, had remained quiet up to now. He said, "Why'd you let Bat go to that woman? I think we all should go up to the house."

"He's right," Harlan said. "Let's go have some dinner."

Clyde tried to rise, but fell back down and rolled over on his back. In the distance he could hear screaming. The breeze felt hot on his face, then pleasantly warm, and the screaming lowered itself into a distant wailing. Then everything went silent.

Harlan and the others arrived to find the first outlaw ripping Eva's clothes off. She was on the porch, her hands over her face, crying and screaming.

He dismounted. "Bat, you ain't had dinner yet. Leave her until after we've eaten."

Lick felt his excitement growing at watching Bat tearing at the woman's clothes. She was older but she still excited him. Anyway, she wasn't that old; a lot of the whores he had visited were older.

"I said leave her be." Harlan grabbed Bat by the back of his open pants and pulled him free. "You ain't first, anyway. You ought to know that."

Eva slid down the wall to the floor, sobbing, trying to cover herself with her torn dress. Harlan pulled her up by the arm. "Don't fret now," he said. "We ain't had dinner." He tied the torn and tattered pieces together so that the dress at least stayed on. "There, that don't look so bad. Dry your eyes, now." The four sat down to the table and Eva, trembling so badly she could barely stand upright, filled a platter with fried chicken and a large wooden bowl with biscuits.

The outlaws ate while she stood beside the stove and, no longer able to control her fear, vomited. None of the outlaws seemed to notice, so busy were they with eating. If they did see her, or could smell it, it didn't bother them.

Bat kept turning to watch her. His pants were still open. He finished his meal first and turned in his chair to stare at her.

"I told you," Harlan said, "you ain't going at her first. In fact, you're last."

"Why?" he asked.

" 'Cause you took it upon yourself to embarrass her. See how bad she feels?"

"That ain't no reason to make me last. Lick should be last. He's youngest."

"I said you're last," Harlan said, shaking a chicken leg in his face, "and that's reason enough."

Everyone finished and Harlan said to Bat, "No need to feel so bad about it. There's enough dessert for all of us."

Eva let Harlan take her by the hand and into the bedroom. What good would it do to fight? She would pretend that he was a young man she had loved so many years before.

So she let herself drift away, to be someone else, uninvolved, while they used her in turn, each one worse than the last. She drifted to faraway places and saw faraway things, looking for fields of flowers and meadows where the sun shone brightly.

She found such a place and lingered there, far from the foul men whom she knew had killed her brother and who would likely kill her. But now it didn't matter to her if she lived or died because she had found this place where, in her mind, she would stay. Yes, no matter what happened, she would never let her mind return.

Twenty-Four

JUSTIN AND Isaac heard the shots faintly—distant popping noises. Since no more followed, they had no concern. It had been a grand day for both of them, riding together through the autumn countryside, viewing mountain hillsides shimmering with golden, quaking aspens.

They had ridden a good way up the canyon, toward two high peaks that stood up along the mountain front in the distance. Isaac didn't know the names of the peaks but commented that if they weren't named already, they soon would be, and likely after someone who had made a name for himself.

"Someday you'll be famous, Justin," he had said. "Wouldn't that strike your fancy?"

"Old Calf Woman told me that the day she died," Justin said. "Now you and Ma have been saying it ever since."

"It's bound to come true, son. Wait and see."

Justin thought it curious that he would hear the same thing over and over. Maybe it could happen. Maybe he could make his pa and his ma both proud of him.

It was something he wanted for himself. Both of them had worked so hard to do good by him and now it was his turn. As soon as he had time he would start thinking about how to become famous, even if it meant going down to Denver for schooling.

He had discussed it with his ma many times. Secretly, he

had always wanted to be able to go to a good school and learn things most boys his age didn't know. He hadn't told anyone for fear of being laughed at; boys his age back in Tennessee would certainly think it funny, and he believed that Nathan Rains would also.

But somehow his ma had known all along. Maybe it was from all the questions he asked, prying to the core of matters. And he had taken to reading more and more, finding books at the local school that dealt with the Knights of the Round Table and a man named Paul Revere, who brought news of the British coming to fight the colonists.

There were many other books on many subjects but not as many, he knew, as there would be in Denver. Should his ma bring it up again, Justin thought he might like to try school down there. He knew from Nathan Rains that all they taught in LaPorte was basic reading and writing, and some numbers. He already knew the basics and wanted to go on.

He was torn, though, as his pa would likely want him to stay. They had enjoyed the ride together but Justin was already seeing that it had taken a lot of strength from him. He just wasn't saying much about it. He needed more and more rest all the time. And with the cold weather not far off, they wouldn't get outside much anyway.

He now thought about telling his pa about it when he saw a bear—very large and tan in color, with a hump on its back. They had stopped to water the horses and Justin pointed it out. He had a rifle that belonged to Isaac and was eager to try it out.

"We could use a bear rug," Justin said.

"We don't need no mad bear coming at us," Isaac said. "Now, put the rifle down."

Justin saw the logic to the demand. The bear, now that he looked at it closely, was far too big for one shot. There was no telling what it could do to a person.

"Is it one of those grizzlies that Burnham talks about?" he asked.

"It could be. It's not worth the risk." The bear loped off and Isaac said, "It's been a grand day, son. Let's hurry back. Your ma should have some news about the meeting."

Isaac coughed hard, the worst fit of the entire day. Justin frowned. Maybe they had hiked too far. He enjoyed the outings with his father but worried that they put too much strain on him.

Within two miles of the ranch they noticed vultures wheeling in the air. Justin mentioned the two popping sounds they had heard earlier, and Isaac said they might have been gunshots at that.

"Likely someone wounded a deer and it got away and died," he said.

Upon reaching the ranch, they saw that the corral gate was wide open. Not a single horse remained, not even Clyde Watson's prize stallion. Instead, the round corral was filled with vultures, hopping and squawking for position around something lying in the corral.

"Justin, you stay here," Isaac said. "Something bad's happened. I just know it."

"I'd rather come with you," Justin said, remembering his narrow escape from Bad Face when his mother had gone to check on what had been scaring the horse.

Together they rode to the round corral and dismounted. Clyde Watson's corpse was covered with feeding vultures.

Isaac shot one and it toppled sideways, flopping. The others rose in a squawking flurry for the nearby bluffs.

Justin turned from the grisly scene. He hadn't liked Clyde Watson, but no one deserved to die and be torn apart by buzzards.

"Who do you think killed him?" Justin asked.

"Likely Musgrove's gang of thieves."

"They would come like this in broad daylight?"

"There's nothing to stop them," Isaac said. Hoping his assessment was wrong, he added, "Maybe he had an accident, but I doubt it. The horses being gone tells me that the thieves for sure made a visit."

"You suppose Uncle Harlan was part of it?"

"He told your mother he was coming for a visit. Remember?"

Justin remembered, thinking, how could he forget? The incident in front of the saloon in LaPorte, when Harlan had taken their horses, still left him shaking. His ma had said during their ride to the ranch that Harlan had promised to come see them. He didn't think that meant he wanted to kill them all, though, and leave them for the buzzards.

"Bring me a tarp from the tack shed, son," Isaac said. "I'll cover him proper."

Justin did as he was told. The buzzards circled above as Isaac covered the torn remains.

They went toward the house to check on Eva, leaving the buzzards, fighting among themselves, to tear at the tarp. She was sitting in a rocker on the porch, looking out toward the river.

Justin realized instantly that something was terribly wrong. Her dress, ripped to ribbons, was soaked with blood, and her eyes held a distant stare.

"Son, this is nothing for you to see," Isaac said. "When someone's dead it's one thing; when they're dead in the mind it's another."

Justin didn't know what his pa could do for her, or what she could ever do for herself. Clyde Watson would go in the ground, the same as anyone whose life had ended. But someone who had no mind? What would happen to them?

He watched while his pa knelt down and spoke softly to her. She stared blankly at him as if he were a stranger, pulling away at first, then crying, then laughing like a strange animal. Justin felt his blood run cold.

The house had been ransacked, everything strewn in all directions. The dresser drawers had each been pulled out and their contents dumped.

"What were they looking for?" Justin asked.

"Valuables. Anything they could steal."

"They made a terrible mess."

"Check the cabins, son," Isaac said. "Make certain nobody else is dead. I hope to God they all went to town."

Justin headed for the cabins with weak knees. He felt relieved, believing everyone else had left, for there were no signs of horses or hitched buggies anywhere. Likely the thieves would have made off with the horses, but they had no use for a buggy.

Certainly Burnham and Tillie were in LaPorte, and he knew it was too soon for Emilio, Rosa, and his ma to have gotten back from the stockgrowers' meeting.

But the cabins, too, were littered with clothes and other belongings. The thieves had taken the beds apart, looking under the mattresses.

"Horses is all they got," Isaac said when he joined his son. "And maybe a few mules."

"It's a good thing they didn't know where your gold was," Justin said.

"That's why I don't put my pokes under the mattress, as some folks would," Isaac said.

"You think they'll come back?"

"I can't say, son."

"We'll be ready for them if they do come."

Outside, Justin noticed an empty whiskey bottle near the round corral.

"This is the kind Uncle Harlan drinks," he said.

"A lot of folks drink that kind," Isaac said. He was silent

a moment. "But then, I don't suspect a lot of other folks would have been out here thieving and killing, either."

Holly and Emilio rode into the yard to find Justin and Isaac standing together in front of the house. Eva was on the porch, rocking slowly, staring into the distance. Overhead, buzzards sailed the air currents.

Emilio stayed on his horse. He didn't like being around the dead or even worse, someone whose mind had left her.

"I'll go into town and be with Rosa," he said. "I'll look after her for a while."

"You won't be leaving the country, will you?" Holly asked.

"I won't be leaving, no. I just want the thieves to be caught so it will be safe here for my wife and baby."

"We'll do what we can to see that it happens."

"Miss Holly," Emilio said, "if you need help to go after them, I will come with you."

Emilio rode off and Holly joined Isaac.

"Musgrove must have been here," he told her. "And maybe Harlan with him."

"It couldn't have been Musgrove," Holly said. "As soon as we got out of the meeting, word came that he had struck the stage stop right there in town, taking all the horses."

"Well, maybe it was Harlan and some others in the gang," Isaac said. "Justin found this whiskey bottle."

Holly knew immediately that Harlan had used the bottle. He had a nervous habit of scratching at the label with his fingernails.

"He killed Clyde and might just as well have Eva," Isaac said. "She'd be better off that way than she is now."

Holly knew what had occurred. She couldn't even get Eva to recognize her or say a word that made sense.

"I suppose she'll want to quit the country," Isaac said. "There's not a thing left for her here."

"We'll leave that up to her relatives," Holly said.

They buried Clyde in a heavy tarp, in case his relatives wanted to exhume him later for reburial in Denver. Eva sat in the rocker on the porch, staring in the other direction, saying nothing to anyone. She fought Holly when she tried to help her into the house and remained on the porch throughout the night.

Emilio had already taken the news to LaPorte, and Abner Loomis, along with some other ranchers, stopped by to hear the story. The hard ride upriver with Justin and the shock of the events upon reaching the ranch had put Isaac back in bed, and he told his version flat on his back, coughing most of the time.

Loomis and the others didn't stay long. It was obvious what had taken place. Together with the raid in town—where, thankfully, no casualties had been suffered—this atrocity had to be rectified if they didn't want more to follow.

Before the afternoon ended, a committee of ranch women arrived to take Eva to town. This time she didn't fight, but climbed into a buggy without a word. Someone had wired her relatives and they were coming by stage to take her back to Denver. Clyde could stay in the ground where he had died. It seemed no one was that fond of him in the first place, and they blamed him for Eva's tragedy.

That evening, Holly suggested to Isaac that he take a room at a boardinghouse in LaPorte, in case his brother considered coming back.

"He's already got the horses," Isaac said. "Why would he come back?"

Justin answered, "You know why, Pa. The gold."

"Justin's right," Holly said. "He has to know you've got some stashed someplace, and he certainly knows that you don't fancy using banks. He could come back here and demand you give it to him. We don't want to be here if that happens."

"But we can't leave the house and buildings," Isaac argued. "They're not worth getting killed over," Holly said. "Did you ever see a house or cabin that couldn't be rebuilt?"

Isaac reluctantly agreed. They helped him into a wagon and, late that evening in LaPorte, rented a room for him. There was no way to tell how long he would need to be there, but certainly until Musgrove and his gang were captured, and Harlan with them.

As Holly stepped out of the room, the landlady said, "I don't run no hospital here, you know."

"I'll double your rent," Holly said. "He'll need his meals brought to him."

"What about his medicine?"

"He handles that himself. And you won't have to care for him. He can get up and around."

"Do you expect him to die soon?"

"We'll have him back at the ranch before long," Holly said.

Holly notified Burnham and Tillie, who insisted on visiting him immediately. Isaac didn't seem to recognize them right away, as he had filled his veins with laudanum. This saddened everyone, especially Justin, who blamed himself for having insisted on the long horseback ride.

"Don't blame yourself," Holly told him. "That was the most fun he's had in a lot of years, certainly since the war."

"But I might have killed him," Justin said.

"You did no such thing. Besides, he's not getting any stronger, no matter what he does. Better he should be doing things that make him happy. Wouldn't you say?"

Justin realized what his mother was telling him: His pa wasn't long for this world, so he had just as well enjoy the time he had. But that didn't make it easier. There would be no more mountain rides.

After two days in town, Holly grew restless. Justin had gone to stay with Nathan Rains and his family, who had quit ranching and had moved close to town to start a vegetable farm. Folks needed produce, and the family expected to make a handsome living at it.

It relieved Holly to see Justin welcomed at the Rainses', but without the boy and with Isaac in bed, oblivious to his surroundings most of the time, she had little to do.

She left early the next morning, headed back to the ranch.

"You'll get yourself killed." Burnham said to her before she left. "Leave it up to the stockgrowers."

"I'm a stockgrower," she said. "I've got to save what I can of our livestock."

"Land sakes, lass!" Tillie was standing next to Burnham. "Isaac's got enough gold buried on that place to buy a thousand more head."

"But only he knows where it's buried," Holly said.

"You'd best ask him where it's at," Burnham said, "before it's too late."

"I'd rather he offer me the information," Holly said, mounting her horse.

At the ranch, she dressed in her buckskins and checked her pistol and rifle. Clyde's blood stained the ground in the round corral, and the memory of Eva rocking on the porch remained vivid. Harlan had gone too far.

She had no trouble finding the outlaws' tracks. There had been no rain, and she followed the hard-packed trail up the valley bottom and off through a rock-walled canyon that led north from the river, across open foothills and into the rough country west of Owl Canyon.

She had never been to Bonner Spring, where it was said the gang hid out, but she knew she would have no trouble finding it. The tracks were so plain that any schoolchild might have followed them.

She rode slowly and cautiously. She had decided not to meet the gang head-on by herself. Burnham and Tillie were right: There was no advantage to getting killed over livestock, especially when Isaac had enough gold to buy horses and cattle for two more ranches.

She had to wonder why someone hadn't stopped Musgrove long ago. As time passed, he was bound to pick up gang members willing to help him, and it was certainly no surprise that Harlan would throw in with such a group. He had never wanted to work for anything in his life; *taking* was his sole means of existence.

By early afternoon, Holly spotted smoke and made her way to the hideout. She backtracked and left the trail, deciding to check out the area around the hideout to learn ways of getting in and out. She guessed the access was limited and that anyone who showed up uninvited might not get a chance to leave.

She hitched her pony to a pine and worked her way along a wooded ridge. Below sat a small cabin, smoke curling from its chimney, and nearby a crude corral, the back of which was a long rock wall. At one end of the corral, four men worked on the horses, tying them in the fashion she had seen Emilio do, taking them down, and using a running iron to rework the brands.

The horses' squeals and the smell of burned horseflesh drifted up to her. She eased her way back to her pony, who was becoming uneasy with the commotion below.

After tying her horse on the other side of the ridge, where the smoke and noise had given way to the wind, she made her way back, getting closer this time, and sat down to watch.

The Diamond Rock horses were there among other stolen stock, all but Clyde's white stallion. Such a prize wouldn't be kept with the others for long and had likely already been sold.

She was amazed at how quickly and deftly the men worked, each of them skilled. She looked closely for Harlan, but he was not there. They seemed to have no fear of getting caught, as they hadn't even posted a sentry to watch the trail.

She wanted in the worst way to make a run at them. With surprise in her favor, she could get two or three of them easily. But she wanted the horses worse than the men, and going at them would get her killed.

She waited. As evening fell, more men arrived with more horses. This time Harlan rode with them.

She went back to her pony and led him to her spot. He nibbled at pine grass while she sat in the dusk, nervous, fingering the Colt revolver. A cool fall wind swept through the trees and a rain shower came and went, leaving the air even cooler.

She crept closer to the cabin. Inside, the men were gambling. She could hear them plainly, arguing and cursing, accusing one another of cheating. Often the conversation would turn to women and they would talk about Eva and laugh. Now and again someone would throw an empty bottle outside the door, or chuck one through an open window. It went on until late into the night.

With the moon up and the wind settled, she crept down to the corral, leading her pony behind. The horses paced nervously. She opened the gate and jumped on her pony.

She didn't have to drive the horses from the corral. One discovered the open gate, followed by another and another, and soon the entire herd pounded along the trail through the darkness, out from Bonner Spring.

She pushed them hard and was well out of range by the time the gang had awakened and started shooting into the darkness. By daylight she had the herd back through the rock canyon and down into Pleasant Valley. She forded the river with the early sun shining off the rippling water, the horses drinking deeply.

Not all of the herd had stayed together in the darkness— some had split off—but she had most of the Diamond Rock horses and wished that Emilio was there to help her cut them out and start them back to the ranch.

Twenty-Five

LANE HODGES stood in the Denver courthouse with five other men, being sworn in as a deputy United States marshal. His feelings were mixed: He would have liked to have left the army under better circumstances and would have liked to have had another chance at redeeming his reputation; on the other hand, he could do that as a lawman.

That day in Red Cloud's village would haunt him the rest of his life. Likely he couldn't have gotten Justin Porter out of that village anyway, so it had been lucky for the boy that Holly had shown up to get him.

Holly Porter was the most unusual woman he had ever met and one of the most courageous to ever travel the Bozeman Road, or any other trail, for that matter. He had to admit she had touched something deep inside him. He had known women and as a young man, before joining the army, had nearly married. But the war had ended that romance.

After the attack on the wagons—when he had believed both Holly and Justin were gone for good—he lay awake at night thinking about what he had done wrong. "Pursue and destroy all hostile Indians" had been his orders, "under any and all circumstances." But had that meant at the peril of the emigrants left behind? His decision tormented him endlessly.

But that had passed and he had seen and talked to Holly, the legendary Wolf Woman, before the storm and buffalo stampede had struck the village. Though the destruction had been terrible, no one had been seriously hurt, and Hodges had left with his soldiers while Red Cloud and his people had begun their journey to the Sun Dance grounds.

Later, on the way back to Fort Phil Kearny, he had run into the company who had been bringing the horses to ransom Justin in Red Cloud's village. Afoot, they had told him the story of the renegades and the raid that had cost them the fifty horses for Red Cloud, plus their own.

Bad Face. Hodges knew at once and realized he should have guessed from what the renegade had said during the council. But now the damage had been done and Red Cloud had become angrier than ever.

The record of his journey to Red Cloud's village didn't exist. The army would never document such a failure in writing.

Hodges had been forced to resign over the matter, for "the good of the service," as a superior officer explained it. He had done what he could for the army and the men under him throughout his career, and yet everything had gone bad. He had never belonged in the army, he concluded, and would never look back.

Instead, he would look ahead and believe he could do some good in his new profession.

He had filled in the forms and offered personal information to the U.S. Marshal's Office only to the extent that he had served at Fort Laramie as a lieutenant and had escorted wagon trains through hostile Indian territory. As a result, he had been told he would likely be given assignments for extra pay that involved Indian problems.

There was more than enough to do, and the judge said as much. "I only wish there were tenfold of you standing before me," he said. "There's a lot of country to cover for so few men."

Hodges supposed the rest of the new deputy marshals were in the job for good reasons, although he doubted one of them, a man with a scraggly beard who smelled of strong drink. No matter, his concerns now lay with ridding the country of thieves and murderers, of which there were plenty. What the others did was their own business.

The swearing-in ceremony was swift and to the point. Back at the main office, U.S. Marshal Graves called a meeting of the new deputies and those who had been on the job for a while but not on assignment.

The marshal looked through his stack of letters and "wanted" posters and, while the new deputies waited, read to himself from the list of requests for marshal services in the region.

There were so many he didn't know where to begin or how to arrange priorities. Shootings and lootings were common, and seemingly one-time affairs could not be looked into. It was the problem thieves who had to be stopped, the ones who maintained a state of disturbance at one location over an extended period of time.

"We've got to address the situation along the Overland Trail before long," Graves told the men. "This Musgrove character and his Bonner Spring Gang have been making it rough on the ranchers. It seems they've been doing some killing along with the thieving."

Hodges listened carefully. He knew that Holly and her family might somehow be involved, and likely Isaac's brother, Harlan, who had boasted at Fort Laramie that he intended to make a good living off the ranchers near LaPorte and old Fort Collins.

"They want our help," Graves continued. He looked up with a smile. "It seems, though, that after one of the raids, a ranch wife stole their horses back. Maybe we should deputize her."

"Do you know who the woman was?" Hodges asked.

"No, the letter didn't give any women's names. But one of the stockgrowers up there, Abner Loomis, is willing to work with us. We need to help them out. It's worse this year than last, and we've got to put an end to the killing."

The marshal pointed to a man named Lowell, one of the more experienced men. "You went up there last year and found them. I'll need to send you back."

"Not alone, you won't," Lowell said. "I almost got myself killed last time."

"I can't send all of these men with you. We've got other problems to attend to."

"I didn't say I wanted everybody to go with me. Maybe just two more."

"One more."

"I need at least two more men. This Abner Loomis is a rancher, not a gunman. I need men with me who've shot and been shot at."

"I said you can have one man," Graves said.

"And how many thieves are there?"

He checked the letter. "It says here eight to ten."

"Listen," the deputy said, "I've had my fill of going out after gangs of killers all by myself. Even two more men won't be enough."

"Maybe you'd better turn your star in, then."

"Is that what you want me to do?"

Graves looked at his list and said, "There's a robber down out of Pueblo but he's by himself mostly, they say, and there's a man in town who used to be a lawman in Texas who'll help us get him. Go down there."

Lowell took the warrant and left. Hodges spoke up. "I can take the assignment up north."

Graves studied him. "I've got something more in your line, since you've had experience with Indians. I'm sending you to Kansas to see if it's Indians or Jayhawkers causing trouble there."

"I could probably do more good up north."

"There's no more Indian problems up north. There's Indian problems in Kansas. I'm sending you there."

A man named Haskell spoke up. "I'll go up north."

Graves handed Hodges a collection of letters and warrants. "Get started for Kansas."

"How long will it take?" Hodges asked.

"As long as it takes," Graves said. "Get it done to everyone's satisfaction there. Bring the wrongdoers back here for trial if you can do it. Hope you're back by Christmas."

Hodges left the office and stuffed the papers into his saddlebags, wondering if he might use them to light a fire along the trail. What good could one man do against a bunch of renegade Indians or Jayhawkers?

He mounted and turned his horse toward the edge of town, veering north. His mission was in Kansas, but Kansas could wait a couple of weeks. He planned to see if Holly and her son had actually found Isaac and if the ranch of her dreams was being plundered by outlaws.

The talk at the stockgrowers' meeting centered around the deputy marshal on his way up from Denver. According to the U.S. Marshal's Office letter, a man named Haskell had been detailed to look into the trouble. When he would arrive was not specified.

"I don't fancy waiting too long for him," one of the ranchers said. "We're in the middle of roundup, and losing horses now would make it tough."

Holly, who had attended again, had been sitting quietly. Davis, the big rancher who had mocked her before, spoke up.

"Why don't we send the little Injun lady after them?" he said. "Seems she got the horses back once. Maybe this time we could talk her into getting rid of the whole gang."

The laughter was sparse. No one felt in a joking mood.

Though Holly had never admitted to getting the horses back from the outlaws, everyone believed she had done it. Emilio was certain, but he only smiled when he spoke of it and had said to her, "Good thing they were all well broken."

Emilio hadn't come to the meeting, as Rosa was near giving birth. Still, he told her that he wished he could come with her, if only for moral support.

"Your place is with your wife at this time," she told him. "You're a good man to realize that."

Holly sat silently while the men talked among themselves. One of them said it was good that the horses were back, but that he for one wouldn't have tried it.

"What do you say little Injun, horse-thieving lady?" Davis said. "You up to getting rid of Musgrove and his bunch? We'd pay you good for it."

"Why don't you do something about it yourself?" Holly asked him. "You're big enough to talk but not big enough to make a difference."

Davis frowned. "You asked for it, Gus," Abner Loomis said. "Maybe you'd best not talk for a while and just listen."

The meeting continued, strained, while they discussed what to do if Deputy Haskell didn't show up soon. Though they didn't speak up, some of the ranchers sided with Davis. A lot of them blamed Holly for getting the gang on the prod by stealing the horses back from them instead of waiting for a lawman to solve the problem.

Musgrove had announced in a LaPorte saloon that he was looking for whoever had taken his horses and meant to make an example of him. He had been told it was a *her,* a woman who had caused his troubles, but he refused to believe that any woman could have gotten the best of him.

"We got our horses back," one rancher said, "but how long are we going to keep them?"

"He's right. Sooner or later Musgrove and his bunch are

going to start raiding hot and heavy," another stockman said. "We've got to be ready for that, deputy or no deputy."

"I suggest that we wait a little while and see if this deputy shows," Loomis said. "I've agreed to work with him, as I know Musgrove and believe that he might fall into a trap for me. I'd like to handle it that way if you all agree."

The vote was taken in favor of Loomis's proposal. The meeting ended with none of the ranchers talking to Holly, not even Loomis. She supposed he didn't want her fouling up his plan to get Musgrove.

She had wanted to ask him how he expected to get the entire gang with just himself and a single deputy, but she had refrained. Maybe he had his strategies and cared to share them only with the deputy. Maybe he thought if he got Musgrove, the rest would disband and leave the country.

She found justice in this land interesting: Should someone run afoul of the law—short of murder and continuous horse thieving—there was no retribution if the wrong was righted. So for an instant she thought maybe some of the gang would switch to an honest living. But she knew better, at least in the case of Harlan Porter.

He had gotten a taste of the outlaw life in grand style, and he liked it. Even more, he had fulfilled his desire to kill, something Holly had seen in his eyes many times. As much as Isaac spoke about his brother's troubled past, there could be no accepting what he had done and would continue to do if not stopped.

In LaPorte, Holly found Justin fishing the river with Nathan Rains. The two boys had each caught some fine trout and were talking about frying them up for supper.

"You'd be welcome, Mrs. Porter, if you'd like to come join us," Nathan said. "Ma is always wanting to visit with you."

Though she knew it disappointed Justin, Holly thanked Nathan but declined. Nathan was right: June Rains was always interested in seeing her, but not as a friend. Instead, she enjoyed viewing Holly as the woman most talked about in the valley, even more than some of the whores who had moved in to take advantage of the increasing traffic.

The first and last time Holly had had a meal with the Rainses, June had spoken softly to her while they had washed the supper dishes. "What's it like to be with an Indian man?" she had asked. "I've seen them and I have to admit, I wonder."

Holly could never get her to understand that her time had been spent with an elderly Blackfoot woman. June didn't want to hear that; she wanted to envision someone she knew bedding with a large warrior.

"You sure you won't have some fish with us, Ma?" Justin asked.

"I'd best spend some time with your pa," she said. "Maybe another time."

At the boardinghouse, Holly found Isaac sleeping soundly, despite the fact he had a visitor standing at the foot of his bed.

Lane Hodges tipped his hat. "Good to see you again, Holly. It's been awhile."

"Lieutenant Hodges?" she asked. "Why are you out of uniform?"

"I'm no longer in the army." He showed her his badge. "You know I've always wanted to do this."

"And the army approved of that decision?"

"Wholeheartedly. In fact, they pushed me into it."

"I see." Holly understood his meaning. "I'm sorry your career didn't work out like you wanted."

"I'm better off for it," he said. "I'm basically my own boss and I come and go as I please."

"That would suit you."

"I heard things have been hard up here," he said.

Holly stood beside Isaac and patted his fevered brow with a wet cloth. "It's not been easy," she said. "I expect it will get worse."

Hodges eyed the laudanum bottles. "Did you think that would do him any good?"

"I didn't put him on the stuff," she said. "A woman who thought I was dead took it upon herself to ruin him."

"How's Justin getting along?"

"He's found a good friend, and I'm thinking of sending him to Denver to school."

"He's a smart young man," Hodges said. "With good schooling, who knows how far he could go. And Burnham? Tillie?"

"They're both getting along, living here in town." She stepped forward. "Tillie's got me making dresses now. I have to say that I like it."

He smiled. "You're good at it, too." He stared out the window, past the foothills to the west. "Who's minding the ranch?"

"Not a soul," Holly said. "Everyone's either been killed, raped, or scared out."

"That's not good. You need someone to help you."

After a silence, Holly said, "You seem to be a good tracker. You found us, at least."

Hodges smiled. "Everyone knows about the woman who lived with the Indians. You're the talk of the town. They say you outdid the outlaws at their own game."

"You can't believe everything you hear."

"When it comes to you," he said, "I could believe about anything."

"I thought they were sending a man named Haskell."

"They are. I'm headed to Kansas, a little out of my way." He rolled his hat through his fingers. "The truth is, I was worried about you. Guess I shouldn't have been, considering you can take care of yourself better than most."

"Are you saying you think I was foolish to take the chance I did?"

"It wasn't a good idea."

"You went out of your way to warn me against getting my own stock back?"

"No. You did something that came to you naturally. That's who you are. It's just dangerous, going against a gang of outlaws alone."

"Can you promise me that the law will work?"

"I can promise you that I will do the best I can by the law. And after I get done in Kansas, I'll stop back."

As he opened the door, Holly told him, "Be careful in Kansas."

Twenty-Six

LANE HODGES had been gone three days when Holly heard the news about Abner Loomis and how he had helped U.S. Deputy Marshal Haskell in capturing the outlaw leader, Musgrove. Everyone rejoiced, believing the thieving and killing had ended.

Loomis had ridden into the Bonner Spring stronghold on his own to tell Musgrove of a prized stallion that had wandered onto his ranch, and that the horse could be found in a pasture along the river. The outlaw followed Loomis to the pasture and, to his pleasure, discovered the stallion grazing peacefully.

"I thank you for telling me," Musgrove said. "I lost him and couldn't figure where he'd gotten off to."

Musgrove's mistake had been in accepting a dinner proposal from Loomis. While they were eating, Haskell had stepped into the room with a large gun and Musgrove had been forced to surrender.

Holly had wondered if the stallion had been Clyde Watson's, but had learned the horse had been a deep chestnut color and had belonged to the big rancher Gus Davis, who had been working with Loomis in order to catch Musgrove.

Burnham had heard the story a number of times and still couldn't understand it.

"Craziest thing I ever heard of," he said, watching Holly and Tillie work on dresses. "You'd think Loomis would have gotten himself shot."

"Maybe Musgrove had planned on killing Loomis," Holly said, "and he didn't get it done before the deputy got the drop on him."

"You've got to give him credit, Mr. Loomis is a brave man, he is," Tillie said.

Holly thought about the event and wondered what had happened to the remainder of the outlaw bunch. Musgrove had been captured, but there had been no word on Harlan or the others.

"I don't expect the thieving to be over yet," she said. "Not as long as Harlan's on the loose."

"Don't you suppose he and the others will disband?" Tillie said. "With their leader headed for Denver and the law watching out, they'd be foolish to continue."

"Nobody ever accused Harlan of having good sense," Holly said.

Tillie got up to look out the window. "Stage is here," she said. "Where's Justin?"

"I'd say he's close by," Holly said. "He's been anxious to go down there with you."

To her great surprise, the boy had eagerly accepted an offer by Tillie to live in Denver for a while and try his hand at a good school.

"I know you've been wanting me to think about it," he told his mother, "and I've thought a lot about it. Maybe it would be good for me."

Holly had been delighted. She hadn't expected his reaction to the offer.

"I'll be back for the holidays," Justin said. "Maybe by then Pa will be strong enough to go for another ride along the river."

In truth, Justin knew better. His pa wasn't going to get any better and the doctor had said he would be surprised if Isaac made it through the winter.

Still, everyone talked about the two of them going riding again. Isaac had said as much himself, not only to go with

Justin but also to search out his brother, Harlan. Musgrove had been captured and Isaac worried that Harlan would soon be caught and maybe killed by lawmen searching for him.

"I'd like to mend things up between us," he kept telling Holly. "We should be like brothers ought to be."

Holly had long since tired of talking about Harlan. Whenever Isaac brought the matter up, she would try and change the subject. But Isaac would just continue on. He was becoming so obsessed with his brother that she worried about his intentions.

"I aim to somehow make things right by him," he told her one night, feverish. "I want it to be soon."

"You don't mean to let him in on the ranch, do you?" she said. "You know it's not a good idea."

"Still, he's my brother," Isaac said.

"He pulled you out of that river a long time ago. You've made amends to him since then."

"I've not done enough for him, Holly."

"Give him a poke of gold and send him on his way."

"I haven't decided yet what I want to do. I'm thinking, though, that he could help on the ranch."

Holly set the dress down and walked outside. The stage had pulled in across the street and Justin was coming along the boardwalk with Nathan Rains.

"He's my best friend," Nathan said as Justin came in the door to get his things. "I'll miss him."

"I'll be back at Thanksgiving," Justin said. "If the river's not froze over, we'll catch us some fish."

He had already said good-bye to his father, after a fashion. Isaac had been sleeping and was hard to awaken. When he did open his eyes, he couldn't sit up for long and fell asleep while talking.

The boy had handled it well. "Can't blame him none," he told his mother. "He's a sick man."

Holly walked with Justin and Tillie to the stage. Tillie would go down and, with money from Holly's sewing profits, make the arrangements for Justin's room and board, then come back within a few days. Her dress business was going so strong that she couldn't be gone long.

Justin gave his mother a hug. "It won't be long till I'm back for a spell," he said.

"You do yourself proud," Holly said as he climbed through the door of the waiting coach.

It was Tillie's turn to give Holly a hug. She wiped at tears. "I'll see to it that he gets set in school," she said. "Don't you worry a bit about it."

"I'd go along," Holly said, "but I don't want Isaac going to look for Harlan, or Harlan coming to look for him."

"I understand, lass. Don't you worry about a thing."

She watched the stage roll out of sight, an emptiness overwhelming her. What if Isaac died before the boy returned for the holidays? She wished she hadn't been so insistent on getting him into school. She could have waited until the next year, but that would have put him that much further behind.

In the dress shop, she busied herself but kept thinking about the changes sure to come. It bothered her so much that she couldn't work. She paced back and forth, stopping only when customers came in. She sold them her dresses, wishing all the while that things were already settled—that Harlan was out of their lives, that Isaac would regain his health, and that it was safe again to live at the ranch.

Before another day had passed news came that Musgrove had been hanged. He had been taken down to Denver in chains but had no sooner gotten settled in jail than a lynch mob had strung him up from the Larimer Street bridge.

Holly said nothing to her husband about it, knowing he

would be all the more worried about his brother. But Isaac heard it from the landlady and told Holly he wanted to talk to her about his future plans.

"I've been thinking about it," he said, "and I intend to give Harlan half my gold."

"Half?" Holly said. "That's being too generous, Isaac."

"No, that's fair. I wouldn't be here if it weren't for him."

"You're sure it's what you want?" Holly said.

"I ain't got much time left, Holly. Take me out to the ranch. Let me stay in that big house I always wanted to stay in. Do that for me."

Holly had no desire to stay in Clyde and Eva's house, yet she couldn't deny Isaac's request. She would take him out and make him as comfortable as possible.

For the first time, she wished her husband would pass on peacefully, before she was forced to meet Harlan once again. She could not bear to think of giving him any of Isaac's gold. She had discussed it with Burnham and he had told her to forget about doing anything for Harlan.

"You can take Isaac out to the ranch," he said, "but don't go looking for Harlan. That would be foolish."

On a clear fall day she drove a buggy to the ranch and helped Isaac into the house. He admitted for the first time that he had paid for the house and had intended it for his own family.

"I had a feeling you'd show up someday," he said. "But I kept getting sick and Eva kept giving me more laudanum. I guess I should have spoke up."

"Well, you're here now and that's what counts," Holly said.

"If I could just make things right by Harlan," he said, "I'd die a happy man."

Each day Isaac would ask if she had located his brother. "Maybe he's left the country," Holly would say. "He's not an easy man to find."

"You ain't looked all that hard, I'll bet," Isaac said one evening. "You should at least do me one last favor and find my brother."

Tillie got back from Denver that night, within the same hour that Rosa had her baby—a little girl she and Emilio named Luisa Marie. Emilio had busied himself keeping the ranch horses in good riding condition as well as checking on the cattle. It was a big country, and if not checked, the cattle could wander as far north as Wyoming Territory.

The next day, Tillie and Burnham packed some bags and moved into the big house. Holly preferred the cabin but knew that Isaac wouldn't stand for it, as he had requested to live in the house—and would likely die there.

Now that it was getting close to Thanksgiving, the weather grew colder and snow fell more frequently, usually in the late evening or in the darkness, melting off by midday. Burnham often sat in the rocker on the porch, watching the sky. He said that when his bones ached, a big storm was on its way.

Isaac lay in a feather bed near the fireplace. Holly and Tillie took turns caring for him at night, each one alternating, while Burnham cut firewood and kept the house warm. When she wasn't watching her husband, Holly slept in an upstairs bedroom.

Waiting for the holidays had become wearisome, and even more so with Isaac badgering her about his brother. In less than a week Thanksgiving would arrive, and it would be a dreary day. Even with Justin coming the following morning to stay through the holidays, the mood wouldn't be festive.

And the matter of Harlan just wouldn't go away.

"When you going to find him?" Isaac kept asking. "I want to see him happy for once in his life."

"We'll wait until after the holidays," Holly said, hoping that would satisfy him.

Then one evening Holly got a cold chill when she saw a lone rider watching the ranch from a high hill. The next evening, even though the fire was stoked up high in the fireplace, her chill returned and she moved out to the front porch, her rifle in the crook of her arm.

Feathery snow had fallen throughout the day, clinging to the trees and covering the ground in a cottony layer of white. The evening sky looked pink through the clouds when Burnham came to the porch, wearing a buffalo coat, and settled into the rocker.

"It'll get worse tonight, when the sun falls," he said. "That wind'll come up for sure."

"Why don't we go inside?" Tillie said. "I'll set to fixing supper."

"You go ahead. I want to be here when they come," Holly said.

"When who comes?"

"I saw Harlan last night. I know it was him. I'm expecting him and his bunch tonight."

Within the hour, four riders came into view, with Harlan Porter leading them. Holly readied her rifle and Tillie took her arm from behind.

"Don't go doing nothing foolish, lass."

"I won't start it," she said. "But I'll for sure answer if he starts."

Holly felt herself burning inside. She hadn't been so determined about anything since setting out for Red Cloud's camp to find Justin. To her, Harlan posed a threat to the future of her family, and she was determined to stop him.

Burnham had gone inside and now returned with a rifle he had brought from town. "I don't figure you need to stand alone on this," he said.

"There's no ranch worth all this," Tillie said.

Holly motioned inside the house. "Keep Isaac in bed if you can."

"I'll see to it," Tillie said.

Harlan rode to the front of the house, the other three close behind. "A fine evening," he said, tipping a bottle.

"What brings you out here?" Holly said.

"Just a neighborly visit. You ain't been home for a spell."

"Isaac's been ill."

"Yeah, too bad. Where is he?"

"Resting."

Harlan offered the bottle to Holly. "How about a little holiday cheer?"

"You're not offering any cheer, Harlan," Holly said. "State your business and be on your way."

"You know my business, woman. This ranch is part mine by rights. I aim to see that it's legal." He pulled a piece of paper from his coat. "My brother needs to sign this."

Isaac suddenly appeared in the doorway, supporting himself against the door frame.

"Well, it appears my brother's finally showed up," he said. "Harlan, I've been wanting to talk."

"Isaac, we can settle this another time," Holly said.

Harlan got down from his horse and stepped onto the porch. "You and me need to talk, Isaac."

"No one invited you off your horse," Holly told him.

He ignored her. "We're brothers, Isaac. What would Ma think if she knew you'd left me outside in the winter without even inviting me in?"

Isaac looked confused; Holly knew his fever had risen again.

"I came to talk over old times," Harlan said. "Patch things up between us. Let me come in, me and the boys. I got some rock candy for the boy."

"The boy's not here," Holly said. "Save your rock candy."

Harlan smiled. "I'll bring it in for when he gets back."

Harlan walked off the porch and began whispering to the other three.

"Don't let him in, Isaac," Holly said. "Please don't do it."

"She's right," Burnham said. "He's a pack of trouble, that one."

But Isaac was already holding the door open for his brother.

"What about my friends?" Harlan asked. "It's cold out."

"You can all come in for a spell," Isaac said weakly.

The four entered the house, grinning, passing Holly's cold stare.

"I heard you're a wild one," one of them said to her under his breath. "My name is Lick and I'm wild, too." He laughed.

Inside, Harlan and the other three knocked snow from their boots and found chairs to sit in. Tillie stoked the fire, her faced lined with fear.

"You did right well up there in Montana," Harlan said. "Got luckier than most."

"Enough for a pretty good layout and a good herd of cattle," Isaac said, struck by a coughing fit.

"You don't sound good," Harlan said.

"Well, I figure to get better."

Harlan and the other three grinned.

Holly turned to Harlan. "The storm's getting worse. Maybe you boys had better get moving."

"We're not done visiting yet," he said. "Maybe one of the ladies could brew some coffee and fix a little supper."

Isaac turned to Tillie. "Could you do that while we talk?"

Tillie headed into the kitchen, and Holly spoke up. "Isaac can't be up long, Harlan. You know that."

"Sure." He grinned crookedly and turned to Isaac. "It's been a spell since we seen each other. A lot's happened. You've put together quite a spread here. If you got your gold in Montana, then why'd you come all the way back down here?"

"They said the Indians were tamed down here," Isaac said. "That makes it a sight easier to ranch."

"You're right," Harlan said. "They're still good and wild up there. One of the boys here got by lucky, though. Show 'em, Bat."

Bat puffed out his chest to Holly like he was some kind of hero. He opened his shirt to show an arrow wound.

Tillie brought the coffee and the four began to slurp noisily from their cups.

"What about the grub?" Harlan said.

"I'll see what I can find." Tillie started for the kitchen.

"They don't have time for supper," Holly said.

Harlan turned to Isaac. "Too bad about Clyde Watson. He must have been a good partner."

"He was fine." Isaac's eyes had become glassier.

"And your other wife, Eva, was she fine, too?"

The four of them hooted, and Holly said, "Isaac needs to rest now."

"About Clyde," Harlan said, ignoring her. "Some say Indians got him. But I don't believe it."

Burnham had been quiet up to now. "Who would you say did it?" he asked.

"I'd say that Musgrove Gang went and killed him," Harlan replied.

"How would you know it was Musgrove?" Holly asked.

"That's what folks are saying."

"Nobody in town seems to be sure who did it," Burnham said.

"Oh, it was Musgrove," Harlan said. "He was doing that right along—until that bunch in Denver strung him up."

Burnham grunted. "The thieves that ran with him are bound to get hung, too, they say."

Harlan took the paper back out of his coat. "Tell you what, Isaac. Maybe you could just sign this and make it legal like."

"He's not signing anything," Holly said.

"I wasn't talking to you," Harlan said.

"He's in no condition to sign anything," Holly said. "It's time for you and your men to leave here."

Isaac began coughing again. "I'd best take some medicine," he said.

Holly helped him to his feet. With Tillie on the other side, the two of them took him over to the bed.

Harlan's voice rose. "You going to let those two women haul you away when we're talking? That ain't like you, Isaac."

"He needs rest," Holly said. "Come back another time."

Harlan stood up. "Isaac, remember what I said about Ma? She wouldn't want us quarreling like this, and you letting them women send me out in the snow."

"We've got to patch things up," Isaac said.

"We should've done it a long time past." Harlan found a pen in an inkwell on a nearby table and handed the paper to Isaac. "Sign here."

"Don't sign anything, Isaac," Holly said. "You're not thinking straight."

"I do owe him something for having pulled me from the river," Isaac said. He took the pen and signed the paper.

The other three outlaws smiled and Burnham turned away. Tillie left for the kitchen, tears in her eyes.

"That was right good of you, Isaac," Harlan said, folding the paper.

"You got what you wanted," Holly said. "Now it's time to leave."

"It's still storming out there," Harlan said.

"We'll let them stay in the back cabin till morning," Isaac said. "That's what I want, Holly." He pointed to a kerosene lantern and said to his brother, "You can find your way out, and we'll have breakfast come first light."

"That's more like it, Isaac," Harlan said. "Ma would be proud of you."

Twenty-Seven

IN THE kitchen, Tillie wept bitterly. "He's taken it from you, he has," she told Holly. "Lord help me, I wish you'd have shot him."

"It's not over," Holly said.

"I've half a notion to head out to those cabins," Burnham said.

Tillie wiped her eyes with her apron. "You'd be foolish if you did. We're all alive, and that's a sight more than I can say for Clyde Watson. And Eva. I guess she's worse off than dead."

"We've got some time," Holly said. "Like as not he'll wait until the snow and cold leave to try and take his part of the ranch over. Maybe the law will show up before then."

"The law already got Musgrove," Burnham said. "They don't have anything on Harlan."

"It's true, but it don't seem right," Tillie added.

"He's got an easy time of it now," Burnham said. "He can use this ranch as his headquarters. There's no way he'll stop his thieving and killing."

Holly knew Burnham was right: With Musgrove gone, Harlan had taken over the gang. As soon as Isaac passed on, he would want the entire ranch for himself.

Later, she lay in the darkness, listening to Isaac's coughing downstairs. Outside, the wind had died down. Her mind raced and she found no way to calm herself.

Unsettled, she rose to check on Isaac. Tillie and Burnham

were wrapped in a buffalo robe downstairs, but she wanted to check on him herself, despite Tillie's advice to get plenty of rest and let them tend to Isaac.

"You need your strength for tomorrow," Tillie had said. "No telling what will come to pass when Harlan and those hooligans come awake. They may want Isaac to sign over the whole place."

"That's what's got me worried," Holly had said.

She rolled from her blankets and found her buckskin dress. It was easy to slip in and out of and warm enough to allow her comfort in the cold upstairs bedroom. Once she got downstairs, the warmth of the fire would relax her.

At the foot of the stairs, she discovered Tillie stoking the fireplace.

"What on earth are you doing up, lass?"

"I couldn't sleep. I came down to check on Isaac."

"It's too cold up there for you, isn't it?"

"It's cold, but nothing I couldn't sleep through," she said. "That feather tick you made would keep a body warm at fifty below."

"It won't get down to that, Lord willing.

Holly sat down in a chair next to Isaac's bed. "I don't know what to do now. I don't know why he signed that paper."

"It wouldn't be so bad if Harlan had ever treated him decent," Tillie said. "Isaac thinks so much of him, for pulling him out of the river so long ago. You'd think he'd see how his brother's changed since then."

"Will you promise me something?" Holly said. "When Isaac goes, will you promise to stay on and help me here with my half of the ranch?"

"Lass, you'd be better off to start your own dress shop, in Denver or thereabouts."

"No, this ranch was Isaac's dream. And it's always been my dream to live beside a river out here, just like we did back in Tennessee. I love to see the sun fall on the water."

"There's a river in Denver where you can see that," Tillie said. "And you don't have to risk your life to do it."

"Yes, but I've always lived in the open, not shut in. I love to make dresses too, but that means staying inside most of the time. I couldn't stand being in the middle of a city."

"What I'm trying to say, lass," Tillie argued, "is that you can live in town and we'll travel out to see the sunsets. It's safer that way."

"No, it's not the same. Safer or not, it just doesn't feel the same. I like to be standing on ground I live on when the river goes by. Can you understand that?"

"I like to be standing on safe ground," Tillie said. "There's precious little of that nowadays."

From nearby came a groan. Holly and Tillie both moved to Isaac's side.

"Can you hear me?" Holly asked him.

He sat up in bed, eyes wide. "The Yanks got Johnny. Shot him in the guts. I can't make him stop crying."

"Bad dreams again," Tillie said.

"I hope to God that Harlan don't get shot," Isaac said. He lay back down, tears pouring from his eyes. Holly covered him but he thrashed the blanket off, saying he didn't want to be pinned down.

Before his leaving Tennessee, Isaac had spent a good many nights fighting the war again, worrying about the men he fought beside, as well as Harlan. Holly had sat up with him, working through the dreams.

"The medicine won't stop the pain anymore," Holly said.

"We can't give him no more, it'll kill him," Tillie said. She hurried to the stove and placed a pot filled with milk to simmer. When it had warmed sufficiently, she filled a tin cup.

"This should put him to good sleep quicker than anything," she said, adding a pinch of whiskey to the milk.

Holly held Isaac up and he took the milk as if he were a small child. A few dribbles rolled down his chin, which she dabbed up with a cloth. Soon he was asleep, snoring loudly.

She tasted the mixture. "I could take to that myself," she said.

"You get on back upstairs," Tillie said. "Get yourself some rest. It'll be light before you know it."

Holly made her way back to her room, disconsolate, feeling a weight she could hardly bear. Tomorrow would be hard to face. She knew Harlan would try and talk Isaac out of the other half of the ranch, and there seemed little she could do about it.

She lay in bed, wondering what to do. With the feather bed closing in warm around her, she closed her eyes. For the time being, she could escape it all.

Smoke and shouting awakened her. And shooting. She jumped out of bed and hurried into her buckskin dress, fumbling in the dark for her pistol before bolting down the stairs.

Below, Tillie was pulling Isaac out of a flaming bed. He choked and swore, batting at the flames with his hands and arms. Holly stood on the stairwell a moment and stared in shock.

"For the love of God, help me, lass!" Tillie bellowed. "He's burning alive."

She rushed down the stairs. The odor of kerosene was everywhere, and already the flames were licking through the living room and into the kitchen.

"They came in the back," Tillie said, "and just threw the lantern on his bed. Then they torched the kitchen as well."

"Let's get Isaac outside!" Holly yelled. She opened the door to rifle fire, and a bullet cracked into the door frame. Another buzzed past her ear, into the open space of the living room.

Burnham, who had been shooting through a window, said, "You'd best take him out another way. They'll pick us off going out there."

"We can't get out the back way," Holly said. "It's all on fire."

Tillie had Isaac on the floor, pounding his smoking bed-clothes with a coat. Holly lifted her Henry rifle from the corner behind the door. She levered a bullet into the barrel and leapt outside, rolling off the porch.

Bullets puffed the snow around her as she wriggled through the shadows. Her hands and face quickly grew numb from the cold, but she held her rifle steady.

Flashes of light from rifle barrels appeared from just in front of the tack shed. They hadn't even bothered to spread out, so cocky were they in their plan to kill Isaac and destroy the house, with everyone in it.

She fired toward a spot in the darkness where one of the rifles flashed, and she heard a grunt. She fired again and again. She heard cursing and men running through the snow. If she could find their horses, she told herself, she would put an end to all of them.

But when she heard the sounds of snorting horses running across the meadow, she realized they had escaped. All but one. She discovered him lying in the snow, breathing hard, holding his foot.

"Did Harlan and the others run off and leave you?" she asked him.

"Don't kill me."

"How bad you hit?"

"It's my ankle. It's ruined."

"Drag yourself over to the house."

"But it's afire."

"I said, drag yourself over, or I'll put a bullet into your crotch."

"I'm going," he said. "Don't shoot me, please."

As he crawled, spitting snow and sniffling, Holly wanted to end it for him. She wanted in the worst way to place her rifle barrel against the back of his head and pull the trigger.

In front of the house, Burnham and Tillie tended to Isaac in the wet snow.

"Stop your crawling and look at me," Holly said to the outlaw.

He turned over on his back, wincing from the pain. He was the one Harlan had called Lick, the one who had whispered to her that he was a wild one.

"Do you feel pretty wild right now?" Holly asked him. "Do you remember when you went into the house tonight and whispered into my ear?"

"Ma'am," he said, "my ankle hurts real bad."

"You expect me to feel sorry for you? Look what you've done here. Look what you've done to my husband. Look!"

"It weren't me that threw the lantern. I was again' it."

"Who did it?"

"Harlan. He's the one. You ain't going to shoot me, are you?"

"Maybe I'll just strip you naked and leave you out in the cold."

"Listen, I can help you."

"How?"

"I can tell you where Harlan's hideout is. Them other three's headed there for sure. They left me for dead, anyway, so why should I do them any favors?"

"I don't need you to find the Bonner Spring hideout," Holly said.

"No, Harlan moved out of there," Lick said. "Too many people know about it."

"Then maybe you can take me to the new hideout, come first light."

"I'd just as soon tell you and you can find it on your own. I ain't fit for riding."

"You can figure on riding or sitting naked in the snow. Which will it be?"

"I figure I can ride," he said.

Burnham came over, holding his rifle. He cocked the gun, staring coldly at Lick.

"Don't do it," Holly said.

"Oh, I wasn't about to shoot him. I was going to take him over to the trees and hang him."

"Hold off on it," Holly said. "He says he can lead us to Harlan."

"And you believe him?"

"He's got but two choices. He makes the wrong one and he's dead."

"Listen, it weren't my idea to come here," Lick said. "I told Harlan it was a crazy-fool thing to do."

"But you came along," Burnham said.

"I had to. Don't you see, he would have shot me otherwise. Any of them would have."

"How many more are in the gang?" Holly asked.

"Two others. They stayed to tend some horses we took from down on the Big Thompson."

"How far's the hideout?"

"A morning's ride is all."

"You'd better be telling the truth," Holly said.

Burnham motioned toward where Tillie was tending to Isaac. "He's in a bad way. You'd best go to him."

While Burnham covered the outlaw, Holly hurried to her husband's side. His face was red and he coughed loudly while Tillie pulled strips of burned fabric off his chest and sides.

"It's bad," Tillie said. "God forgive me but I hate those men."

"I warned him," Holly said. "I told him to send them away. Now look what it's cost him."

"You can't blame him, poor man. He was out of his head."

Holly knew she was right. His condition had riddled him with guilt over his relationship with Harlan. It hadn't mattered to him that Harlan wanted no relationship, just anything that Isaac had.

"We'll load him in a wagon and take him down to the doctor," Tillie said.

"The horses are loose in the hills," Holly said. "Harlan ran them all off."

"So what do we do?"

"I'll catch one, then ride down and fetch the doc up here. That would be quicker than taking him down in a wagon, anyway."

"First, help me get him to the bunkhouse," Tillie said. "He'll freeze to death if we don't move him now."

They dragged Isaac's unconscious body into the bunkhouse, where the room was still warm from the fire. The outlaws had ransacked the place, taking anything valuable they could find before setting the blaze.

"I knew better than to give in to Isaac's wishes," Holly said. "I should have spoken up."

"It don't matter, lass. There'd have been trouble no matter how it was laid out."

Holly paced the room, trying to cool her temper. "I should have done something."

At the bed, Tillie bent over Isaac.

"He's awake," she said. "He wants to talk to you."

Holly took his hand, kneeling at the bedside. "Isaac, you're going to be fine. Just fine."

"No, Holly, I ain't." His raspy voice was low and Holly had to lean close to hear. "Take care of the boy."

"We'll take care of him together."

"Tell him, Holly . . . " He paused for a breath. "Tell him I wished I could have been here to see him grow to be a man. Tell him I wanted to in the worst way."

"Isaac, I'm going to fetch you a doc."

"No, I can't make it. I'm sorry for it, but I guess it's the Lord's will."

Holly's eyes flooded with tears. She tried to speak, but words wouldn't come.

"You've been the best, Holly," Isaac said. "The best wife and ma to the boy that a man could ever find. I know there were times when I never held up my end."

"Isaac, you've been the best husband a woman could want."

"You're a good woman and there's very few like you. I just want you to hear me say this, 'cause I know I haven't ever said it enough. I love you, Holly."

Isaac's breath left him and he lay still.

"Isaac? Isaac?" She turned to Tillie.

"He's gone, lass. God rest his soul."

Holly fell across her husband's chest, sobbing, releasing the pent-up frustration and worry and anger of nearly three years.

"He didn't have to die like this," she said. "He could have gone in his bed, just slipped away."

"Likely he felt no pain since we took him outside," Tillie said. "When he talked to you, he was nearly gone, so he felt nothing."

Holly ran her hands over Isaac's face, closing his eyes fully with her fingers, brushing his hair into place.

"He was a good man, Tillie."

She walked outside and saw Burnham standing over the outlaw.

"Burnham, Tillie needs you."

He looked her way and he knew. He had already hog-tied the outlaw and left him in the snow, coming over to Holly.

"He's gone, ain't he?"

"He's gone, Burnham."

"I'm sorry it had to be this way." He stared at the burning building. "I guess we're whipped."

"Not hardly," Holly said. "I'm going to find Harlan and then we'll start over."

"You sure?"

"I have never been more sure of anything."

Twenty-Eight

THE SUN lit the eastern sky, framing the smoke that rose from the ruins of the house in a ball of gold. In a nearby pine, chickadees chattered and flitted about. Somewhere nearby a blue jay squawked into the morning.

Holly sat with a rifle across her knees, staring into the blackened timbers. Isaac had been ready to die, there had been no doubt, but to see his brother hasten that death would haunt her forever.

At early daylight, she had caught two horses that had wandered back to the ranch, then had set fire to some logs near a big cottonwood tree along the creek. When the frosty ground had warmed she and Burnham had dug a grave for Isaac. She would wait to bury him until Justin got home, which would be the following day. By then she should be back from finding Harlan.

For now, Isaac lay in the tack shed, wrapped in his favorite coat. Tillie and Burnham had arranged him there, as Holly had wanted some solitude. She would visit him soon, but not with him laying among the saddles and bridles.

She rose and started for the two horses hitched in front of the bunkhouse. Tillie came out, frowning.

"You don't plan to go after them, surely," she said. "Leave it to the law."

"There is no law here," Holly said.

"Denver has law. They'll send someone again. Maybe that deputy Haskell, who helped Ab Loomis out."

"I can't wait for him. Harlan will be back for the rest of us."

"I thought you said Lane Hodges had stopped by. Maybe he'll swing back on his way through."

"Tillie, I just can't depend on that."

"Oh, won't you listen to me, lass? There's no sense in what you're doing. Give it a day of thought, or maybe two, then you'll see the folly."

"I have this ranch," Holly said. "I'll rebuild and I'll make it work."

"Women don't run ranches, lass. They cook and sew and clean, but they don't run ranches."

Holly looked at her silently.

"Sell out," Tillie went on. "Round up your cattle and sell them to the highest bidder. Do what I asked and start your own dress shop. Don't you see, lass, it's the best thing for you."

Holly turned to watch the sunshine on the mountains. The maps to the buried pokes of gold had been destroyed in the fire and Holly had no way of knowing where to dig. Besides, the snow had piled up nearly six inches, and turning a shovel in cold ground would be very difficult. Any woman in her right mind would listen to Tillie.

"You hear me, lass?" Tillie said.

"I hear you, Tillie, but this is where I belong. There needs to be an outlaw cleanup around here, and with that done I can stay here and do well. Emilio and Rosa will come back and in the summers Justin can be of help."

"It's hard to talk sense to you," Tillie said. "You're not of fit mind, not with what's happened."

"Well, I've set my mind. When I get back we'll talk about the future."

She walked into the bunkhouse, where Burnham stood watching the outlaw, Lick.

"You sure you don't want me to come along?"

"You need to be here with Tillie," Holly said.

"Do you remember enough Indian tricks to get them all by yourself?"

"I remember plenty, Burnham," she said.

Lick stood on one leg, balancing against a bedpost. His ankle was dark and swollen to the size of a melon. He looked like he might welcome death to the pain he was feeling.

"You won't take me to a doc?" he said.

"Not until you lead me to Harlan Porter."

"What if I die along the way?"

"I guess there's a few wolves around here who could use a good breakfast."

Burnham had fashioned a crutch from a pine limb. He shoved it into Lick's hand. "Take that and get out of my sight," he said. "Go on, before I find a rope."

Holly pulled on her wolf coat, remembering when Old Calf Woman had presented it to her. "The wolf is strong and brave," the old woman had said. "This coat, if you wish to believe, can make you quick in thought, like the wolf, and able to evade danger. It will give you an edge."

She had found the coat to be invaluable. Red Cloud and his warriors had feared her because of it, as had Bad Face's renegades. She hoped that besides warmth, the coat would once again give her the edge she needed.

She pushed Lick into the saddle and tied him in. She climbed on her pony and with Burnham and Tillie looking after them, they started across the meadow toward the trail Lick said would take them to the new hideout.

Lane Hodges rode into LaPorte, hoping he had not arrived too late to help Holly. His trip to Kansas had been a waste of time.

Snowstorms and confusing stories had given him little to base arrests on. Everyone said that Jayhawkers had been bothering them and that they had to be stopped. Everyone had said the same thing about renegade Indians.

He had found a lot of graves and a lot of grieving widows with small children, but no one to support him when he wanted to find the killers.

"Ain't no ten men armed to the teeth going to stop what's going on here," a shopkeeper told him. "It's going to take the army to help out, and the army's moved west to chase Injuns that don't need chasing. That's what's caused these to be renegades in the first place."

Hodges heard more than he wanted to about the army—what they had done and what they had refused to do. Against his better judgment, he decided to pursue the matter of thievery and killing on his own, nearly losing his life in the process.

He had tried to stop a gang of Jayhawkers from looting and burning a homestead in southeastern Kansas. There had been twelve of them and they had laughed at him, giving chase. His only salvation had been finding a herd of cattle pushing through the late fall, headed across to the railheads, and a few brave drovers who had offered to protect him.

There had been a shootout. He had killed three Jayhawkers, and the drovers had gotten three more. A bullet had clipped one drover's shoulder, but neither Hodges nor any of the others had been scratched.

"If you were thinking to take any of them back for trial," one drover said, "then you'd better take them in a coffin. Didn't you know that's the only way they'll go?"

"I'm new at this," he confessed.

"If you want to get old," the trail boss said, "you'd better choose another profession, and I don't mean pushing beeves up the trail. That's worse than marshaling."

"I didn't know anything was worse than marshaling," Hodges said, "based on the way I've been treated."

"The law don't fare well in these parts," another hand told him. "Those that care for the law won't help, and those who don't are in the majority."

One of the drovers had then left the fire and returned with a couple of ropes.

"If you want to enforce the law," he said, "learn to tie a hangman's noose."

After a dinner of beef and beans, Hodges had thanked the trail boss and the drovers and made his way back toward Colorado, intent on looking in on Holly Porter and her family. He didn't know if Deputy Marshal Haskell had done any good, but he did know that one man, wherever he happened to be sent on any given assignment, could never be enough.

He reached LaPorte in a snowstorm. The town was bustling with activity. Most of the travel north had slowed down, owing to the winter coming on, and those who had businesses were counting their summer profits.

Hodges left his horse at a livery and found the boardinghouse where Isaac had stayed. Wearily, he put his saddle on the bed.

"Lucky man, you are," the landlady said. "This is the last room left."

"What happened to Isaac Porter?"

"They took him out to the ranch to die," she said. "I never saw a man so weak hang on for so long."

"I'm glad you decided to rent me the room," Hodges said. "I didn't want to go all the way down to Denver in the dark."

"So you didn't come up from Denver?"

"No," Hodges said.

"I see. I was hoping you had."

Hodges remained silent, knowing the woman's meaning.

"Folks in these parts are hoping the law will show up one more time," she said. "It seems there's still some outlaws around, even though Musgrove and most of his gang are gone."

Hodges considered telling her he was a deputy, but thought better of it, deciding that it would complicate matters. The woman would then have a number of questions for him to answer that he didn't have time for. He was officially in Kansas and wanted it to stay that way.

The following morning he rode up the river and saw that the main ranch house had been burned to the ground. Burnham and Tillie met him at the door of the cabin.

"You should have been here last night," Tillie said. "You could have stopped Isaac's brother from burning the place down, and Isaac with it." She pointed to the freshly dug grave.

Hodges peered over at the dark hole in the ground awaiting a body. "Where's Holly? After Harlan, I suppose."

"She left a couple of hours ago," Burnham said. "There's no one who could stop her."

"She believes she can do it all alone," Tillie added.

"I'll be going to find her, then," Hodges said.

"You'd better do it quick," Burnham told him. "I know it will be either Harlan or Holly who'll go next. One of them won't be alive much longer."

Holly had ridden most of the day, leading Lick on his horse behind her. The going had been slow, as Harlan's tracks had filled in with snow and she had to depend on Lick for directions. The farther up the canyon they rode, the more she suspected that he was taking her into nowhere.

"I'm telling you, it's up here," he told her when she questioned him. "It ain't far now. You'll see."

"Why would you go up so high? It's nearly winter and you can't work horses in deep snow."

"Who said anyone would work them?" Lick said. "This is just a place to hold them for a while. Go on, ride up the trail. We'll find them, I promise."

Holly stopped her horse and studied the trail ahead, which curved into a narrow rock canyon dense with pine on both sides.

"Is there another way to the hideout besides through there?" she asked.

"Not that I know of."

"I think we'll find another way," Holly said.

She had no sooner turned her pony than a volley of rifle fire zipped past her and into the snow around her pony's heels. She heard the pony grunt and felt it falter under her.

She grabbed her rifle and jumped off, allowing the groaning pony to roll onto its side. A bullet had passed through its stomach. With a single pistol shot behind the ear, she put the animal out of its misery.

Lick had kicked his horse into a run and was doing his best to stay on. But the snow slowed the pony considerably and it struggled to keep from slipping.

A straightaway shot, Holly leveled her rifle and fired. Lick rolled off to one side and lay thrashing.

Laying low behind the pony, Holly could see the outlaws riding toward her through the trees above the canyon. She counted six of them, though she couldn't tell which one was Harlan.

She leveled her rifle at one of the riders. The bullet slammed into his chest, knocking him from the saddle. The others moved back out of range. They sat and talked among themselves, while the fallen rider slid down the hill through the snow and lay still.

She decided the late afternoon sun was on her side, as it would soon fall over the mountains and darkness would work to her advantage. She believed Harlan had to know that, as the outlaws began to split up, working to close her in from all sides while they could still see her.

Even with the pony for cover, her back was exposed. She

had to move or they would surround her and pick at her as if she were a duck alone on a pond. To her left was a small, pine-studded hill that rose above the trail. They might surround her, but should she make that hill, they would have a hard time shooting at her through the timber.

She made certain her pistol was strapped tightly and, grabbing her rifle, ran close to the ground toward the pine hill. Bullets ripped the snow around her, and though she zigzagged as she ran, one narrowly missed her face.

I'm running like a wolf would run, she thought. I'm a very hard target.

She reached the hill and dug herself in at the top, where she could see in every direction. To one side a single outlaw moved toward her, hiding himself in the brush that covered the hillside. She cocked the hammer back on the rifle and waited for him to bob up. His head appeared and she fired, then watched him tumble over on his back and lie still.

She kept low as bullets pelted the timber around her. The reports came ever closer and she knew they were nearly on top of her. Darkness or not, she would need a good amount of luck for them not to overrun her.

Knowing this, she decided not to die on the hill. She could make a run for it and maybe get one or two of them before making another stand somewhere else and hold out until dark.

She began creeping down the back of the hill. Then shots sounded from the other side and she could hear men yelling. In front of her, two men rose up to see what was happening. One of them was Harlan.

He saw her rise, rifle leveled, and turned fast enough to avoid being shot through the middle, though the bullet caught his left leg just above the knee. The other outlaw lost himself in the brush and timber before Holly could fire again.

She approached Harlan cautiously, her rifle ready. Though hit bad enough to keep some men down, he was not easily stopped. His rifle was too far away to reach but he pulled his pistol. She shot him in the shoulder. He fell back, cursing.

"You've reached the end, Harlan," she said.

His eyes were ablaze. "I'm not done in yet."

"I could do it now," she said.

"You could but you won't."

She considered pulling the trigger. That would be too easy for him. He needed to be paraded in the streets.

"I'm going to show you off to everyone," she said. "They'll all see that a woman brought you down."

"I'm not going anywhere with you," he said.

"You'll ride, or I'll drag you behind a horse through the snow."

Harlan looked around, waiting for one of his men to show up. Instead, Lane Hodges rode over the hill, leading a horse behind him, a wounded outlaw tied in the saddle.

"I'm glad I found you."

"I'm glad, too," Holly said. "I was in a bad way here."

"How many times have I told you not to do this?"

"Plenty. This is the last time."

"That's what they all say," Hodges said with a slight grin. "You think we should take these two back?"

"I told Harlan the town would see that we caught him," Holly said. "What happened to the others?"

"One's down and one got away," he said. "I don't think he'll hang around. I saw him ride over the divide into the next basin."

"Let's take these two back, then," Holly said.

Harlan laughed. The pain twisted his face. "It's a waste of time. You can't take us to no jail. You've got nothing to charge us with."

"You killed Isaac," Holly said. "That's plenty enough."

"Did you see me throw the lantern into the house? It could have been one of the others."

"Tillie saw you."

"She's an old woman," Harlan said. "Who's to say what she really saw, it being smoky and all?"

"He's got a point," Hodges said. "It might be hard to prove a case against him."

"You're giving up pretty easy, I'd say," Holly told him. "That's not like you."

"I'm just saying it would be hard to prove he murdered anyone."

Harlan smiled. "Yeah, that's right."

"You want me to let him go?" Holly asked.

"I got some extra rope over in Kansas, from some cowhands trailing cattle," Hodges said. "Maybe we can put it to good use."

Harlan's face whitened. "You just said you couldn't prove murder against me."

"Yes, but you're a horse thief. You'll have to pay the price."

"You can't do that."

Holly rolled Harlan onto his back, pushing his face into the snow. As she tied his hands he tried to resist, but his wounded leg and shoulder filled him with pain and he submitted. By the time she had caught his horse, Hodges had two nooses formed and tossed over two separate pines.

"Let's get it done," he said.

The other outlaw sat in silence, crying softly as Hodges led his horse to the tree and set the noose around his neck.

"Anything you want to say?" Hodges asked him. "Maybe send a letter to someone?"

"I ain't got no one," he said. "Just do it."

Hodges slapped the horse on the rump and the young outlaw swung back and forth, kicking for a time before going limp.

Hodges worked with Holly to force Harlan into the saddle. After seeing the young outlaw hang he struggled violently and begged for mercy.

"Holly, I'm Isaac's brother. We came up the trail together."

"I remember it well," Holly said.

"I'll give my half of the ranch back and I'll quit the country. You'll never see me again."

"It's too late for that, Harlan."

"Then be damned!" he said. He spat at her.

At the tree, he cursed continually until the horse jumped out from under him. He jerked at the rope's end and finally fell limp, swaying gently back and forth.

Hodges stepped over and took Holly into his arms and held her while she wept.

Twenty-Nine

THEY RODE silently through the darkness, reaching the ranch well after midnight. Hodges left her at the cabin and rode on back to LaPorte, while she told Burnham and Tillie what had happened.

"He was bound to go that way," Burnham said. "It was just a matter of time."

"Thank God you're safe, lass," Tillie said.

"Thank God it's over," Holly said.

Holly had no trouble drifting off to sleep. She dreamed of Isaac, a sound man dressed in a gray uniform who came to her with a smile on his face. He told her not to be sorry about anything, that it had all turned out for the best.

"You did what you felt was right," he said. "You can't ask more of a person."

He told her to bury him with a quick service when Justin came home and not to dwell on his death.

He was as Holly had remembered him—strong and anxious to fight for the cause he believed in. She hoped that wherever he was headed, he wouldn't have to face war again.

"No more fighting for me," he told her. "I'll wear this uniform because you always fancied me in it, but there'll be no bloodstains now."

She looked into his eyes and saw great peace there.

"I doubt I'll be back to see you again," he said. "But you never know."

"Why wouldn't you come again?" she asked.

"You'll be in good hands." He smiled.

She arose in her bed, feeling a warmth in the room. The darkness caressed her and she had no fear. With a deep breath she lay down and fell back to sleep.

Hodges rose the next morning and took breakfast with the other boarders. Everyone had heard about the fire at Diamond Rock Ranch and the outlaws who had set it. They had also heard rumors of vigilantes forming and discussed it at the breakfast table.

"Somebody will get to them and they'll all either get hung or shot," one boarder was saying. "When the law don't get here quick enough, folks has got to do it themselves."

Those at the table agreed. No one was particularly high on having a woman operating a ranch but none of them thought it fair she should be burned out and her husband killed.

After breakfast, Hodges rode to the ranch and found Holly standing beside the hole where Isaac would be buried.

"Justin's coming with Tillie and Burnham soon," she said. "You want to stay?"

He thought a moment. "It's best that Justin see his pa for the last time without me," he said. "I'll go on down to Denver now. You going to be all right?"

"I'm going to be fine," she replied. "What are you going to tell the marshal?"

"I'm not going to tell him anything. I just came back from Kansas and I'll have my hands full with the report from those parts."

"But they will hear about it down there."

"He should have sent a group of lawmen up here and it wouldn't have happened."

"Where will you go next?"

"I can't say, but there's no shortage of thieves and killers."

"Maybe one day you'll get tired of trying to solve everyone else's problems."

"I'm already tired of it," he said. "But I took the job and I'll stay with it, at least for a while."

After Hodges rode off, Holly thought about other things she might have discussed with him, but that could come at another time. She believed she would see him again.

She was still at Isaac's grave when Tillie and Burnham arrived with Justin. The buggy creaked to a stop and Justin jumped out.

"I'm sorry, Ma," he said. "I heard what happened."

She detected a hint of relief in his voice.

"Aunt Tillie said he went right away and didn't suffer much."

"She's right, he didn't suffer much," Holly said.

Burnham and Holly brought Isaac's body out and laid it in the grave, then quickly covered it. Tillie read from her Bible.

That night they sat by a fire in the bunkhouse and Justin read from a schoolbook. He was learning a lot in Denver and was anxious to learn more.

"You'll go on back down after the holidays," Holly told him, "and you'll learn so much that I won't know who you are."

Justin laughed. "I doubt I'll change that much."

"You're learning more all the time, and it's good for you."

"I've got to say, I do like it," he said. "There's more to this world than I ever dreamed of."

Two days later, Holly traded a neighbor a new dress for a turkey gobbler. Burnham and Tillie took the bird back to the ranch and the following day, they dined on the bird, with dressing and sweet potatoes and fresh rolls.

The little cabin was filled with people, with Holly and

Justin, and Burnham and Tillie. In addition, Emilio and Rosa arrived with their new baby, whose round black eyes took in everything.

"She'll be big before we know it," Rosa said. "And she already likes horses."

"By the time she's old enough to ride," Holly said with a laugh, "we'll need another horse wrangler."

"You'll make this ranch grow, lass," Tillie said. "If anybody can do it, you can. And maybe you can still make a dress now and then."

"Oh, I can make more than one now and then." She smiled at Emilio. "I'll have a good foreman here to watch over the operations. That will free me up to do a lot of things."

Later in the day Nathan Rains and his mother arrived with a fresh pumpkin pie.

"I'm glad to see that you're enjoying the holiday," June Rains said. "I was worried about that. Do you know who hanged the outlaws?"

"There's a lot of talk," Holly said. "Nothing is certain, though."

"I'd like to have you make me a dress when you can, if you would do that."

"I'd be happy to," Holly said.

Holly had discovered that June Rains had changed and now wanted her as a real friend, not just someone she could gossip about with the other women. Holly was pleased, as she knew it would open the door for friendships with other ladies.

Perhaps they had been afraid of her before, she reasoned. It wouldn't be surprising, their thinking she had taken on Indian ways and would much rather live in a tepee. But her making dresses had caught their attention. Sewing nicely made a woman stand out on the frontier, and Holly Porter could stitch with the best of them.

With Thanksgiving over and Christmas on its way, she turned her attention to dressmaking for gifts. She had a backlog she knew she couldn't handle alone and, though Tillie had large orders of her own to fill, the two worked together, getting much more done than either would have separately.

"I don't see how you two can talk so derned much and yet make so many dresses," Burnham observed.

As the days passed, Justin grew more relaxed as well. With the death of his father behind him, he was free to put his mind to other things. He spent a lot of time with Nathan Rains, and the pair searched the river often for open holes where fish might bite.

They caught a great many, and soon everyone had tired of fish.

"We can't have fish for Christmas," Justin remarked one day. "But there sure are a lot of geese in these parts."

The day before Christmas, Burnham surprised Justin with a ten-gauge shotgun. That afternoon Justin went out with Nathan Rains, and the boys got themselves a Canada goose. The birds were everywhere along the river and down into the valley around LaPorte.

"It'll make a fine Christmas meal," Tillie said.

Holly and Justin, with Burnham and Tillie's help, cut a small tree for the cabin, and they all wrapped popcorn garlands around the branches and tied red ribbons from top to bottom. Holly thought of Christmastime in Tennessee, when Justin had been small. She and Isaac had shared a few good holidays together, holding the baby and discussing the future.

An early Christmas present arrived in the form of Nathan Rains's dog, which came with Nathan during a visit and, while digging out a mouse at the corner of the cabin, had unearthed a poke of gold.

"That's got to be one of the biggest ones," Justin remarked. "You've got a good dog there, Nathan."

When Christmas arrived, everyone gathered in the cabin again, laughing and exchanging gifts. Besides the shotgun, Justin received new pants and shirts, made especially by Holly for him to wear to school. He displayed them with a wrinkled nose: Clothes were good enough presents, but there could have been other things that would have struck his fancy.

He was thinking of what they might be when Lane Hodges rode into the yard and unloaded a pile of presents he had tied to his saddle. He had a checkerboard for Burnham, who delightedly set up a game, and scarves and bonnets for Tillie and Holly.

Among the presents was a set of books for Justin, about faraway people and places, one of them being *Robinson Crusoe*.

Then Tillie brought out a cedar-lined hope chest for Holly. With a twinkle in her eye, she said, "Thought you might have good use for this."

They sat down to dinner and toasted the new start with hard cider.

"We'll build the new house when the weather breaks for good," Holly said. "Come spring roundup I want everybody to see the new place."

They talked about their plans and in a short while the goose, along with a lot of potatoes and gravy, had vanished. June Rains had sent over two pies with Nathan, and they started in on them.

"This country's filling up with people," Burnham said. "I expect Denver is growing even faster."

"It is for certain," Hodges said. "Even though I'm based out of there, I travel a lot, and every time I come back, it's grown again. It won't stop, I don't believe."

"Did you ever feel you'd like to settle down somewhere?" Justin asked.

"In time," Hodges said, having trouble with the words. "I would like to do that in time."

He noticed Justin looking over at Holly.

"There's plenty of pie left," she said. "Lane, how about you?"

"Thanks, but I've got to be heading back," he said.

"All the way to Denver?" Justin asked.

"Likely I'll stay in LaPorte tonight. I'll go on down tomorrow."

"Maybe you could go the next day," Justin said. "Tomorrow we could ride the river, all of us, being the weather's·so nice."

And so they rode the river the next day, Holly laughing more than she had in a long time. When Hodges left she placed her wolf coat in the hope chest and closed it, thinking of the times she had worn it, hoping she would never have to bring it out again.

When spring arrived, Holly rode the valley up and down, assuring herself that the Diamond Rock herd was still in existence and that the cowhands she would soon hire—with Emilio's help—would share her desire to make the outfit one of the best along the Front Range.

Before the roundup, she would start the project of building the new house, trading labor with the husbands of town and country ladies alike who wanted her dresses. They would arrive in good numbers, and the house would be up in no time.

And she looked forward to Lane Hodges returning. In a letter, he said he had never been a carpenter but was certainly willing to learn. He had talked about leaving his job as a deputy U.S. marshal and doing something else.

He wouldn't rush into anything, he said, but take things slow and easy.

Justin had said in a letter home that he hoped Lane Hodges would help build the house. "Things are better when he's around," the letter had read. "He should be around more."

Holly agreed and decided that when the time was right, the two of them would spend many a pleasant evening along the river she had come to love and call her own.